CON MEN

MUNDIN: Young idealist trapped in a corporate
slave state where murder signs the
memos.

NORVELL: Mild-mannered executive exiled to
a brutal ghetto.

LANA: Ultraviolent leader of a battle-hardened
clan of barbarian children.

RYAN: Erratic masterbrain with an insatiable yen
for mind-bending drugs.

GLADIATOR-AT-LAW
The sensational novel of the ultimate sting

GLADIATOR-AT-LAW

by
FREDERIK POHL
and
C. M. KORNBLUTH

GLADIATOR-AT-LAW

*A Bantam Book / published by arrangement with
the authors*

Bantam edition / January 1977

ISBN 0-553-06422-3

Published simultaneously in the United States and Canada

*Bantam Books are published by Bantam Books, Inc. Its trade-
mark, consisting of the words "Bantam Books" and the por-
trayal of a bantam, is registered in the United States Patent
Office and in other countries. Marca Registrada. Bantam
Books, Inc., 666 Fifth Avenue, New York, New York 10019.*

PRINTED IN THE UNITED STATES OF AMERICA

Chapter One

THE ACCUSED was a tallow-faced weasel with "Constitutional Psychopathic Inferior" stamped all over him. He wailed to Charles Mundin, LL.B., John Marshall Law School:

"Counselor, you got to get me off! I been up twice and this time they'll condition me!"

Mundin studied his first client with distaste. "You *won't* plead guilty?" he asked again, hopelessly. He had been appointed by the court, and considered that the court had played a filthy trick on him. This twerp's pore patterns were all over Exhibit A, a tin cashbox fishhooked from a ticket window at Monmouth Stadium. *Modus operandi* coincided with that in the twerp's two previous offenses. An alleged accomplice, who had kept the ticket clerk busy for almost all of the necessary five minutes, was all ready to take the witness stand—having made his deal with the prosecutor. And still the twerp was stubbornly refusing to cop a plea.

Mundin tried again. "It won't be so bad, you know. Just a couple of days in a hospital. It's quite painless, and that's not just talk. I've seen it with my own eyes. They took us around in my junior year——"

The twerp wailed, "Counselor, you just don't understand. If they condition me, my God, I have to go to *work*."

Mundin shrugged. "You're acting against my advice," he said. "I'll do what I can for you."

But the trial was over in a matter of minutes. Mundin tried for a reversible error by objecting to the testimony of the accomplice. He claimed feebly that the moral character of the witness made his testimony inadmissible in a conditionable offense. The prosecutor, a grandee from Harvard Law, haughtily smacked him down by pointing out that the essence of the conditionable offense lay in the motivation of the accused, not the fact of commission, which was all the accomplice had testified to. He snapped a series of precedents.

The judge's eyes went blank and distant. Those inside the rail could hear confirmation of the precedents droning faintly into his ears through the headphones under his elaborate wig. He nodded and said to Mundin, "Overruled. Get on with it."

Mundin didn't even bother to take an exception.

The prosecution rested and Mundin got up, his throat dry. "May it please the Court," he said. His Honor looked as though nothing had pleased that Court, ever. Mundin said to the jury box, "The defense, contending that no case has been made, will present no witnesses." That, at any rate, would keep Harvard Law from letting the jury know of the two previous convictions. "The defense rests."

Harvard Law, smiling coldly, delivered a thirty-second summation, which in three razor-sharp syllogisms demonstrated the fact that defendant was guilty as hell.

The court clerk's fingers clicked briskly on the tape-cutter, then poised expectantly as Mundin stood up.

"May it please the Court," said Mundin. That *look* again. "My client has not been a fortunate man. The product of a broken home and the gutters of Belly Rave, he deserves justice as does every citizen. But in his case I am impelled to add that the ends of justice can be served only by an admixture of mercy."

Judge and prosecutor were smiling openly. The hell with dignity! Mundin craned his neck to read the crisp yellow tape that came clicking out of the clerk's encoding machine. He could more or less read jury-box code if it was simple enough.

The encoded transcript of his summation was simple enough. The tape said:

O-O . . . O-O . . . O-O . . .

"Defense rests," he mumbled and fell into his chair, ignoring a despairing mutter from the twerp.

The judge said, "Mr. Clerk, present the case to the jury box.

2

The clerk briskly fed in the two tapes. The jury box hummed and twinkled. If only you could fix one of those things! Mundin thought savagely, staring at the big seal on it. Or if you could get one of those damned clerks to cut the tape—no, that was out too. They were voluntarily conditioned. Like voluntary eunuchs in the old days. Gave up manhood for a sure living.

The red window lit up: GUILTY AS CHARGED.

"Work!" the twerp muttered, his eyes haunted.

The judge said, shifting his wig and showing a bit of earphone under it, "Mr. Bailiff, take charge of the prisoner. Sentencing tomorrow at eleven. Court's adjourned."

The twerp moaned, "I hate them damn machines. Couldn't you have got me a human jury, maybe get an injunction——"

Mundin said wearily, "A human jury would have crucified you. Why did you have to steal from the Stadium? Why not pick on something safe like the Church or the judge's piggy bank? See you tomorrow." He turned his back on the defendant and bumped into Harvard Law.

"Nice try, young man." The grandee smiled frostily. "Can't win them all, can we?"

Mundin snarled, "If you're so smart why aren't you a corporation lawyer?" and stamped out of the courtroom.

He was on the street before he regretted the crack. Harvard's face had fallen satisfactorily, but the jibe was another O-O. Why, indeed? The same reason Mundin himself wasn't, of course. He hadn't inherited one of the great hereditary corporation-law practices and he never would. Even grinding through Harvard Law School can't get you conveniently reborn into the Root, or Lincoln, or Dulles, or Choate families. Not for Harvard (or for Charles Mundin) the great reorganizations, receiverships, and debenture issues. Not for them the mergers and protective committees. Not for them the golden showers that fell when you pleaded before human judges and human juries, human surrogates and human commissions. For them—the jury box and the trivia of the criminal law.

A morose fifteen-minute walk through Monmouth's sweltering, rutted streets brought him to his office building. His wallet nerve twinged as his eye fell on the quietly proud little plaque beside the door of the building. It announced that its rental agents were sorry but could offer no vacancies. Mundin hoped it would stay that way, at least as far as his own office was concerned.

He got an elevator to himself. "Sixteen," he told it. He was thinking of his first client, the twerp. At least he would get a fee; you got a fee on conditionable cases. The twerp was terrified that he'd find himself unable to steal. Maybe Counselor Mundin himself might soon be driven to dangling a hook and line over the wall of a ticket window at Monmouth Stadium. . . .

Or he might get really desperate, and find himself one of the contestants in the Field Day inside.

His mail hopper was empty, but his guaranteed fully automatic Sleepless Secretary—he was still paying for it—was blinking for his attention. The rental agents again? Lawbook salesman? Maybe even a client? "Go ahead," he said.

In its perfect voice the machine said: "Telephone call, 1205 hours. Mr. Mundin is out, Madam. If you wish to leave a message I will take it down."

The voice was the voice of Del Dworcas, chairman of the County Committee and purveyor of small favors. It said: "Who the hell are you calling madam, sister?"

The secretary: "Gug-gug-*gug*—ow-*wooh*. Sir."

Dworcas, his voice annoyed: "What the hell——? Oh. One of those damn gadgets. Well, listen, Charlie, if you ever get this. I sent somebody over to see you. Named Bligh. Treat him right. And give me a call. Something to talk about with you. And you better get that damn machine fixed unless you want to lose some business."

The secretary, after a pause: "Is that the end of your message, madam?"

Dworcas: "Damn your guts, yes! And stop calling me madam!"

The secretary: "Gug-gug-*gug*—ow-*woooh*." And *click*.

Oh, fine, thought Mundin. Now Dworcas was sore at him and nothing could be done about it. The secretary's confusion between the sexes and banshee howl didn't seem to be covered by the service contract.

And Dworcas was chairman of the County Committee,

4

which handed out poll-watching assignments to deserving young attorneys.

The mailtube popped while he was blaspheming Dworcas and the salesman who had flattered him into buying the secretary. He eagerly fished the letter from its hopper, but when he caught sight of the return address he dropped it unopened. The Scholarship Investors' Realization Corporation could have nothing of interest to say to him; he knew he owed them the money, and he knew by virtue of the law course they had paid for that they couldn't do anything drastic to make him pay.

Then there was nothing to do until someone showed up—this Bligh or the man from the sheriff's office. Sing hey for the life of a lawyer, gabbling at machines you naggingly suspected thought you were not so bright as they were.

The Sleepless Secretary said: "Sir or madam as the case may be. Gug-gug-*gug*. Regret to advise." Mundin kicked it savagely. It burped and said: "A gentleman is in the outer office, Mrs. Mundin."

"Come in!" Mundin yelled at the door. Then he said, "Oh, excuse me. Mr. Bligh?"

The man blinked at him and came in cautiously. He looked around and picked out a chair. He wore a hearing aid, Mundin noticed; perhaps that was why he cocked his head a little.

He said, "That's right; Norvell Bligh. I—uh—asked Mr. Dworcas if he could recommend a first-class attorney and he—uh—suggested you."

Mundin said aloofly, "What can I do for you?"

"Well." Bligh's eyes roamed nervously around the room. "My wife—that is, I would like to get some information on adoption. I have a step-daughter—my wife's daughter by her first marriage, you see—and, well, my wife thinks we should arrange about adopting her."

Good old Del Dworcas, Mundin thought savagely. He *knows* I belong to the Criminal Bar, and he goes right ahead ——He said, "I'm sorry, Mr. Bligh. I can't help you. You'll have to find a civil attorney to handle that for you."

Bligh touched the control of his hearing aid. "Beg pardon?"

"I said," Mundin enunciated loudly, "I—can't—do—it."

"Oh, I know you can't," Bligh said. "Mr. Dworcas explained that. But he said that the civil attorneys would charge an awful lot, and you—— That is, since you were a friend of his and I was a friend of his brother, it would be done on a friendly basis. All I need to know, really, is what to do. I don't think I'd have to have a lawyer in court, do you?"

Mundin pondered hopefully. "Maybe not." It was questionable practice, no doubt of it, and small thanks to Dworcas for getting him into it. Still, if it was just a matter of advice and information—thank God, the corporation boys didn't have *that* sewed up yet.

He leaned back, covertly looking Bligh over. Not the most imposing figure he had seen, but tolerably well dressed, certainly not a deadbeat. He'd be some kind of contract worker, no doubt, getting his regular pay, living in a G.M.L. house, suffering his wife's obvious nagging. Mundin said:

"Tell me the story. First of all, how much—? That is, the court will want to be sure you can earn enough to support the child."

"Well, I've *been* supporting her for three years. Excuse me, Mr. Mundin, but can we keep this short? I'm on my lunch hour, and Mr. Candella is very fussy about that."

"Certainly. Just give me the facts—age of the child, where the father is and so on."

Bligh coughed self-consciously. He said, "My name is Norvell Bligh. I'm an associate producer for General Recreations, in charge of Field Day procurement, mostly. My wife is named Virginia. She was married before I met her to a man named Tony Elliston. They—uh—didn't get along too well. It was a pretty tough experience for her. They had one daughter, Alexandra. Virginia and her first husband, they got divorced, but I understand he's dead now. Anyway, she got custody, complete. I have the papers here. Alexandra is ten now. Is that all?"

Mundin scribbled rapidly—purely pretense, since the Sleepless Secretary was recording the whole thing automatically. On second thought, he told himself, maybe not pretense at that. "That's enough for the time being," he said. "I'll have to look up—have to discuss this matter with one of my colleagues. If you would care to come back, say, Friday at this time? Fine."

As Bligh left, looking vaguely alarmed, the Sleepless Secretary told him. "Pending the receipt. Ow-*woooh*. Mrs. Mundin is out of town."

Mundin turned it off.

Two clients in one day, he thought wonderingly. Anything was possible. Perhaps he wouldn't, after all, have to let the factory reclaim the secretary and the Scholarship people garnishee his salary and the landlord toss him out on the street.

Perhaps.

Chapter Two

HE DIDN'T seem to be much of a lawyer, Norvie Bligh told himself on the way back to his office, but at least this fellow Mundin probably wouldn't charge much. Arnie had as much as promised him that; Arnie had said, "You go see my brother, Norvie. Del's quite an important man and, if you don't mind my saying so, one of the most powerful minds in government today. He'll put you on the track of somebody good. And he'll make the price right, too."

Anyway, who needed a legal eagle to put adoption papers through? The whole thing was pretty silly. If only Ginny weren't so touchy lately, you could explain to her that it was just an unwarranted expense, nobody was going to take Alexandra away from them; there wasn't even any question about inheriting if he died.

He tasted that for a moment. Virginia had certainly seemed to take that part of it seriously, he thought. She had mentioned it half a dozen times: "Don't forget to ask him about inheriting." And, of course, he had forgotten. Well, there would be another chance on Friday.

And you couldn't blame Virginia if she was a little, well, insecure. Life with that Tony must have been pure hell, living in Belly Rave from hand to mouth, no future, no security. That was why she was such a devoted wife now.

Of *course* she was a devoted wife now, he told himself.

Right now, though, the important thing was whether Candella was going to say anything about his being fifteen minutes late. Candella was pretty difficult lately. Of course, you couldn't blame him; he was naturally jumpy with the big fall Field Day coming up and all.

Of course you couldn't blame Candella. Of course you couldn't blame Virginia, or Arnie when his promises didn't jell, or Alexandra when she was a little touchy, like any ten-year-old, of course.

Of course you couldn't blame anybody for anything. Not if you were Norvell Bligh.

Fortunately, Candella didn't notice what time he came back from lunch. But in the middle of the afternoon his secretary came worriedly out to Norvie's desk and said, "Mr. Candella would like to discuss your Field Day program with you."

He went in with a feeling of uneasiness, well justified.

Old Man Candella slapped the papers down and roared:

"Bligh, maybe you think a Field Day is a Boy Scout rally where the kids shoot arrows and run footraces around the tennis court. Is that right? Maybe you think it's a Ladies' Aid pink tea. Maybe you just don't know what a Field Day is supposed to be, Bligh. Is that it?"

Norvie swallowed. "No, sir," he whispered.

"'No, sir,'" Candella mimicked. "'No, sir.' Well, if you do know what a Field Day is, why doesn't it show? Why isn't there at least one good, exciting idea in this whole bloody script? I take back that word 'bloody,' Bligh. I got to give you that, nobody would say this script was bloody. There might be some complaints in the other direction, but I guarantee there wouldn't be any complaints that there was too much blood." He jabbed at the program with a hairy forefinger. "Listen to this. 'Opening pageant: Procession of jeeps through gauntlet of spearmen. First spectacle. Fifty girl wrestlers versus fifty male boxers. First duet: Sixty-year-old men with blowtorches.' Ah, what's the use of going on? This is supposed to be the big event of the year, Bligh, did you know that? It isn't a Friday-night show in the off season. This is the one that counts. It's got to be *special*."

Norvie Bligh shifted miserably. "Gosh, Mr. Candella, I—I thought it was. It's a classical motif, do you see? It's like——"

"I can tell what it's like," Candella bellowed. "I've been producing these shows for fifteen years. I don't need anybody to tell me whether a script will play or it won't. And I'm

8

telling you this one won't." He stabbed a button on his console. Norvie felt the seat lurch warningly underneath him, and scrambled to his feet as it disappeared into the wall. "Take this script away," Candella growled. "We've got to start casting on Monday. Let's see if we can have something above the level of an Odd Fellows' smoker tomorrow night." He didn't even look up as Norvie cringed out the door.

The whole afternoon was like that.

Norvie dictated and erased five tapes. He sent his three assistants on three different errands of research, to find the best spectacle on the highest-rated Field Days in every major city. Nothing they brought back was any help. When Miss Dali came in to pick up the afternoon's dictation and he had to face the fact that there was no afternoon's dictation, he grumbled to her:

"What do they expect in that moldy gym they call a stadium here? Look at Pittsburgh—we're twice as big, and *they* have armored halftracks."

"Yes, sir," said Miss Dali. "Mr. Stimmens would like to see you."

"All right," he said ungraciously, and dialed a chair for his junior scriptwriter.

"Excuse me, chief," Stimmens said hesitantly. "Can I see you for a moment?"

"You're seeing me," Norvie had picked that bon mot up from Candella the week before.

Stimmens hesitated, then spoke much too rapidly. "You've got a great organization here, chief, and I'm proud to be a part of it. But I'm having a little trouble—you know, trying to get ahead, hah-hah—and I wonder if it wouldn't be better for you chief, as well as me if——" He went through a tortuous story of a classification clerk's mistake when he finished school and an opening in Consumer Relations and a girl who wouldn't marry him until he got a Grade Fifteen rating.

Long before Stimmens had come anywhere near the point, Norvie knew what he wanted and knew what the answer had to be; but Candella's bruises were fresh on his back and he let Stimmens go on till he was dry. Then, briskly:

"Stimmens, if I'm not in error, you signed the regular contract before you joined us. It has——"

9

"Well, yes sir, but——"

"*It has*, I say, the usual provision for cancelation. I believe you know the company's policy in regard to selling contracts. We simply cannot afford to sell unless the purchase price is high enough to reimburse us for the employee's training time —which, I might say, in your case is all the time you've spent with us, since you have clearly failed to master your job. I'm surprised you come to me with a request like that."

Stimmens looked at him. "You won't let me go?"

"I *can't* let you go. *You're* at liberty to cancel your contract."

Stimmens laughed shortly. "Cancel! And go back to Belly Rave? Mr. Bligh, have you ever been in Belly Rave?" He shook his head like a man dispelling a nightmare. "Well, sorry, Mr. Bligh," he said. "Anything else for me to do today?"

Norvie looked undecided at his watch. "Tomorrow," he growled. As Stimmens slumped away, Norvie, already feeling ashamed of himself, petulantly swept the chair back into the wall.

It was almost quitting time.

He made a phone call: "Mr. Arnold Dworcas, please. Arnie? Hello; how're you? Fine. Say, I saw that attorney of your brother's today. Looks like everything will be all right. Uh-huh. Thanks a lot, Arnie. This evening? Sure, I was hoping you'd ask me. All right if I go home first?—Ginny'll want to hear about the lawyer. About eight, then. S'long. . . ."

Arnie Dworcas had a way of interminably chewing a topic and regurgitating it in flavorless pellets of words. Lately he had been preoccupied with what he called the ingratitude of the beneficiaries of science. At their frequent get-togethers he would snarl at Norvie:

"Not that it matters to Us Engineers. Don't think I take it personally just because I happen to be essential to the happiness and comfort of everybody in the city. No, Norvie, We Engineers don't expect a word of thanks. We Engineers work because there's a job to do, and we're trained for it. But that doesn't alter the fact that people are lousy ingrates."

At which point Norvie would cock his head a little in the nervous reflex he had acquired with the hearing aid and agree: "Of course, Arnie. Hell, fifty years ago when the first bubble-cities went up women used to burst out crying when they got a look at one. My mother did. Coming out of Belly Rave, knowing she'd never have to go back—she says she bawled like a baby when the domes came in sight."

And Arnie: "Yeah. Not that that's evidence, as We Engineers understand evidence. It's just your untrained recollection of what an untrained woman told you. But it gives you an idea of how those lousy ingrates settled down and got smug. They'd change their tune damn fast if We Engineers weren't on the job. But you're an artist, Norvell. You can't be expected to understand." And he would gloomily drink beer.

Going home from work and looking forward to seeing his best friend later that night, Norvie was not so sure he didn't understand. He even felt a little grieved that Arnie had insisted on it. He even felt inclined to argue that he wasn't an artist like some crackpot oil painter or novelist in a filthy Belly Rave hovel, but a technician in his own right. Well, kind of; his medium was the emotional fluxes of a Field Day crowd rather than torques, forces, and electrons.

He had an important job, Norvie told himself: Associate Producer, Monmouth Stadium Field Days. Of course, Arnie far outstripped him in title. Arnie was Engineer Supervising Rotary and Reciprocal Pump Installations and Maintenance for Monmouth G.M.L. City. . . .

Not that Arnie was the kind of guy to stand on rank. Hell, look at how Arnie was always doing things for you—like finding you a lawyer when you needed one—and—well, he was *always* doing things for you. It was a privilege to know a man like Arnie Dworcas.

Knowing a fellow like Arnie made life a great deal more enjoyable for a fellow like Norvie.

Norvie smiled internally at the thought of Arnie, right up to the moment when he arrived at the door of his bubble-house and the scanner recognized him and opened the door, and he went in to join his wife and child.

Chapter Three

CHARLES MUNDIN, LL.B., entered Republican Hall through the back way.

He found Del Dworcas in the balcony—the Hall was a busted, slightly remodeled movie house—telling the cameramen how to place their cameras, the sound men how to line up their parabolic mikes and the electricians how to use their lights. For that was the kind of hairpin Del Dworcas was.

Mundin stood on the sidelines faintly hoping that one of the cameramen would take out a few of Dworcas's front teeth with a tripod leg, but they kept their tempers admirably. He sighed and tapped the chairman on the shoulder.

Dworcas gave him the big hello and asked him to wait in the manager's office for him—he had to get these TV people squared away, but it wouldn't take more than a few minutes. "Did you see that fellow Bligh?" he asked. "Yeah? Good. Soak him, Charlie; you got to make a living, you know. Some friend of my kid brother's. Now go on down to the office. Couple of people there for you to talk to." He looked palpably mysterious.

Mundin sighed again; but that, too, was the kind of hairpin Del Dworcas was. At the foot of the stairs he yelled in astonishment: "Great God Almighty! Prince Wilhelm the Fourth!"

William Choate IV jerked around and looked confused, then stuck out a hand for Mundin to grasp. He was a pudgy little man of Mundin's age, classmate from John Marshall, heir to a mighty corporate practice, tidy dresser, former friend, solid citizen, four-star jerk. "Why, hello, Charles," he said uncertainly. "Good to see you."

"Likewise. What are *you* doing here?"

Choate made a mighty effort and produced a shrug. "Oh," he said, "you know."

"Meaning that even a corporation lawyer has political dealings once in a while?" Mundin helped him out.

12

"That's it exactly!" Choate was pleased; it was just like old times. Mundin had always helped him out, all the way through John Marshall Law.

Mundin looked at his former protégé with emotions that were only distantly related to envy. "It's a pleasure to run into you, Willie," he said. "They keeping you busy?"

"Busy? Whew! You'll never know, Charles." That was an unfortunate remark, Mundin admitted to himself. Busy——

"You know the I. G. Farben reorganization?"

"By reputation," Mundin said bitterly. "I'm in criminal practice right now. Incidentally, I had an interesting case to-day——"

"Yes," Choate said. "Well, you might say I've won my spurs. The old man made me counsel for the Group E Debenture Holder's Protective Committee. Old Haskell died in harness, you know. Think of it—forty years as counsel for the Protective Committee! And with a hearing before the Referee in Receivership coming up. Well, I won my spurs, as you might say. I argued before the referee this morning, and I got a four-year stay!"

"Well," Charles Mundin said. "To use a figure of speech, you certainly won your spurs, didn't you?"

"I thought you'd see it that way," Choate beamed. "I simply pointed out to old Rodeheaver that rushing through an immediate execution of receivership would work a hardship on the committee, and I asked for more time to prepare our suits for the trust offices. Old Rodeheaver just thought it over and decided it would be in the public interest to grant a stay. And, Charles, he congratulated me on my presentation! He said he had never heard the argument read better!"

"Well done," said Charles. It was impossible to resent this imbecile. A faint spark of technical interest made him ask, "How did you prove hardship?"

Choate waved airily. "Oh, that was easy. We have this smart little fellow in the office, some kind of cousin of mine, I guess. He handles all the briefs. A real specialist; not much at the "big picture," you know, but very good in his field. He could prove old Green, Charlesworth were starving in the gutter if you told him to. I'm joking, of course," he added hastily.

Poor Willie, thought Mundin. Too dumb for Harvard Law,

too dumb for Columbia, though he was rich enough to buy and sell them both. That's how he wound up at John Marshall, a poor man's school which carried him for eight years of conditions and repeats until sheer attrition of memorizing had worn grooves in his brain that carried him through his exams. Mundin had written most of his papers, and nothing but goodheartedness and a gentle, sheep's gaze had got him through the orals.

And poor dumb Willie glowed, "You know what that little job is worth? The firm's putting in for two hundred and twenty-five thousand dollars, Charles! And as counsel for record I get half!"

That did it. Mundin licked his lips. "Willie," he said hoarsely, "Willie——"

He cut it off there. His mind played out the conversation to its end: The abject begging, *Willie, you owe me something, give me a job, I can be a smart little fellow as well as anybody's cousin.* And the dismally embarrassed, *Gosh, Charles, be fair, the old man would never understand, what would you do if you were in my place?*

Hopeless, Mundin knew the answer. In Willie's place, he would keep the lucrative practice of corporate law right in the grip of the Choate family. He would sit on top of his practice with a shotgun in his lap. And if anybody tried to take it away from him he would blast with both barrels and then club him with the butt until he stopped twitching. . . .

"Yes, Charles?" Willie was patient and expectant.

"Nothing," said Mundin heavily. "You were saying there's more work to do?"

"More work?" Willie beamed. "Why, with any luck I'll hand the Group E Debenture Holders' Protective Committee down to William Choate the Fifth! The reorganization's only been going for forty-three years. Soon lots of principals in the case will be dead, and then we'll have trusts and estates in the picture. Sub-committees! Sub-sub-committees! I tell you, Charles, it's great to be on the firing line of the law."

"Thank you, Willie," Mundin said gently. "Must you go now?"

Willie said, "Must I? Oh. Yes, I guess I must. It's been good seeing you, Charles. Keep up the good work."

Mundin stared impotently at his pudgy back. Then he

14

turned wearily and went on to Dworcas's office, not very optimistically. But it was the only thing he could think of to do, apart from suicide. And he wasn't ready for that, yet.

Dworcas had still not arrived. The manager's office, back of the closed-up ticket booth, was tiny and crowded with bales of literature. The people waiting there were a young man and a young woman, obviously brother and sister. Big sister, kid brother; they were maybe twenty-eight and twenty-two.

The girl got up from behind one of the battered desks. Mannish. No lipstick, cropped hair, green slacks, a loose plaid shirt. She gripped his hand crunchingly.

"I'm Norma Lavin," she said. "Mr. Mundin?"

"Yes." Mannish. Now, why was good old Del passing this screwball on to him?

"This is my brother Don."

"Pleased to meet you." Don Lavin had something weird and something familiar about him. His eyes drew attention. Mundin had often read of "shining eyes" and accepted it as one of those things you read that don't mean anything. Now he was disconcerted to find that he was looking into a pair of eyes that did shine.

"Please sit down," he said to them, clearing a chair for himself. He decided it was simply Lavin's habit to blink infrequently. It made his eyes look varnished, gave the youngster a peering, fanatic look.

The girl said, "Mr. Dworcas tells us you're a lawyer, Mr. Mundin, as well as a valuable political associate."

"Yes," he said. He automatically handed her one of the fancy penny-each cards from his right breast pocket. Don Lavin looked somewhat as if he had been *conditioned*. That was it. Like a court clerk or one of the participants in a Field Day—or, he guessed, a criminal after the compulsory third-rap treatment.

"Yes," he said. "I'm a lawyer. I wouldn't swear to that other part."

"Umph," she said. "You're the best we can do. We got nowhere in Washington, we got nowhere in Chicago, we got nowhere in New York. We'll try local courts here. Dworcas passed us on to you. Well, we have to start *somewhere*."

"Somewhere," her brother dreamily agreed.

15

"Look, Miss Lavin," Mundin began.

"Just Lavin."

"Okay. Lavin, or Spike, or Butch, or whatever you want me to call you. If you're through with the insults, will you tell me what you want?"

Del Dworcas stuck his head in the door. "You people getting along okay? Fine!" He vanished again.

The girl said, "We want to retain you as attorney for a stockholders' committee. The G.M.L. Homes thing."

G.M.L. Homes, Mundin thought, irritated. That's silly. G.M.L.—why, that means the bubble-houses. Not just the houses, of course—the bubble-cities, too; the real estate in practically continental lots; the private roads, the belt lines, the power reactors. . . .

"Nonsense." It wasn't a very funny joke.

The shiny-eyed boy said abruptly, "The 'L' stands for Lavin. Did you know that?"

Something kicked Mundin in the stomach. He grunted. Suppose—just suppose, now—that maybe it isn't a joke, he thought detachedly. Ridiculous, of course, but just suppose——

G.M.L. Homes.

Such things didn't happen to Charles Mundin, LL.D. To squash it once and for all, he said, flat out, "I'm not licensed to practice corporate law, you know. Try William Choate the Fourth; he was——"

"We just did. He said no."

They make it sound real, Mundin thought admiringly. Of course, it couldn't be. Somewhere in the rules it was written down inexpungibly: *Charles Mundin will never get a fat case.* Therefore this thing would piffle out, of course.

"Well?" demanded the girl.

"I said I'm not licensed to practice corporate law."

"That's all right," the girl said contemptuously. "Did you think we didn't know that? We have an old banger we dug up who still has his license. He can't work, but we can use his name as attorney of record."

Well. He began hazily. "It's naturally interesting——"

She interrupted. "Naturally, Mundin, naturally. Will you get the hell off the dime? Yes or no. Tell us."

Dworcas stuck his head in again. "Mundin. I'm awfully

sorry, but I've got to have the office for a while. Why don't you and your friends go over for a cup of coffee?"

Hussein's place across the street was pretty full, but they found a low table on the aisle.

The old-timers stared with dull, insulting curiosity at the strange face of Don Lavin. The kids in zoot hats with five-inch brims looked once and then looked away quickly. You didn't stare at a man who had obviously been conditioned. Not any more than in the old days you stared at the cropped ears of a convicted robber or asked a eunuch what it was like.

Norma Lavin got no stares at all. Young and old, the customers looked coldly right through her. The Ay-rabs blamed women like her for the disconcerting way their own women were changing under their very eyes.

Hussein himself came over. "Always a pleasure, Mr. Ur-murm," he beamed. "What will you have?"

"Coffee, please," Mundin said. Don Lavin shook his head absently. Norma said nothing.

"*Majun* for the lady?" Hussein asked blandly. "Fresh from Mexico this week. Very strong. Peppermint, raspberry, grape?"

Norma Lavin icily said, "*No.*" Hussein went away beaming. He had delivered a complicated triple insult—by calling her a lady, offering her a narcotic and, at that, a narcotic traditionally beloved by Islamic ladies denied the consolation of love by ugliness or age.

Mundin masked his nervousness by studying his watch. "We have about ten minutes," he said. "If you can give me an idea of what you have in mind——"

Somebody coming down the aisle stumbled over Don Lavin's foot.

"I beg your pardon," Lavin said dreamily.

"What's the idea of tripping me?" asked a bored voice. It was a cop—a big man with an intelligent, humorous face.

"It was an accident, officer," Mundin said.

"Here we go again," Norma Lavin muttered.

"I was talking to this gentleman, I believe," the cop said. He asked Don Lavin again, "I said, what's the idea of tripping me? You a cop-hater or something?"

"I'm really very sorry," Lavin said. "Please accept my apology."

17

"He won't," Norma Lavin said to Mundin, aside.

"Officer," Mundin said sharply, "it was an accident. I'm Charles Mundin. Former candidate for the Council in the 27th, Regular Republican. I'll vouch for this gentleman."

"Yes, your Honor," the cop said, absently saluting. He turned to Lavin. "Suppose we show some identification, cop-hater."

Lavin took out a wallet and spilled cards on the table. The cop inspected them and muttered: "Dreadful. Dreadful. Social Security account card says you're Donald W. Lavin, but Selective Service registration says you're Don Lavin, no middle initial. And I see your draft registration is with an Omaha board but you have a resident's parking permit for Coshocton, Ohio. Tell me, did you ever notify Omaha that you're a resident of Coshocton?"

"Of course he did," Mundin said quickly.

Lavin said dreamily. "I'm extremely sorry, officer. I didn't. I registered in Omaha because I happened to be passing through on my eighteenth birthday. I simply never got around to changing."

The cop decisively scooped up the cards and said, "You'd better come along with me, Lavin. Your career of crime has gone far enough. It's a lucky thing I tripped over you."

Mundin noted that he had dropped the pretense of having been tripped. "Officer," he said, "I'm taking your shield number. I'm going to tell my very good friend Del Dworcas about this nonsense. Shortly after that, you'll find yourself on foot patrol in Belly Rave—the two-to-ten shift. Unless you care to apologize and get the hell out of here."

The officer grinned and shrugged. "What can I do?" he asked helplessly. "I'm a regular Javert. When I see the law broken, my blood boils. Come along, Dangerous Don."

Lavin smiled meagerly at his sister, who sat with a thunder-cloud scowl on her brow, and went along.

Mundin's voice was shaking with anger. "Don't worry," he told Norma Lavin. "I'll have him out of the station house right after the meeting. And that cop is going to wish he hadn't been born."

"Never mind. I'll get him out," she said. "Five times in three weeks. I'm used to it."

"What's the angle?" Mundin exploded.

18

Hussein came up with coffee in little cups. "Nice fella, that Jimmy Lyons," he said chattily. "For cop, that is."

"Who is he?" Mundin snapped.

"Precinct captain's man. Very good to know. The uniform is just patrolman, but when you talk to Jimmy Lyons you talk right into the precinct captain's ear. If you pay shakedown and two days later other cop comes around for more shakedown, you tell Jimmy Lyons. The cop gets transferred to Belly Rave. Maybe worse. You know," Hussein grinned confidentially, "before I come to America everybody tells me how different from Iraq. But once here—not so different."

Norma Lavin stood up and said, "I'm going to get my brother sprung before they start switching him around the precincts again." Her voice was leaden. "I suppose this is the end of the road, Mundin. But if you still want to consider taking our case, here's the address. Unfortunately there's no phone." She hesitated.

She began, "I hope you'll——" It was almost a cry for help. She bit off the words, dropped a coin and a card on the table and strode from the coffee shop. The Ay-rabs looked icily through her as she went.

Mundin managed to see Dworcas for a minute. "Del," he said, "what's with these Lavin people? What do you know about them?"

Dworcas's face was open and friendly—Mundin knew how little that could be relied on. "Not much, Charlie. They wanted a lawyer. We've worked together; I thought of you."

"Right after you thought of Willie Choate?"

Dworcas was patient. "What the hell, Charlie? Choate wouldn't touch it, I knew that. But they wanted to talk to somebody big."

"Sure." Mundin hesitated, but already Dworcas was beginning to pick at papers on his desk. "Del, one thing. Some cop named Jimmy Lyons picked the boy up in Hussein's, no reason that I could see. The—the boy was conditioned, I think."

"Um. *Jimmy* Lyons? He's the captain's man. I'll call." Dworcas called, while Mundin thought about the complications of life on the firing-line of the law. There had not been, at John Marshall, a course in How to Get Along with Wardheelers. But there should have been, thought Mundin, there should have been. Let us put you up to take a fall in the year when we aren't going to win the Council, and your name turns up on the slate of poll-watchers. Give us a hand at speeches, and when a case drops in our lap, we'll think of you. . . . Dworcas came up smiling.

"The sister bailed him out. They just wanted to cool him off—the kid gave Lyons some lip, evidently, and Lyons got sore. What the hell, cops are human."

"Del, the kid didn't give Lyons any lip. Lyons was looking for it."

"Sure, Charlie, sure." Del's eyes were beginning to rove. Mundin let him go.

He plucked the girl's card out of his pocket and turned it over, bemused. G.M.L. Homes, he thought. Corporate practice. A shrewd, hard cop looking for trouble. It's not generally known that the "L" stands for Lavin.

And a cry for help.

The card said *Norma Lavin*, with an address in Coshocton, Ohio, and a phone number. These were scratched out, and written in was *37598 Willowdale Crescent*.

An address in Belly Rave!

Mundin shook his head slowly and worriedly. But there had been a cry for help.

Chapter Four

IT HAD BEEN a trying evening for Norvie Bligh. When he walked in on Virginia and the girl they had been perfectly normal—sullen. His news about the lawyer, Mundin, and the prospects of adopting Alexandra had produced the natural effect: "You forgot to ask about the *inheritance*. Leave it to Norvie! He'd forget his Social Security number if it wasn't tattooed on him."

Before he finished dinner he was driven to the point of getting up and stalking out.

It wasn't anything they *said*. It was just that neither of them said anything to *him*. Not even when, pushed past the threshold of control, he had shrieked at his wife and slapped the child.

But there was always Arnie.

He killed time for half an hour—Arnie didn't like it if you got there too early; hell, you couldn't blame him for that—and then hurried. He was almost out of breath as he got to Dworcas's door.

And Arnie was warmly friendly. Norvell began at last to relax.

It wasn't just a matter of plenty of beer and the friendly feeling of being with someone you liked. Arnie was going out of his way, Norvell saw at once, to get at the roots of Norvell's problems. As soon as they had had a couple of beers he turned the conversation to Norvell's work. "They must be really beginning to roll on the Field Day," he speculated.

Norvell expanded. "Sure. I've got some pretty spectacular things lined up for it, too," he said modestly. "Of course, Candella hasn't given me the final go-ahead"—he frowned at a submerged memory—"but it's going to be quite a program. One gets a big charge out of doing one's best on a big job, Arnie. I guess you know that. I remember a couple of years ago——"

Dworcas interrupted. "More beer?" He dialed refills. "Your place has quite a good reputation," he said with sober approval. "This afternoon, in the shop, We Engineers were talking about the technical factors involved."

"You were?" Norvell was pleased. "That's interesting, Arnie. This time I was talking about——"

"Especially the big shows," Dworcas went on. "The Field Days. Say, you know what would be interesting, Norvell? Getting a couple of the fellows to go to one, to see just how the thing looked from the engineering viewpoint. I'd like to go myself—if I could get away, of course; we're pretty busy these days. Might invite a few of the others to come along."

"You would?" Norvell cried. "Say, that would be fine. There's a lot of engineering connected with a Field Day. Like this time a couple of years——"

"Excuse me," Arnie interrupted. "Beer. Be right back."

While Dworcas was gone, Norvell felt actually cheerful. Arnie was *so* concerned with his work; you didn't find many

21

friends like Arnie. Warmed by the beer, Norvell re-examined his recent blinding depression. Hell, things weren't too bad. Ginny was a bitch, he told himself. All right, so she's a bitch. Lots of men live with bitches and make out all right. Besides, if a woman's a bitch doesn't it say something about the man she's married to? And the kid, of course. Kids reflect what's around them. And as for Candella— he thought briefly about Candella, and retreated tc the safer ground. Virginia. Suppose he went back home tonight, not saying a word of anger or reproach—— No, it was better to have things out. Well, suppose he went right up—she'd be asleep—well, went right up and woke her up. "Ginny," he could say, "we've made a lot of mistakes." Cancel that. "Ginny, I've made a lot of mistakes, but I love you. I want to live happily with you." He thought for a second, then amended it: "With you and Alexandra." Maybe he should wake up Alexandra too.

He had almost decided to have a swift cup of black coffee and go home when Arnie came back. Dworcas entered, beaming.

"Well, what say, Emotional Engineer? Want a couple of real live slide-rulers to look over your show?"

"What? Oh, sure, Arnie. Just let me get this Field Day out of the way. We'll throw a real party—one of the Friday-night shows. There's a lot of complicated stuff under the stadium; you'd be interested——"

Dworcas was pursing his lips. "I don't know," he said thoughtfully, "if the fellows would be interested in one of the second-rate shows. Maybe we ought to skip it."

"No, no," Norvell said earnestly. "The regular shows are just as interesting technically. Why, just last week something came up. You'll be interested in this, Arnie. We had a broken-field run—barbed wire and castrator mines—and, half an hour before the show started, the director came around crying that he didn't have enough men for the spectacle. Well, Candella—that is, we—put in a quick call to the cops and they sent a squad down to Belly Rave. Got twenty-five volunteers in fifteen minutes. The orderlies lined 'em up and gave them million-unit injections of B_1." He chuckled. "Arnie, you should have seen some of those guys when they sobered up. We——"

Arnie was shaking his head. "I don't think you understand," he said seriously. "That sort of thing isn't what We Engineers are interested in. It's the big effects."

"Oh. You mean like in the Field Day next week." Norvell thought vaguely about the Field Day. "Yeah," he said uncertainly, "There certainly are plenty of headaches when you run a Field Day. Can I have another beer, please?"

As he dialed another glass, Dworcas said sunnily, "Suppose you can fit us in, then? After all, you've got eighty thousand seats. There ought to be five somewhere that the man who runs the whole damn thing can give to a friend."

"Sure," Norvell mumbled. "Uh—now it's my turn. Excuse me, Arnie. All right?"

When he came back the room wasn't spinning quite so dizzily, but the warmth in his body wasn't so gratifying either.

He stared so long at the glass of beer by his chair that Arnie thought it was flat and pressed a replenishment button. "Oh, thanks," Norvell said, startled.

He picked up the glass and took a sip, then put it down hard. Half of it slopped over. Over the whistle of the suction cleaners draining the spilled beer, Norvell said with sudden misery, "Arnie, I'm in trouble."

Dworcas froze. After a moment, he said carefully, "Trouble?"

"Yes, trouble. The dirtiest, damnedest, lowest-down trouble I've ever been in in my life. It scares me, Arnie. I swear to God, if it weren't for people like you—hell, if it weren't for you *personally*—I don't know what I'd do. Arnie, I think I'm going to go out of my head! It isn't just one thing, it's everything. The job, the wife, that slimy little kid—everything." He told Dworcas about the grisly dinner with his wife and stepdaughter; about the countless run-ins with Candella; about all of the fights and frustrations that had come to him. "The worst was this morning, just before I went to that lawyer. Candella—God, I could've killed him! Or myself. I was reaming out that little punk Stimmens when Candella walked into the room. He must've heard every word I said, because when I turned around and saw him he said, 'Excellent advice, Mr. Bligh, I hope you'll follow it yourself.' And Stimmens just stood there laughing at me. I couldn't do a thing. For two cents I would have gone in and asked him for my contract."

Dworcas nodded precisely. "Perhaps you should have," he said gravely.

23

"What? Oh, no, Arnie, you don't understand. General Recreations is lousy on that. They won't sell unless they can get their pound of flesh and plenty more besides. We had a vice-president once, a couple of years ago, got in dutch with the board and wanted out. Well, they set a price of *four hundred thousand dollars* on his contract. He had some rich relatives, I guess, or anyway he got some money somewhere and tried to bribe another firm to buy him, but of course they wouldn't pay that kind of money. He had a family, couldn't give up his job, give up his house, just like that, you know. He killed himself, finally. It was that or cancel."

"That's a point to remember, Norvell. In any engineering problem there are always two components, at least, to any vector."

Norvell chewed his lip a second. "Oh, I see what you mean," he said unconvincingly. "There's no way out."

Dworcas shook his head. "No, Norvell, that's what I just said. There are *always* two ways out."

Norvell said, "Well——"

"At the shop," Arnie said, leaning back, "these problems don't arise, of course. Not like with you temperamental artists. But, of course, I know what I would do."

"What?"

"I don't want to interfere——"

Norvell sighed. "I guess you're right."

"—don't *want* to interfere in your life, but if it were my decision, I'd cancel."

Norvell goggled. He was suddenly sober.

"That's right, Norvell. I'd cancel."

Norvell looked at him unbelievingly, but Dworcas's gaze was grave and considerate—except, perhaps, for a tiny glint that was enjoying Norvell's consternation very much. Norvell looked away. He took a deep drink of his beer as Dworcas said:

"I know it's a tough decision to make, Norvell. Heaven knows, I'd find it hard to make myself without half an hour or more of serious thought. But what is your alternative?"

Norvell shifted uncomfortably in his chair. He put his beer down; neither man said a word for a long time, while Norvell's mind raced from Candella to Dworcas to the lawyer, Mundin, to Virginia to Stimmens to a fire-red mystery marked "Belly Rave" to the old man who had sat weeping out loud while he waited for the broken-field event to start; he had slid through the wire and missed every mine, but the man next to him wasn't so fortunate and the old man had fainted dead away when he heard the blast.

At last, with a sigh, Norvell surrendered to the terrifying theme.

"I don't think I ought to," he said faintly.

Dworcas inclined his head. "It's your decision, Norvell," he said courteously.

"I just don't see how I can, Arnie. I'd lose the house, Virginia would raise holy——"

Arnie stopped him. He shrugged. "You may be right. Who knows? There's certainly no security in the world for a man without a contract job. You'd have to leave your home, true, and move to the suburbs——" Norvell blinked "——at least temporarily. It's a hard life there. Hard work, few amusements, a constant challenge to prove yourself—to make your way in spite of hell or high water—or fall by the wayside." He looked speculatively at Norvell, and dismissed the subject. "Well," he said generously, "I just wanted to give you the benefit of my thinking on the point. You do as you see fit. I guess you'll want to be getting home."

"Sure," Norvell said. And remembering: "Oh, Arnie, I meant to thank you for steering me to that lawyer. I don't know what I would have——"

"Think nothing of it. I'm always glad to do anything I can for you, you know that. You won't forget about the tickets."

"Tickets?" Norvell asked wildly.

"The tickets for the Field Day. Not general admission, you know. As close to the Master's box as you can get them."

Norvell's eyes opened wide. He said in a thin voice, "Arnie, you were bragging to your boss that you could get tickets even though they've been sold out for six weeks. Isn't that it?" They stared nakedly at each other; then Norvell's eyes fell. "Just kidding," he mumbled. "I'll try to get them."

He got home, somehow. Virginia was still awake, but there was only a minor squabble over the music coming from behind Alexandra's locked door. Norvell made the mistake of commenting that it was past midnight, and a ten-year-old should be——

His wife said raucously, "Should be this, and should be that, and should do everything Mr. Bligh wants her to. Sure! Norvie, did you ever stop to think that she's a *person?* This whole house isn't organized around you, you know; it's *our* home too, and——"

Norvell had had all he could take. He yelled, "It's *our* house now, but it's the *company's* house too, and one more word out of you and I give it back to them. Then you two prize packages from Belly Rave will be right back where you belong."

The words "Belly Rave" did it, more than the threat. Virginia's face stiffened in shocked surprise. Norvell stalked out and down the steps and poured himself a drink.

He sat with it in his hand for a long minute of wordless anger and finally set it down untasted. Belly Rave; hell, it couldn't be *too* bad. He looked in sudden wonder at the room around him.

Such a difference between a bubble-city G.M.L. house and Belly Rave? Why did they take it so hard? He decided he'd have to visit Belly Rave one of these days, anyhow. Not for anything nasty. Thank God *he* didn't care for that sort of thing. Just to get a look. But what could the difference be? A house was a house. It had warm resilient floors; it had walls; it had utilities. If you didn't like the floor warm you dialed it to cool. If you didn't like the wall color or pattern you turned the selector wheel to something else. If you didn't like a room plan you unclipped the wall and clipped it somewhere else. Hell, that's what a house *was*.

Norvell dialed a bed and set the house to full automatic. As he lay down his pillow chimed softly, but he didn't need sleepy music that night; with a curse, he reached over his head and turned it off. In the copper plexus at the house's core transistors pulsed; solenoids barred the doors; microswitches laid traps for intruders; thermocouples tasted the incoming air and cooled it an additional four degrees. Commutator points roved around a hidden dial until they reached the stations where a sweeping clock hand would boil the water for the coffee, heat the griddle for the eggs, set the breakfast dishes. But by then Norvell was already asleep.

Chapter Five

REVERSE YOUR TELESCOPE. Point the small end at a sign that is neither here nor now, a long way off in space and as many years past as it has been since the end of World War II.

The sign is in a dozen chromatic colors, a picture of a vine-covered cottage with a curl of smoke winding from a fieldstone chimney, and an impossibly long-legged girl waving from the door. The giant letters read:

> BELLE REVE ESTATES
> "Gracious Living for America's Heroes"
> VETS! OWN YOUR OWN HOME!
> $350 cash, $40.25 monthly, pays all
> F R E E !
> 3-speed washer, home freezer
> FIFTEEN-FOOT PICTURE WINDOW

Before the paint on the sign was dry, three cars were parked in the muddy ruts in front of it and three couples were being guided through the model home by Belle Reve salesmen—estate managers, they preferred to be called.

Their technique was identical. If any one of them had lost his voice, or been blasted to charcoal by a resentful God, any of the others could have taken his place in mid-syllable. And their movements were as exact as a ballet troupe; when salesman A brought his charges into a room, salesman B was just on the way out. The rooms were handsomely made and cutely furnished, but the sales director didn't like to have too many people in a room at one time—gave the impression the rooms were *small*.

When the salesman had finished, a prospect got back to the sparkling kitchen, where the closing desk was, under the dizzy impression that somehow he could move into the place tomorrow, furnished as it was, simply by signing his name and handing over the twenty-dollar binder. And a swimming pool would be on their lawn the day after to be shared with another nice couple like them, and the children could gambol on the grassy sward unmenaced by city traffic, and they would spit right in the eye of the city apartment-house janitor after telling him they were getting out of the crowded, evil-smelling, budget-devouring, paper-walled, sticky-windowed, airless, lightless, privacyless hole in the wall forever. They were going Home to Belle Reve. They signed and paid.

Time passed.

Belle Reve receded before them always like a mirage. The four-color circulars continued to arrive, and the statements of their down-payment balance due. Plus title-search fee. Plus handling charge. Plus interest. Plus legal fee. Plus sewer assessment. Plus land tax. Plus road tax. They paid.

Time passed.

Their house was built; their hour had struck! The kids wailed, "Is *that* it?" and began to cry. Whichever was weaker, the wife or husband, sagged shoulders and stared in horror at the sea of mud, the minute house riding it like an ark, like one ark in a fleet of identical arks drawn up rank by rank for review by a snickering deity. Whichever was stronger, the husband or wife, squared shoulders and said loudly, "It may not look like much now, but give us a few weekends and we'll have it just like the demonstration place. And we'll be working for ourselves, not some landlord. This place isn't an expense; it's an asset."

Time passed.

Sod was laid on the mud. It sank in curious hummocks and swales when it rained. Takes a little time to settle, honey. Fill was dumped on the sod, and topsoil on the fill. Grass was planted on the topsoil to burn and die in the summer. Honey, we can't water it this year because of the water rates. In a normal year, sure, but we have a few non-recurring charges, and once they're out of the way—— The sewer assessment. The road assessment. The school tax. And we ought to do something about the foundation, I guess. You catch these little cracks early and you never have trouble again. Every house settles a little, honey.

Time passed.

The place isn't an expense, honey; it's an *asset*. Do you realize we have an equity of *eight thousand dollars* in this house we can recover at the drop of a hat if we can find somebody to buy the place and if there was some place else to go? It makes a man feel mighty good to know he has eight thousand dollars to his name. I know it runs a little higher than anybody figured, but things are up all over. Insurance, sewer assessment, road tax, fuel oil, interest, assessment in that stockholders' suit whatever it was about—it isn't more than a hundred twenty-five a month, if that. If I get the raise and swing that note on the car we can have the roof repaired before the November rains, and then get right to work on the oil heater—please don't cry, honey. Besides. There's. No. Place. Else. To. Go.

Time passed.

You've got to talk to her, dear. Coming in past midnight after she was out with God-knows-who and telling me there isn't any use asking her to entertain at home because we'd be right on top of her because the place is so small you can't sneeze without blowing somebody's hat off you've got to talk to her I'm going out of my mind with worry she could get in trouble and so are all the other mothers I know the place isn't very attractive but can't you get it painted somehow even if you aren't as young as you once were she's ashamed of the place and she's right about it being too small and the washer's broken again and I'm not as young as I once was and I can't keep hauling water all my life and when are we going to fix the picture window it looks horrible with a big crack right down the middle not that I blame the Elliston boy the poor kid doesn't have any place to play trapped like a rat here in Belle Reve like the rest of us in chicken coops crumbling around us while we watch but they never quite fall down as long as we keep patching and patching and patching and paying and paying and paying. . . .

Time passed.

Over the back fence (patched and peeling; leaning this way and that, inadequate to keep the children in the yard or the prowling, huge rats out): I heard of them and I saw the ads. I don't read much these days because of my eyes but he came home with the paper, for once he wasn't gray and tired. G.M.L. Houses, he said. Wonderful G.M.L. bubble-houses— a complete departure. He said he knew it had to come some day, a complete break with tradition the way it said in the ad. It has something to do with contracts. They lease the machines

29

to the companies, I think, or something, and the companies build the houses for people who work for them. It gets around taxes or something. He was sure the company would lease the machines and we could get a G.M.L., but it didn't come to anything because he doesn't have a contract and they just build them for their contract people. But heavens he's lucky to *have* a job the way things are going; the boy's been looking and looking and there doesn't seem to be anything, I don't know how we'd get by if it wasn't for the allowance. . . .

Time passed.

Steady, pop, don't snop your top. I swear I'll cool ya if ya give me more than a sufficiency of that cack. Me get a job? Some cack, ya old frack! What have I got that a little black box hasn't got more and better? Gimme that "fifty years with the company" once more and you'll be flat on your bat. You get the allowance for me, don't ya? If ya didn't have crap in your cap you'd be a contract man and we'd be in a bubble for double instead of my being a lousy slave from Belly Rave. Me hitch to the city and look for work? Pterodactyl cack! Tell ya what I'm gonna do. I'm gonna have a big breakfast and hitch a ride to the Stadium. Good show today—Rocky Granatino, Rocky Bolderoni, Rocky Schistman and Kid Louis in a blindfold free-for-all with spiked gloves after the regular bouts. Then I'm gonna pick up a surrounded cavity and we'll find a nice, empty dump here in Belly Rave and shove some love. Maybe the Wexley place down the street so you won't worry about me getting lost. Old Man Wexley made contract grade last week after fifteen years in night school, so he took off for Monmouth G.M.L. City like he had a fire in his rire. I bet the beds are still made, which might come in handy. Any questions?

No; there were no questions. And the boy swaggered out across the screeching floorboards, the house trembling to his stride. The old man said, "Fifty years with the company," and began to cry. He had been replaced last Friday by a little black box that never made mistakes, never got tired, never took a coffee break. From now on the allowance check would be tripled; as head of a family he had that coming to him. And he owned the house outright, almost. In just a few years it would be his, as soon as he cleared up the sewer assessments outstanding. I'll sell, he schemed craftily, forgetting to cry. At the top of the market. Not right now; things were too dull. A few of the places on the street were empty, abandoned by owners who had made contract grade and won entitlement to a G.M.L. house. A kind of funny element was moving in; not the kind of people you talked to much. Bad for the children. He was sure that passing the abandoned Samuels place he had smelled something like the raw reek of alcohol and glimpsed shining copper pots and tubing through the ill-shuttered picture window. Sometimes police cars and copters descended on Belly Rave and left loaded—but that was on the outskirts, the neighborhood would pick up, the old man told himself sternly. And then he'd sell at the top of the market.

Time passed. . . .

More than a century.

Chapter Six

FOUR TAXI DRIVERS flatly refused to take Mundin to Belly Rave. The fifth was a devil-may-care youngster. "Just took this heah job waitin' for the draft call," he confided. "How can I lose? Anything goes wrong in this heah Belly Rave place, maybe Ah get beat up so bay-yud the ol' army won't take me." He laughed. "But seriously, I figger it cain't be as tough as they say."

Mundin did not contradict him and away they went.

There was no sizable city which did not have the equivalent of Belly Rave. The festering slums of Long Island were another New York problem; Boston had its Springfield; Chicago its Evanston; Los Angeles its Greenville. None was worse than Belle Reve Estates. Mundin noticed that the battered streetlights of Belly Rave didn't light; as they rolled past the first weed-grown yards and boarded-up houses he noticed ramshackle structures in the back. Occasionally they passed a burned-out area, but not often. The plots were generous enough in size to keep a normal fire from spreading from house to house. Unfortunately.

There was life in Belly Rave: a furtive, crepuscular life

31

called into being by the unpoliceable wilderness of tall weeds, endless miles of crumbling battered driveway unmarked by street signs or house numbers. The taxi wasn't alone. Zooty little cars prowled along the crumbling concrete, occasionally pulling to the curb where a dim figure swung a phosphorescent handbag. They passed one block of houses that was a blaze of light and noise. The doorman trotted along beside the taxi urging: "Anything goes, mister. Spend the night for five bucks, all you can drink and smoke included. Why pay taxes, mister?"

Sometimes the Alcohol & Hemp Tax Unit's men raided such joints. Not often.

The driver asked the doorman, "We anywheah close to 37598 Willowdale Crescent?" He stopped the cab.

"What you need is a guide," the doorman said promptly. "Jimmy!" Somebody jelled out of the dark. Mundin heard a fumbling at the door of the cab.

"Step on it!" he yelled at the driver, snapping the door lock and running up the window. The driver stepped on it.

The ambush left behind, they cautiously approached bag-swingers for directions. In half an hour they were on the 37-thousand block of Willowdale Crescent, counting houses.

"This must be it," said the driver, no longer devil-may-care.

"I guess so. Wait here, will you?" Mundin said.

"Nossir! How do I know you ain't going to slip through a back door and stiff me? You pay me what's on the clock an' Ah'll wait."

The meter read a whopping eight dollars. Mundin handed over a ten and started up the crumbled walk.

Vroom! The taxi was on its way before he had taken half a dozen steps. Mundin cursed wearily and knocked on the door. He studied the boarded-up picture window while he waited. They were all broken, all boarded up. Inevitably in the years that had gone by since they were eased and puttied carefully into place, the rock had been flung, or the door had been slammed, or the drunk had lurched into the living room.

The man who came to the door was old and sick.

"Is this the Lavin place?" Mundin asked, blinking against a light haze of woodsmoke. "I'm Charles Mundin. She asked me to call in connection with a legal matter. I'm an attorney."

The old man started at the word. "Come in, Counselor," he said formally. "I'm a member of the bar myself——"

He broke off into a fit of coughing, leaning against the doorframe.

Mundin half-carried him into the living room and eased him into a sagging overstuffed chair. A Coleman lamp, blowing badly, cast a metallic blue-green glare into every corner of the room. A fire smoldered on the hearth, billowing against a closed register. A tinny radio was blaring, "—nately was kept from spreading, though the four houses involved in the arson attempt were totally destroyed. Elsewhere in Belly Rave, warfare broke out between the Wabbits and the Goddams, rival junior gangs. One eight-year-old was killed instantly by——"

Mundin clicked it off and opened the register. The smoke began to clear from the room and the fire to flicker. The old man was still folded up in the chair, his parchment face mercilessly picked out by the flaring light. Mundin fiddled aimlessly with the valve and accidentally got it to stop roaring. There was a green glass shade; he put it on and the room was suddenly no longer a corner of a surrealist hell but simply a shabby room.

"Thank you," the old man muttered. "Counselor, would you please see if there is a small, round tin in the bathroom cabinet?"

The bathtub was full of split kindling and the cabinet shelves loaded with the smaller household staples—salt, spices, and such. There was an unmarked tin, which Mundin pried open. Small, gummy-looking pills and an unmistakable odor: Yen pox. He sighed and brought the old man the opened tin.

The old man took it without comment and slowly swallowed five of the opium pills. When he spoke his voice was almost steady. "Thank you, Counselor. And let this be a lesson to you: Never get a belly-habit. It's weakening, humiliating. You said you had an appointment with Norma? She should have been here hours ago. Naturally—the neighborhood—I'm worried. I'm Harry Ryan. Member of the S.E.C. Bar, and other things. Of course——" he stared at the tin of yen pox— "I'm retired from practice."

Mundin coughed. "I believe Miss Lavin mentioned you. As I understand it, you would be attorney of record and I'd do the legwork in some sort of stockholder's suit, if we work it

33

out." He hesitated and went on to tell the old man about the arrest of the boy.

"Yes," Ryan said matter-of-factly. "I told her it was a mistake to go to Mr. Dworcas. It is inconceivable that Green, Charlesworth would not get wind of it."

"Green, Charlesworth?" Willie Choate had once mentioned the name, in some connection or other. "Are they the investment house?"

"They are. They are *the* investment house, just as you say."

"But she told me her business was connected with G.M.L. Homes. How does Green, Charlesworth get into it?"

Ryan chewed another opium pill and swallowed it. "Mr. Mundin," he said, "you will find that Green, Charlesworth do not *get* into things. They already are in everything. Raw materials, belt-transport patents, real estate, insurance, plant financing—you name it, Mundin."

"Even ward politics in the 27th?"

"Even that. But don't let it disturb you too greatly, Mundin, It is probable that Green, Charlesworth are only casually interested in the Lavins at the present time. They no doubt wish to keep posted on what Don and Norma are up to, but I do not expect they will intervene."

"You think that?"

Ryan explained heavily, "I have to think that." The door knocker rattled and the old man heaved himself from the overstuffed chair, waving Mundin aside. "I'll get it," he said. "Ah—this was just a temporary indisposition. You needn't mention it to——" He jerked his chin at the door.

He came back into the living room with Norma and Don Lavin.

"Hello, Mundin," she said tonelessly, her voice leaden with depression. "I see you found us. Have you eaten?"

"Yes, thanks."

"Then excuse us while we have something. The Caddy broke down five times on the way out here. I'm beat."

She and her brother morosely opened a couple of self-heating cans of goulash. They spooned them down in silence.

"Now," she said to Mundin, "the background. I'll make it short." Her voice was satiric, hate-filled.

"Don and I were born of rich but honest parents in Coshocton, Ohio. Daddy—Don Senior—was rather elderly when

34

we came along; he spent the first fifty years of his life working. He started out as a plastics man with a small factory—bus bodies, fire trucks, that kind of thing. He happened to have gone to school with a man named Bernie Gorman, who happened to have specialized in electronics and electrical stuff. The two of them worked together, when they could find time, dreaming dreams and weaving visions. They were dedicated men. They invented, designed and constructed the first pilot model of the G.M.L. Home, otherwise known as the bubble-house."

Mundin said frostily, "I happen to know a little about G.M.L., Miss Lavin. Wasn't there a man named Moffatt involved?"

"Involved he was, but not until later. Much later. For almost thirty years, Daddy and Mr. Gorman worked like dogs, starved themselves, gave up everything for their dream. Mother said she scarcely saw Daddy from month's end to month's end. Mr. Gorman died a bachelor. They had designed the bubble-house, they had built it, but they didn't have the capital to put it on the market."

"Oh, come now," objected Mundin. "They could have leased the rights——"

"And had them bottled up. Didn't I already say they were dedicated men? They had designed a home that was cheaper than the cheapest and better than the best. It was a break-through in housing, like nothing that had gone before except, perhaps, the synthetic revolution in textiles or the advent of the Model T Ford. Don't you see that even a millionaire could not have owned a better house than the G.M.L.? Daddy and Mr. Gorman wanted to give them to the people at only a reasonable profit; no manufacturer would dream of it until the top-price market had been filled. They weren't big business-men, Mundin. They were dreamers. They were out of their field. Then Moffatt came along with his plan."

Ryan stirred himself. "Most ingenious, really," he said. "Adapted to the tax situation. By leasing manufacturing rights to large corporations, G.M.L. avoided capital outlay; the corporations gave their employees what could not be had else-where—and good-by to labor troubles. At first, G.M.L. leased the rights for money. Later, when they got bigger, the consideration was blocks of stock, equities in the firms."

The girl nodded soberly. "Within ten years, G.M.L. owned sizable shares of forty corporations, and Daddy and Mr. Gorman owned half of G.M.L. Then Daddy found out what was happening. He told Mr. Gorman, and I think it killed him—he was an old man by then, you see. Contract status. One word of back-talk and you get thrown out of your G.M.L. house. Get thrown out of your G.M.L. house and you find yourself——" she hesitated, and her eyes roved around the sordid room "—here."

Mundin said wonderingly, "But if your father was one of the owners——"

"Only twenty-five per cent, Mundin. And Mr. Gorman's twenty-five per cent went to distant cousins after the embolism. So there was Daddy at sixty-five. His vision was a reality; his bubble-homes housed a hundred million people. And they had become a weapon, and he was frozen out of the firm."

Don Lavin said dreamily, "They gave the plant guards his picture. He was arrested as drunk and disorderly when he tried to go to the stockholders' meeting. He hanged himself in his cell." He stared absently at Mundin's shoe.

Mundin cleared his throat. "I—I'm sorry. Wasn't there anything to be done at all?"

Ryan said, with a touch of professional admiration, "Very little Mr. Mundin. Oh, he still had stock. They impounded it. A trumped-up creditors' committee got an order on his safe-deposit box against dissipation of assets when he died. They kept it impounded for twelve years. Then somebody got careless, or somebody quit or got fired and the new man didn't know what the impoundment was for—anyway, G.M.L. blinked. The order expired. Norma and Don Lavin are twenty-five per cent owners of G.M.L."

Mundin looked around the shabby room and didn't say a word.

"There's just one little thing," Norma said bitterly. "Don got the stock out of the box and put it away. Tell us where it is, Don."

The brother's dreamy eyes blinked and widened. His face muscles worked wildly; he said, "K-k-k-k-k-k-k-k-k" in a convulsion of stammering. The idiot stutter went on for long moments, until Don Lavin began raspingly to cry. Norma, stone-faced, patted him on the shoulder.

She said to the appalled lawyer, "When we began making trouble, as they said, Don was snatched. He was gone for three days and he doesn't remember them. We took him to a doctor; the doctor said it looked like at least fifty hours of conditioning."

Mundin said, out of shock and rage, "That's illegal! Private persons can't use conditioning techniques!"

Norma flared, "Of course not! You're our lawyer now, Mundin. Just straighten that out for us, will you? Get an injunction against G.M.L."

Mundin sat back. Habitual criminals—like his twerp—were conditioned in twenty-five hours of treatment over a week or more. Fifty hours in three days!

"Why didn't they just snatch the stock?" he asked.

"That would be illegal," explained Ryan—and hastily held up a hand. "No, seriously. A forced sale could be attacked, and perhaps set aside—by Don himself, or by his heirs or guardians. This way the stock is neutralized, and nothing pinned to G.M.L. They don't need the stock; they've got plenty of stock. They just don't want Don and Norma to have it."

Mundin felt ill. He said, "I see. Sorry I was so stupid. So now Don doesn't know where he put the stock and you want to find it."

Ryan looked at him with disgust. "No, Counselor," he said heavily. "Not quite as simple as that. I may not have practiced at the Big Bar for some time, but I imagine that even I could manage to get duplicate certificates. Unfortunately our position is somewhat worse than that. Donald, as the male heir, was the obvious person——" Norma snorted "—the obvious person, I say, to conduct a suit, so Norma signed an irrevocable proxy of interest to him. That was an error, as it turned out. Donald can't do the job. He can't bring suit; he can't tell us where the stock is; he can't even discuss it."

Mundin nodded sickly. "I see. You're stymied."

Norma made a contemptuous noise. "Great, Mundin," she said. "You've put it in a nutshell. Now that it is established that we're licked, we might as well lie down and die."

Mundin said stiffly, "I didn't say that, Miss Lavin. We'll do what we can." He hesitated. "For instance," he went on, "if it's only a matter of conditioning, no doubt we can have

37

your brother undergo a deconditioning course somewhere else. After all——"

Norma raised an eyebrow. "'Private persons can't use conditioning techniques,'" she quoted. "Didn't you say that just a moment ago?"

"Well, yes, but surely *someone* will——"

All at once Norma seemed to collapse. She said to Ryan, "You tell him. Tell him what he's up against."

Ryan said, "G.M.L.'s assets are not less than fourteen billion dollars, comprising cash in the bank, negotiable securities, plant and properties and equities, as of their last statement, in eight hundred and four corporations. I don't say that they can break the law with impunity, Counselor. But they can sure as hell keep *us* from breaking it."

Chapter Seven

FOURTEEN BILLION DOLLARS. Mundin, trudging apprehensively through Belly Rave's dark streets, felt very small up against fourteen billion dollars. Still, he had accepted the case.

A mournful hooting from the shadows made him quicken his step, but no lurking thugs showed up. Mundin shivered uncomfortably and turned up his coat collar. It had begun to rain.

Luck was with Mundin. He was neither mugged nor lured into one of the clip joints. The footpads were stalking other streets, the roving gangs of armed adolescents plotted in their cellars instead of braving the rain, the cab Mundin spotted, ran after, and hailed was a legitimate cab and not a trap. He got out of Belly Rave without difficulty, and he never knew what he had missed.

The cab ride gave him time to think. But the thinking came to very little. The Lavins, he was convinced, had a legitimate claim. He had promised them he would work on it; he had tried to reassure them that things were not as hopeless as they seemed. He felt uncomfortably sure that the girl had seen through his empty words.

The cab came to territory he recognized, and he stopped it at an all-night restaurant. Coffee might help. While he was waiting for it, he invested a dime in a call to his office; you never could tell, maybe someone had called.

Someone had. The Sleepless Secretary hooted and groaned and came across with the record of a familiar, scared voice: "Mr. Mundin, uh, this is Norvell Bligh. Can you come and get me out of jail?"

Chapter Eight

NORVIE WOKE UP with a start. They were joggling him, with identical, contemptuous smiles. Even in the fog of sleep he felt a little stab of pride at Virginia's beauty, a twitch of unhappiness at the same bony beauty smothered beneath the fat of her daughter.

"What's the matter?" he croaked.

His voice sounded odd, and he realized he wasn't wearing his hearing aid. He groped for it beside the bed. It wasn't there. He sat up.

He yelled at Alexandra, his voice thin and strange to him as it was sustained through the bones and cavities of his body rather than the neat chain of the auditory apparatus: "Where is it? If you've hidden it again I'll break your neck!"

Alexandra looked smugly shocked. She mouthed at him, "Goodness, Norvell, you know I wouldn't do that." The exaggerated mouthing was a mockery of consideration; he had repeatedly told her that exaggeration only distorted the lips.

Virginia tapped him on the shoulder and said something, stiff-lipped. He caught an "eep" and a "larm."

He clenched his fists and said, "What?"

She mouthed at him, "I said, you must have come in too drunk to set the alarm before you went to sleep. Get up. You're an hour late for work now."

He leaped from bed, anguish spearing his heart, Oh, God! An hour late on this day, of all days!

He found the hearing aid—on the floor in the entrance hall,

39

where he couldn't possibly have left it, any more than he could possibly have failed to set the alarm. But he didn't have time for that minor point. He depilated in ten seconds, bathed in five, dressed in fifteen and shot out of the house.

Fortunately Candella wasn't in.

Norvie sent Miss Dali to round up his staff and began the tooling-up job for the integrator keyboard, while the production men busied themselves with their circuits and their matrices, and the job began. This was the part of Norvie's work that made him, he confessed secretly to himself, feel most like God. He fed the directions to Stimmens, Stimmens fumblingly set up the punch cards, the engineers translated the cards into phase fields and interferer circuits. . . . And a World That Norvie Made appeared in miniature.

He had once tried to explain his feelings to Arnie. Arnie had snarled something about the presumptuous conceit of a mere pushbutton. All Norvie did, Arnie explained over many glasses of beer, was to decide what forms and images he wanted to see. It was The Engineers who, in Their wisdom, transmuted empty visions into patterns of light and color that magically took the form and movement of tiny fighters and wrestlers and spear-carriers. The original thought, Arnie explained severely, was nothing. It was the tremendous technical skill that transformed the thought into visual reality in the table-top model previewer that was important.

And Norvie humbly agreed. Even now he was deferential to the production men, those geniuses so well skilled in the arts of connecting Circuit A to Terminal IV, for they were Engineers. But his deference extended only to the technical crew. "Stimmens, you butterfingers," he snarled, "hurry it up! Mr. Candella will be here any minute!"

"Yessir," said Stimmens, hopelessly shuffling the stacks of notes out of Norvell's hands.

Stimmens was coming along well, Norvie thought. A touch of the whip was good for him.

It took twenty minutes and a bit more, and then Norvell's whole design for a Field Day was on punch cards. While Stimmens was correcting his last batch of cards, the production men began the highspeed run-through. The little punched cards went through the scanners; the packed circuits measured

40

voltages and spat electrons; and in the miniature mockup of the Stadium, tiny figures of light appeared and moved and slew each other and left.

They were Norvell's own, featureless and bright, tiny and insubstantial. Where Norvell's script called for the bodies of forty javelin-throwers in the flesh, the visualizing apparatus showed forty sprites of light jabbing at each other with lances of fire. No blood spilled; no bodies stained the floor of the Stadium; only the little bodiless fire-figures that disappeared like any other pattern of excited ions when the current went off.

Somehow, inside Norvell's mind, it was here and not in the big arena that the real Field Days took place. He had heard the cries of the wounded and seen the tears of the next of kin waiting hopelessly in the pits, but they were not real; it was as mannikins that he thought of them always.

One of the production men looked up and said approvingly, "Good show, Mr. Bligh."

"Thanks," said Norvell gratefully. That was always a good sign; the technical crews had seen 'em all. Now the question was, what would Candella say?

He found out.

What Candella said, gently at first, was:

"Bligh, the upcoming Field Day is important. At least, it seems to me that it is. It seems to me that everything we do is important. Don't you think so?"

Norvell said, "Well——"

"I'm glad you agree. Our work *is* important, Bligh. It is a great and functional art form. It provides healthful entertainment, satisfying the needs of every man for some form of artistic expression. It provides escape—escape for the hardworking bubble-house class, escape for the masses of Belly Rave. For them, in fact, our work is indispensable. It siphons off their aggressions so that they can devote their time to—uh—to comparatively harmless activities. Allotments and Field Days! Our society is built on them. You might call our work the very foundation of society, looked at in that way. Do you agree?"

Norvell's voice failed him. He said in almost a whisper: "Yes, sir."

Candella looked politely apologetic. "I beg your pardon?"

"*Yes, sir!*" Norvell, too late, found he was almost bellowing.

Candella looked pained. "You needn't shout." he reproved —gently, smilingly. "There is nothing wrong with *my* hearing." Norvell winced. You unutterable louse, he thought. But Candella was going right on. "—foundation of our society, as I say, but also an art form. The cultured classes appreciate our efforts on the artistic plane; the rabble of Belly Rave— with all respects, my dear Bligh, to the origin of your charming wife—*need* it on the glandular level. *Every* show we produce is important. But the Field Day——"

He hesitated, and the composition of his features changed. His thick brows came down like the ragged anvils of thunder-clouds; his temples pulsed. His voice became a bass roar. He thundered, "The Field Day, you asinine little tin-eared incompetent, is the biggest day of the year! *Not* just because it draws the biggest audience—but because that's the one *I* am judged by! The Board attends. The Mayor attends. The men from G.M.L. attend. If they like it, good. If they don't—it's *my* head that's on the line, Bligh! And I don't want it lopped off because of the idiotic blunderings of a half-witted ass like you!"

Norvell opened his mouth; it hung open, wordless. Candella roared on, "Not a word! I want no excuses. You had the as-signment, and you muffed it. Your notion of what constituted a Field Day was, of course, uninspired. But I thought that, with patching and improvising, we might get by. However, I no longer think so—not since examining the superb presenta-tion that was handed me this morning—at nine o'clock, I might add." He slammed a sheaf of punch-cards on the desk. "By a member of your own staff, Bligh! A brilliant boy whom you have evidently been holding down. Thank God for his guts! Thank God for his loyalty! Thank God he had the cour-age and sense to come to *me* with this masterpiece instead of permitting you to destroy it!"

There was a long pause. At last Norvell was able to croak, "Who?"

Candella said triumphantly, "Stimmens."

Norvell was speechless. The thing was not possible. *Stim-mens?* Wet behind the ears, untried, incompetent even at simple research? Stimmens who didn't even want to stay with the firm, who had the infernal gall to ask for a contract release? *Strimmens?*

His hand stretched out for the cards, and then he stopped, abashed, realizing he had forgotten to ask permission. "Go ahead," Candella said coldly.

Norvell scanned them in astonishment. Why, he thought, this is impossible—and this bit here, we can't——

"Mind if I play these, Mr. Candella?" he asked and, getting an ironic nod, fed the punch-cards into Candella's previewer. The circuits scanned the punched holes and built a scene of electronic slaughter for him. He watched the little fire-figures in growing apprehension.

When he looked up, he said, so bemused that he hardly remembered to be fearful, "Why, it's good."

"Of course it's good!"

"No, *really* good, Mr. Candella." He shook his head wonderingly. "Stimmens, eh? I never would have believed it. Of course, it's rough—the emotional values need bringing out. The comedy stuff with the vitriol pistols ought to follow a tense thriller like Man Versus Scorpions instead of another comedy number like the Octogenarians with Flame Throwers. But that's easy enough to fix. Race Against Man-Made Lightning is out too; Stimmens told me himself we couldn't get the equipment from Schenectady. I suppose he forgot."

Candella was looking at him with an indescribable expression, but Norvell raced on, babbling nervously. "Real originality, Mr. Candella. I—I must say I admire him. Piranhas in the aquatic meet! Wonderful. And the octogenarians are a terrific switch. Number after number I've never heard of! I have to admit it, Mr. Candella, that boy has talent."

Candella said dangerously, "What the hell are you talking about?"

Norvell stammered, "Why, the—the *originality*, Mr. Candella. The *freshness.*"

Candella hardly heard him; he was mumbling to himself as he riffled through sheets of paper. He pounded them with his fist and glared at Norvell.

"Originality! Bligh, do you think I'm nuts? Do you think I'm crazy enough to run untried novelties in a show like this?

43

Every one of these features has been a smash success some-where in the country within the last ninety days."

"Oh, *no!* No, Mr. Candella, honest—I know. I've been get-ting all the reports, and none of this stuff—— Honest, Mr. Candella! I was saying to Stimmens just the other day, 'It's funny how little new stuff is turning up.' Gosh, Stimmens was doing the research himself, he ought to know!"

Candella exploded, *"Look, you fool!"* He tossed a sheaf of reports at Norvell.

They were all there. Names, dates, and places. Norvell looked up in horror. *"Mis-*ter Can-*del-*la," he whispered. "It's a doublecross!" His voice gained strength. "He wants a Fifteen rating. Just yesterday he tried to get me to recommend remis-sion of his contract. I wouldn't do it; this is his way of getting even."

"Bligh! That's a serious charge!"

"Oh, I'll prove it, Mr. Candella. I've got the copies of his reports in my desk, under lock and key. Please, Mr. Candella —come into my office with me. Let me show you."

Candella stood up. "Show me," he ordered.

And ten minutes later he was saying grimly, "Thought I wouldn't call your bluff, eh?"

Norvell stared unbelievingly at the reports, face white as a sheet. They had been in his desk, locked with his key. . . .

And they were not the reports he had seen. They sparkled with novelties; they showed all the magnificent new concepts in Stimmens's outline, and much, much more.

The papers shook in Norvell's hands. *How?* He couldn't have left the desk unlocked. Nobody had a key but him and Miss Dali—and she had no reason to do such a thing. There had been no chance for sleight of hand, no possibility his eyes had deceived him. Had he gone mad? Was it some chemical prank, the reports he saw in disappearing ink, the substituted ones then coming to light? *How?*

Over Norvell's desk set Candella was calling Stimmens in. The boy appeared, looking awed and deferential.

Mr. Candella said briefly, "Congratulations, Stimmens. You're the head of the department from this moment on. Move into your office whenever you like—*this* is your office. And throw this bum out." To Norvell: "Your contract is canceled *for cause*. Don't ever try to get a job in this line again; you'll waste your time." He left without another word.

Norvell was entirely numb.

Stimmens said uneasily, "You could have avoided this. Don't think I enjoyed it. I've been working on it for six months, and I didn't have the heart to go through with it. I had to give you a chance; you turned it down."

Norvell stared, just stared. Stimmens went on defensively: "It isn't as if I just walked into it. Believe me, I earned this. What do I know about Field Days? Sweat, sweat, sweat; I haven't had a moment's peace."

Miss Dali walked in and kissed Stimmens, burbling: "Darling, I just heard! You wonderful Grade Fifteen you!"

"Oh," said Norvell in a sick voice.

They said more, but he didn't hear; it was as if his hearing aid were turned off, but the switch was not in his pocket but in his mind. He was out on the street before he realized what he was doing . . . and what had happened to the contract career of Norvell Bligh.

The thing was, Virginia.

Norvell came up to that point in his thinking as he had come a thousand times before and, like a thousand times before, he backed away from it. He ordered another drink.

No contract status, no bubble-house. It would be Belly Rave, of course. Norvell took a deep swallow of the drink. Still, what was so bad about Belly Rave? You'd be out in the fresh air a lot, at least. You wouldn't *starve*—nobody ever starved, that much everybody knew. He could find something to do, probably. The allotments would take care of eating; his extra work—whatever it turned out to be—would give him a chance to save a little money, make a fresh start, maybe find a place in the old section of the city. Not like the bubble-houses, of course, but better than Belly Rave, from all he'd heard.

He wished one more time that he knew a little more about Belly Rave. Funny, considering that Virginia had been born there; but she had never wanted to talk about it.

And there he was, back on the subject of Virginia again.

How she would take it was another matter. He really couldn't guess. She had been so resolutely, reliably silent on

45

the subject of Belly Rave and all it concerned. Her childhood, her parents and even her husband, the power-cycle stunter whose crash in a long-ago Field Day had left young Norvell Bligh with a tearless widow to jolly out of filing a claim. He had married her instead; and Candella had made an unforgivable joke. . . . No. He faced it. He hadn't married her; *she* had married him—and not even him, really, but a contract job and a G.M.L. house.

He dialed another drink.

He looked around the bar; he had never been in the place before. He didn't even know where he was; he'd found himself wandering through the Ay-rab section of town, footsore. He had turned back and this place had been there, new and shiny and attractive. It looked like a nice place. Someday he might bring Arnie here, if Arnie would still——

He squelched *that* thought before it was properly formed. Certainly he would bring Arnie here! Arnie wasn't the kind of friend to look the other way when you were a little down on your luck—not even that, really, just temporarily in a little bit of a rough time due to a professional misunderstanding and a doublecross. Good old Arnie, Norvell thought sentimentally.

He caught a glimpse of the time.

Better face the music and get it over with. Maybe he could have it out with Virginia, and then go over and spend a little time with Arnie. The thought bucked him.

He swallowed his drink and slipped his wallet into the bar slot. Having it out with Virginia might not be so tough at that. In a way, he thought, the fact that she had been born in Belly Rave was an advantage, if he could only make her see it that way. She would know the ropes. She'd have friends there; she'd have some ideas about pleasant, useful work he could do to supplement the allotment until he got on his feet again. She could save him plenty of time in making contacts, getting——

Something crushed his shoulder and spun him around. "Whaddya think you're up to, Buster?" the policeman demanded in a bass snarl. He shook Norvell's wallet under his nose. "You know the penalty for passing a bum credit card? You Belly Ravers are all alike; get a lapsed card and a front, and try to get a free load. Come along, Buster. The Captain wants to talk to you."

It was all quite horrible.

Of course Candella had canceled his card at once—but it was a simple-enough oversight. Norvell spent a long time trying to make them believe him down at the precinct, before he realized that they did believe him—believed him, and just didn't care.

It was close to dinner time, and they put him in something they called "the Tank" to think things over until the desk sergeant got back from his meal. Norvell didn't like the Tank, and he didn't like the looks of the half-dozen other persons who occupied it with him. But still, he reminded himself, it could have been worse. It was only a question of his lapsed credit card; they could easily have added drunk and disorderly to the charge. And Norvell *could* have found himself logged for being without visible means of support, which meant getting a job, instanter, or getting jugged for quite a while. And there was only one kind of a job a man in police trouble could pick up a phone and get, every time. Usually you didn't have to phone. The cops would drive you down to the Stadium's service entrance themselves; Norvell knew the process, having seen enough "volunteers" delivered.

"Hey, Bligh."

Norvell said, "Yes, sir?"

The cop opened the door. "This way." They came to a dingy room. There was an embarrasing process of holding your hands over your head while someone ran his hands over you; you couldn't blame them for searching you, Norvell told himself, there must be plenty of times they had desperate criminals here. There was a curiously interesting process of inking the fingers and rolling them across a piece of paper. There was a mildly painful process of looking into what seemed to be a binocular microscope; a light flashed, photographing the retina of his eyes, and Norvell had a little trouble seeing for some time afterward.

While Norvell was blinking at the halo in his field of vision the cop said something. Norvell said, "What?"

"I said do you want to call your lawyer?"

Norvell shook his head automatically. Then he remembered: He *had* a lawyer. "Why, yes," he said. He found Mundin's phone number in the book with some difficulty; it was after hours, but he was lucky enough to get an answer—

though Mundin himself wasn't there, and the person who answered seemed, Norvell thought, to be drunk or something. But he left a message, and then there was nothing to do but wait.

Curiously, the waiting was not unpleasant. Even the thought of what Virginia would say or do about this was not particularly terrifying; what could happen worse than had already happened?

So he waited. Past six o'clock, past seven; and for a couple of hours more before he began to worry.

It was almost ten o'clock; if he didn't get out pretty soon, it would be too late to try to see good old Arnie.

Chapter Nine

"THANK YOU VERY MUCH, Mr. Mundin," Norvell said. He looked back at the precinct house and shuddered.

Mundin said, "Don't thank me. I just put in a word with Del Dworcas, and he put in a word with the precinct. Thank him."

Norvell brightened. "Oh, I want to! I've wanted to meet Mr. Dworcas for a long time. Arnie—you know his brother Arnie is a very close friend of mine—has told me so much about him."

Mundin shrugged. "Come on, then," he said. "I'm going to the Hall anyhow."

It was only a short walk to the Hall, and the rain discouraged conversation. Mundin stalked sourly ahead of his client, his mind on G.M.L. Homes. The hope kept hammering at his good sense: *Maybe* he could pull it off—maybe. . . .

Norvell followed contentedly enough. Everything was being ordered for him; he was out of a job, he had been *in jail,* he was hours and hours late for Virginia without a word of explanation—but none of it had been his own decision.

Decisions would come later. That would be the hard part.

Norvell stared around the Hall curiously. It wasn't as impressive as one might expect—though maybe, he thought, you had to admire the Regular Republicans for their common touch. There was certainly nothing showy about Republican Hall.

Norvell stopped, politely out of earshot, as Mundin spoke to a dark, sharp-featured man in shirtsleeves. Some kind of janitor, he guessed; he was astonished when Mundin called him over and introduced him to Del Dworcas.

Norvell said with a certain pride, "I'm really delighted to meet you, Mr. Dworcas. Your brother, Arnie, is very proud of you; we're very good friends."

Dworcas studied him thoughtfully. He asked irrelevantly, "Live around here?"

"Oh, no. Quite some distance away, but——"

Dworcas seemed to lose interest. "Glad to meet you," he said, turning away. "You want to see Arnie, he's in Hussein's across the street. Now, Charles, what was it you wanted to see me about?"

Norvell was left standing with his hand extended. He blinked a little, but—after all, he reminded himself, Mr. Dworcas was a busy man. And Arnie—lucky day!—was in some place called Hussein's across the street.

On the way downstairs he caught a glimpse of the time. After eleven!

Might as well be hanged for a sheep as for a lamb, he told himself recklessly. He turned his coat collar up and plunged out into the rain, almost into the arms of a policeman escorting a scrawny young girl into the Hall. His heart pounded, but the policeman paid him no attention; he crossed the street to the coffee shop.

Arnie was at a table by himself, reading. He looked up as Norvell came close, and hastily put the magazine away. He said nothing, except with his incredulous eyes.

Norvell slipped into a vacant seat, smiling at his little joke on Arnie. "Surprised to see me?"

Arnie frowned. "What are you doing here?"

Norvell lost his smile. "Can—can I have some coffee, Arnie?" he asked. "I came out without any money." Arnie looked mildly outraged, but beckoned the grinning waiter.

Then Norvell told him—about the jail, and Mundin, and Del Dworcas. Arnie took it in without emotion—until Norvell stopped for breath, when Arnie permitted himself a smile.

"You've had a busy day," he said humorously. "I'm glad you met Del, though; he's a prince. Incidentally, I've taken the liberty of asking a couple of his associates to the Field Day. So when you get the tickets——"

Norvell licked his lips. "Arnie——"

"When you get the tickets, will you get three extras?"

Norvell shook his head. "Arnie, listen to me. I can't get the tickets."

Arnie's chin went up. "You *what?*"

"I got fired today. That's why I didn't have any money."

There was a pause. Dworcas began looking through his pockets for a cigarette. He found the pack and put it absently on the table in front of him without lighting one. He said nothing.

Norvell said apologetically, "It—it wasn't my fault, Arnie. This rat Stimmens——" He told the story from beginning to end. He said, "It's going to be all right, Arnie. Don't worry about me. It's like you said. Maybe I should have canceled long ago. I'll make a fresh start in Belly Rave. Virginia can help me; she knows her way around. We'll find some place that isn't *too* bad, you know, and get it fixed up. Some of those old houses are pretty interesting. And it's only a question of time until——"

Dworcas nodded. "I see. You've taken an important step, Norvell. Naturally, I wish you the best of luck."

"Thanks, Arnie," Norvell said eagerly. "I don't think it'll be so bad. I——"

"Of course," Arnie went on meditatively, "it does put me in kind of a spot."

"You, Arnie?" Norvell cried, aghast.

Dworcas shrugged. "It doesn't matter, I suppose. It's just that the fellows at the shop warned me. They said you were probably stringing me along about the tickets. I don't know what I'll tell them that won't make you look pretty bad, Norvell."

Norvell squeezed his eyes shut in an agony of self-flagellation. Loyal Arnie! Concerned about *his* status in the eyes of the other engineers, when it would have been so easy simply to let them think the worst.

"Well, that's the way the ball bounces, Norvell," Arnie went on. "*I* don't blame you. Forget it. I can't blame you for putting your own problems first." He looked ostentatiously at his watch. "I don't want to keep you," he said. "I'd better be getting back to the Hall in any case; my brother has something he wants to consult with me about. Oh, nothing too special—but it's every citizen's duty, of course, to do what he can." He dropped a bill on the table and piloted Norvell to the door.

Under the dingy marquee, he patted Norvell's shoulder. "Drop me a line once in a while, won't you?" he urged. "I'm the world's worst letter-writer, but I'll always be glad to hear how you're getting along."

Norvell stopped dead and planted his feet; the rain spun in on them from the tempest outside. "Write you a letter, Arnie?" he demanded urgently. "I'll be seeing you, won't I?"

"Of *course* you will." Dworcas frowned at the rain. He said patiently, "It's just that, naturally, you won't want to make that long trip from Belly Rave too often. Hell, I can't blame you for that! And for that matter I'll be kind of tied up evenings myself until I get this thing for my brother over with. . . . Look, Norvell, no sense standing here. Drop me a line when you get a chance. And the *best* of luck, fellow!" And he was gone.

Norvell sloshed through the drowned streets. With his credit card canceled and no cash in his pockets, it was a long, wet way home. After the second block he thought of going back and borrowing cab fare from Arnie; but, after all, he told himself, you couldn't do a thing like that, when Arnie had been so nice about the tickets and all. . . .

He had plenty of time to rehearse what he was going to say to Virginia.

He said it.

When it was over, he stared at his wife less in relief than in wonder. His walk home in the gusty rain had been a hell of apprehension. She would scream at him. She might throw things. She would call him names—horrible, cutting, hit-below-the-belt names.

But she didn't.

Fortunately the daughter was asleep; it would have been harder with her around. He changed his clothes without a

51

word to his wife, came down, looked her in the eye and told her—directly and brutally.

Then he waited. The explosion didn't come. Virginia seemed almost not to have heard him. She sat there, blank-faced, and ran her fingers caressingly over the soft arms of the chair. She rose and wandered to the wall patterner wordlessly. Typical of her sloppy housework, the morning-cheer pattern was still on. With gentle fingers she reset the wall to a glowing old rose and dimmed the lights to a romantic, intimate amber. She drifted to a wall and mirrorized it, looking long at herself. Norvell looked too. Under the flattering lights her skin was gold-touched and flawless, the harsh scowl lines magicked away.

She sat on the warm, textured floor and began to sob.

Norvell found himself squatting awkwardly beside her.

"Please, honey," he said. "Please don't cry."

She didn't stop. But she didn't push him away. He was cradling her shoulders uncomfortably in his arms, her head on his chest. He was talking to her in a way he had never been able to before. It would be hard, of course. But it would be real. It would be a life that people could stand—weren't thousands of people standing it right now? Maybe things had been physically too easy for them, maybe it took pressure to weld two personalities together, maybe their marriage would turn into shared toil and shared happiness and——

Alexandra giggled from the head of the stairs.

Norvell sat bolt upright. The girl tittered sleepily, "Well! Excuse *me*. I didn't dream there was anything *intimate* going on."

Virginia got quickly to her feet, bowling Norvell over. He felt his neck flaming a dull red as he got up.

He swallowed and made the effort. "Sandy," he said gently, using the almost-forgotten pet name that had seemed so much more appropriate when she was small and cuddly and not so much of a sl—*hold on!* "Sandy, please come down. I have something important to tell you."

Virginia stood blank-faced. Norvell knew she was trying, and loved her for it.

The child came untidily down the stairs, her much too sophisticated dressing gown fastened with a careless pin. Norvell said firmly, "Sandy——"

The child's face was ancient and haughty. *"Please,"* she interrupted him. "You *know* how I feel about that *humiliating* nickname."

Norvell got a grip on himself. "I didn't mean——" he started, through clenched teeth.

"Of *course* you didn't mean *anything*. You didn't *mean* to wake me up with your drunken *performance* on the stairs, did you? You didn't *mean* to keep Virginia and me in *terror* when you didn't *bother* to let us know you'd be out late." She shot a sly glance at her mother, fishing for approbation. Virginia's hands were clenched.

Norvell said hopelessly, "I only wanted to tell you something."

"Nothing you can say *now* would help."

"No?" Norvell yelled at her, restraint gone. "Well, listen anyway, damn it! We're going to Belly Rave! All of us—tomorrow! Doesn't that mean something to you?"

Virginia said at last, with a wiry edge to her voice, "You don't have to shout at the child."

That was the ball game. He knew perfectly well that she had meant nothing of the kind, but his glands answered for him: "So I don't have to shout at her—because *she* isn't deaf like me, is that it? My loyal wife! My loving family!"

"I didn't mean that!" Virginia cried.

"You never do!" Norvell bellowed over Alexandra's shrill contribution. Virginia screamed:

"You know I didn't mean it, but I wish I had! You! Call yourself a husband! You can't even take care of a family!"

It went on almost until dawn.

Chapter Ten

CHARLES MUNDIN SAID: "Thanks for springing Bligh, Del."

Dworcas said affably, "Hell, any time. Besides, he's a friend of the kid's. Now what's on your mind?"

Mundin said, "G.M.L. Homes. Del, I think you've put me onto something. If it works out—— Well, I won't forget."

53

"Sure, Charles. Look, it's getting late and I've got a couple things to do."

"I'll make it quick. This election, Del—let me out of it, will you? I mean, it isn't as if you need poll-watchers. And I could use the handout—but I can't spare the time."

Dworcas looked at him appraisingly and made his decision. He grinned widely. "Hell, Charles—why should I get in your way? Hop on this deal if it looks so good. I'm not saying it won't leave me shorthanded—I've even got my kid brother helping out. God knows he won't be good for much but he ought to be able to hand out a dodger. So you think this G.M.L. deal is on the level, do you?"

Charles started to answer, but one of Dworcas's handymen stuck his head in the door. He whispered to Del.

Dworcas apologized, "Sorry, Charles, but Jimmy Lyons is here; excuse me a minute."

It really wasn't much more than a minute, even though when Dworcas came back he was walking slowly. He didn't look at Mundin.

Mundin said, "Yes, I do think it's on the level. At any rate, I'm going to give it a whirl."

Dworcas said to the wall, "Wonder if you're doing the right thing."

Mundin was startled. "How do you mean?"

Dworcas shrugged. "It's a pretty serious business, practicing a kind of law you aren't fitted for. It's your business, Mundin. I just don't want to see you getting into trouble."

Mundin said, "Wait a minute, Del! What's this about? It was your idea, wasn't it?"

Dworcas said coldly, "Worried, Mundin? Trying to hang it on me?" He picked up his phone in a gesture of dismissal. "Take off, will you? I've got work to do."

It bothered Mundin all the way home, and it bothered him the next morning when he woke up.

It bothered him even more at the County Courthouse. He walked in with a nod to the duty cop, and the cop looked right through him. He said to the assistant clerk at the counter, "What do you say, Abe? How are the kids?" And the clerk mumbled something and closed his window with a bang.

By then Mundin began to catch on. He got sore, and he got

54

determined. He waited in line at the next window and asked for the records he wanted. He sent back the wrong folder they gave him first; he pointed out that half the papers were missing from the right folder when he got it. He sat in the County Clerk's waiting room for two hours, until the secretary wandered in and said, with aggrieved hostility, "Mr. Cochrane has gone to lunch. He won't be back today." He wrote out a formal complaint on the sheet of paper she grudgingly gave him, alleging that he was being illegally and improperly hampered in his attempt to examine the corporate public-records files of G.M.L. Homes, Inc., and he doggedly left it with her, knowing what would happen to the paper as soon as he got out of the door. It fluttered into the wastebasket *before* he got out of the door, and he turned angrily to object.

The duty cop was standing right beside him, looking eager. Mundin went back to his office to think things over.

Fourteen billion dollars. . . .

But how the devil did they know so fast? Not from Dworcas, Mundin told himself; he could swear that Dworcas didn't know the heat was on until Jimmy Lyons had called him out of the room. And Dworcas had sent him there in the first place. Because—Mundin flushed angrily at the thought, almost certain that it was right—because Dworcas was pretty sure that a two-bit ambulance chaser like himself wouldn't do them any good anyhow? And what had changed his mind if so?

Mundin kicked the Sleepless Secretary and went on pacing. In bell-like tones the Secretary told him that Mrs. Mundin would remit the full balance due by Friday.

He sat down at the desk. All right, so the going was going to be tough. That figured. What else would you expect? And the harder G.M.L. Homes made it, the more scared they were —didn't that figure? And the more scared they were, the more chance that this whole impossible thing was on the level, that Charles Mundin LL.B. stood on the threshold of corporate law.

He took out a piece of paper and began to figure. They could make it rough, but they couldn't stop him. He could get court orders to see the records, that was the obvious starting place, if only to make sure for himself that the Lavins were on the level; and as long as Norma Lavin was willing to call him her attorney-in-fact they couldn't keep him out. There would be a slowdown at the court, naturally. But it couldn't take more than a couple of days, and meanwhile he could get started on some of the other angles. Don's conditioning— might be a criminal charge in that somewhere, if he could get some names, dates, and places.

He reached for his model-forms book and began drafting a power of attorney for Norma Lavin to sign. She'd sign it, of course; she was an independent and, no doubt, a difficult person, but she didn't have much choice. Besides, he thought absently, a lot of that mannishness was undoubtedly protective coloration. In circumstances like hers, what could you expect?

The phone rang; he cut out the Sleepless Secretary hastily and picked up the receiver. "Mundin," he said.

The voice was ancient and utterly lost. "This is Harry Ryan," it quavered. "Norma—she isn't here. Better come out here, Mundin. I think they've picked her up."

Chapter Eleven

NORVELL WAS LYING on a cake of ice. He kept trying to explain to someone enormous that he was sorry for everything and he'd be a good and dutiful son or husband or friend or whatever he was supposed to be if only the someone would leave him alone. But the enormous someone, who couldn't have been Norvell's father because Norvell didn't even remember a father, only put his hand before his mouth and tittered and looked down from a long flight of stairs, and then when Norvell was least expecting it, reached out and swatted him across the ear and sent him skidding across the enormous cake of ice into the tittering face of Alexandra and the jagged, giant teeth of Virginia. . . .

Norvell woke up.

He was very cold, very stiff. He looked dazedly around him. The living room. But——

Yes. It was the living room. With the wall patterns off and

no light except a sickly dawn from outside. All of the walls were on full transparent and he was lying on the floor. The bed he had dialed out to sleep in had folded into the basic cube, dumping him on the floor. And the floor was cold.

No heat. No power. The house was turned off.

He got up, wincing, and hopelessly sidled to the window control. It didn't respond; the windows remained full transparent.

He knew what had happened, and swore between clenched teeth. The skunks. Turning off the place without a word of warning, at daybreak, without even giving him a chance to——

He wearily began picking up his clothes from the floor where a rack had dumped them as it returned to folded storage state. Through the indecently transparent windows he saw the other bubble-houses, all decently opaqued with only their nightlights and entry lights and here and there a warmly lit upstairs window. By the time he was dressed he began to hear a clamor upstairs. His wife and daughter charged down in negligee, commanding him to do something about it.

"Get dressed," he said, and pointedly disconnected his hearing aid.

He rambled about the house while they did. Absently he tried to dial coffee and gave up with a self-conscious laugh when the water would not flow. The closets, drawers, and dressers had rejected all their contents, upstairs and down. Pushers had calmly shoved them out and the doors had closed and locked—to him, forever. He contemplated the disordered piles of clothes and kitchenware, and began to pack a traveling case.

Two bored policemen wandered in while he was doing so; the door, of course, was no longer on lock. He plugged in his hearing aid, taking plenty of time about it. He said to them, "Well?"

They told him he had plenty of time; they weren't in any hurry. Take an hour if you need it, bub. They'd tote him and his family and their stuff out to Belly Rave, help him pick out a good place. And—uh—don't take this too hard, bub. Sometimes when people got busted out of contract status they—uh—got panicky and tried to, well, knock themselves off.

The moving had one golden moment. One of the cops helpfully picked up a suitcase. Alexandra told him to remove his *filthy* hands from——

The cop clouted her and explained what they didn't take none of off of Belly Rave brats.

The police car handed Norvell a jolt. It was armored.

"You—you get a lot of trouble in Belly Rave?" he guessed.

The friendlier of the cops said, "Nah. Only once in a while. They haven't jumped a squad car in six months, not with anything but pistols, anyway. You'll be okay." And they pulled away from Monmouth G.M.L. Unit W-97-AR. There was no sentiment to the parting. Norvell was sunk in worry, Alexandra was incandescent but still. And Virginia had not said two words to anyone that morning.

The car paused at the broad beltway circling the bubble-city, motor idling and the driver impatiently talking into his radio. Finally two more police cars rolled up and the three of them in convoy left the city roads for the cracked asphalt that led to Belly Rave. Once the road they traveled had been a six-lane superhighway, threading a hundred thousand commuters' cars morning and night. Now it wound through a scraggly jungle, the toll booths at the interchanges crumbled into rock piles and rust.

They bumped along for a couple of miles, then turned off into a side road that was even worse.

The first thing that hit Norvell was the smell.

The second thing was worse. It was the horrible feeling of betrayal as he looked on Belly Rave. A man can reconcile himself to anything. If life is doomed to be an eternity of agony with duodenal cancer, or the aching and irremediable poverty of the crippled and friendless, he can manage to survive and make the best of it. But when he has steeled himself to disaster . . . and the event is a thousandfold worse than his fiercest nightmare . . . the pockets of strength are overrun and nothing remains inside him but collapse.

And Belly Rave, in its teeming ruin, was worse than anything Norvell had dreamed.

The police cars swayed around a corner, sirens blasting, and stopped in the middle of a long, curving block. The convoying cars pulled up ahead and behind; a cop got out of each and stood ankle-deep in weeds and refuse, hand idly resting on his gun.

Norvell's driver said, "This one will do. Let's go."

The act of moving their possessions into the house in the driving rain, ringed by an audience of blank-faced Belly Ravers, was mercifully blurred in Norvell's mind. At one moment he was sitting in the police car, staring in disbelief at the wretched kennel they offered him; at the next, the police cars were gone, he was sitting on a turned-up suitcase, and Alexandra was whining, "Norvell, I've *got* to have something to eat before I absolutely *die*, it's been——"

Virginia sighed and stood up. "Shut up," she said levelly to her daughter. "Norvell, help me get the big suitcase upstairs."

She kicked a heap of rattling cans out of her way and headed for a flight of steps, ignoring her daughter.

Norvell followed her up the narrow stairs, the treads, ancient and patched with a miscellany of boards and sheetmetal, groaning under them. The upper floor (Expansion Attic for Your Growing Family) was soggy with rain, but Virginia found a spot where no water was actually dripping in. He dumped the suitcase there. "Go on down and watch the other stuff," she ordered. "I'm going to change my clothes."

Before she got down they had company.

First to arrive were three men in ragged windbreakers. "Police," one of them said, flashing something metallic in Norvell's face. "Just a routine check. You people got any valuables, alcoholic beverages, narcotics, or weapons to register?"

Norvell protested, "The police just left."

"Them's bubble-town police, buster," the man said. "They got no jurisdiction here. If you want to take my advice, you won't give us arguments. Come on, buster, what've you got to register?"

Norvell shrugged feebly. "Nothing, I guess. Unless you count our clothes."

The men moved purposefully toward the bags. "Just clothes?" one of them flung over his shoulder. "No guns or liquor?"

Virginia's high, clear voice came down the stairs. "You're God-damned right we have guns," she said tensely. "You bums turn around and get out of here before you find out the hard

59

way!" Norvell, eyes popping, saw an oldfashioned revolver in her hand.

"Just a minute, sister," one of the "police" objected.

"Beat it!" she clipped. "I'm counting to five. One, two, three——"

They were gone, swearing.

Virginia came down the stairs and handed the gun to Norvell. "Keep it," she said coldly. "Looks better if *you* use it. Just in case you were wondering, there aren't any cops in Belly Rave."

Norvell swallowed. He hefted the gun cautiously. It was surprisingly heavy, far heavier than his unskilled imagination, not considering the mass needed to contain bursting gunpowder, would ever have guessed. "Where did you get this thing?"

Virginia said drearily, "I've always had it. Used to be Tony's, before he died. There's lesson one for you: You don't live here without a gun."

Alexandra came forward with shining eyes. "You were *wonderful*," she breathed. "Those detestable *brutes*—heaven only knows *what* would have happened to me if only *Norvell* had been here."

She started to plant a wet kiss on her mother's cheek. Virginia shoved her daughter away and studied her coldly.

She spoke at last, in a strange, dry voice. "We'll have no more of that cack, Missy. From now on you're going to level with me—and with Norvell, too. Hear me? We can't afford lying, faking, doublecrossing, or temperament. You'd better learn it, and learn it *fast*. The first bad break you make and I'll sell you like a shot."

Alexandra's face was a study in terror.

Her mother said dispassionately, "Sink or swim—you're in Belly Rave now. You don't remember; but you'll learn. Now get out of here. If you can't scrounge something to eat, go hungry. But don't come back here until sundown."

The child stood blankly. Virginia took her by the shoulder; pushed her through the door; slammed it behind her.

Norvell looked through a chink in the boarding of the cracked picture window and saw Alexandra plodding hopelessly down the battered walk, weeping.

He uncertainly asked Virginia—the *new* Virginia—"What was that about selling her?"

She said, "What I said. I'll sell her. It's easy, you can always find a fagin or a madam for a kid. I don't know how prices run; when I was thirteen, I brought fifty dollars."

Norvell, his hair standing on end, said, *"You?"*

"Me. Not Wilhelmina Snodgrass or Zenobia Beaverbottom. Me. Your wife. I guess I was lucky—they sold me to a fagin, not into a house. He ran a tea pad; I helped him roll the clientele. That's where I met Tony. Now, if there are no more useless questions, help me unpack."

Norvell helped her, his head whirling. Without shame or apology she had demolished the story of her life—the story he had painstakingly built up from her "accidental" hints and revelations over the years. She "hadn't wanted to talk about it" . . . but somehow Norvell *knew*. The honest, industrious parents. The frugal, rugged life of toil. The warmth of family feeling, drawn together by common need. The struggling years as a—as a something she had never exactly specified, but something honorable and plain. The meeting with Tony Elliston—glamorous cad from the Field Day crowd. Not a bad fellow. But not love, Norvell—not what *we* have. . . .

He had thought himself clever. He had pieced it together into a connected tale, chuckling privately because she couldn't know how much he knew.

And all the while she had been a pickpocket in a dope joint, sold into it by her parents.

There was a knock on the door.

Virginia said through her teeth, "If that brat's come back before I told——" and swung it open. She screamed.

Norvell, greatly to his surprise, found he had the revolver in his hand. He was pointing it at the middle of the hulking, snaggle-toothed figure in the doorway.

The figure promptly raised its enormous hands over its small, shock-haired head and told him, grinning, "Don't shoot, mister. I'm harmless. I know I'm not pretty but I'm harmless. Came here to help you out. Show you where to register and all. The name's Shep. I'll give you a fair shake. Show you the best places for firewood, wise you up on the gangs. Hear you have a little girl. You want to sell her, I'll get you a price.

You want to go into business? I can put you next to a guy who'll start you out with hemp seed. If you got real money, I know a sugar dealer and a guy with a still to rent. I'm just Shep, mister. I'm just trying to get along."

Virginia said, "Keep the gun on him, Norvell. Shep, you come in and sit down. What do you want?"

"Surplus rations," the giant said with a childlike smile. "Cash, if you have any. Always I'm desperate, but now I'm out of my mind." His arm swept at the open door. "See the rain? I have to catch it. It's the front end of the rainbow, mister. See it? I have to catch it; I never saw it before. And to catch it I've got to have some crimson lake. Some other things too, but the crimson lake. You don't see crimson in it, do you? Well, you won't see crimson in the canvas, but it'll be there—in the underpainting, and because it's there I'll have the pot of tears, the bloody, godawful rainsweep caught gloom-driving down on two hundred thousand desolations."

Norvell, lowering the pistol, said stupidly, "You paint."

"I paint. And for fifty bucks I can get what I need, which leaves me only the problem of getting fifty bucks."

Virginia said, "With your build you could get it."

Shep shrugged apologetically. "Not like you mean, not with rough stuff. Not since I started painting," he said. "You can't be half a virgin. So I run errands."

He put his hands down, peering at them out of his Neanderthal skull. "Any errands? I've got to raise the fifty before the rain stops."

Virginia appeared to come to a conclusion. "Norvell, give Shep fifty dollars." He shot his wife a horrified look; that would leave them with eighteen dollars and sixty-five cents. She said contemptuously, "Don't worry. He won't skip; there's no place to hide for long in Belly Rave." She told Shep, "You'll work for it. One week's hard work. The outhouse is probably brim-full. The chimney looks like it's blocked. We need firewood. This place needs patching all around. Also my husband doesn't know the ropes and he might get in trouble. You'll watch him?"

"For fifty, sure!" he glowed. "Want me to watch the kid?"

"No," she said shortly.

The giant nodded, his eyes dark. "You know what you're doing, lady. It'll be rough on her. Can I have the fifty now?

It'll take two, three days to get the stuff. Ten bucks for the kid who does the running. *I can't miss this rain.*"

Norvell counted out fifty dollars and handed them over. "Okay!" Shep boomed happily. "We'll get my crimson lake out of the way, then registration."

They walked through the driving rain to a tumbledown building guarded by a ratfaced boy of twelve. Shep told him cryptically, "Got a message for Monmouth."

The boy raised his head and hooted mournfully, "Wa-wa-wa-wa-wabbit twacks!"

Norvell blinked his eyes. Kids! Everywhere. From nowhere. Ratfaced, gimlet-eyed, appearing from the rainshroud, silently and suddenly before him as though they had condensed out of the watery air.

Shep told them, "Like last time, but with *crimson lake* too. Got it?"

A haggard girl of perhaps thirteen said dispassionately, "Cack like last time. The Goddams joined up with the Goering Grenadiers. It'll be a busted-bottle job getting through the West Side."

Shep said, "I'm in a hurry, Lana. Can you do it or can't you?"

She mildly told him, "Who said 'can't,' you or me? I said it'd be a busted-bottle job."

The ratfaced twelve-year-old said sullenly, "Not me. They know I was the one got Stinkfoot's kid brother. Besides——"

"Shut your mouth about Stinkfoot's kid brother," Lana blazed. "You stay here; I'll talk to you when I get back." The boy cowered away. Lana called to the kids, "Bwuther wabbits, inspection *harms!*"

Jagged glass edges flashed. Norvell swallowed at what they implied.

"Good kids," Shep cried, and handed Lana the fifty dollars.

"Wa-wa-wa-wa-wabbit twacks!" She hooted mournfully, and the kids were gone, vanished back into the shrouding rain.

Norvell swallowed his questions, trudging after Shep through the floods. He had learned that much, at least.

The Resident Commissioner lived in an ordinary house, to Norvell's surprise. He had expected the man who was responsible for the allowances of thousands of people to be living in a G.M.L.; certainly his rank entitled him to one. There were only twenty commissioners scattered through Belly Rave.

Then Norvell saw the Resident Commissioner. He was a dreary old hack; he told Norvell dimly, "Carry your cards at all times. Be sure and impress that on your wife and the little girl. There's all kinds of work to getting duplicate cards, and you might go hungry for a week before they come through if you lose these. As head of the family you get a triple ration, and there's a separate one for the wife. Is the little girl a heavy eater?"

Norvell guessed so. He nodded vaguely.

"Well, we'll give her an adult ration then. Lord knows there's no shortage of food. Let's see, we'll make your hours of reporting on Wednesdays, between three and five. It's important to keep to your right hours, otherwise there's likely to be a big rush here sometimes, and nobody at all others. Is all that pretty clear? You'll find that it's mostly better to travel in groups when you come down for your allowance. Shep can tell you about that. It—it prevents trouble. We don't want any trouble here." He tried to look stern. And pathetically added, *"Please* don't make trouble in my district. There are nineteen others, aren't there?"

He consulted a checklist, whispering to himself. "Oh. Your ration cards entitle you and the whole family to bleacher seats at all bouts and Field Days." Norvell's heart was torn by the words. The rest was a blur. "Free transportation, of course —hope you'll avail yourself—no use to stay home and brood —little blood clears the air—door always open———"

Outside in the rain Norvell asked Shep: "Is *that* all he does?"

Shep looked at him. "Is there something else to do?" He swung around. "Let's get some firewood."

Chapter Twelve

AS A DISAPPEARING ACT, it was a beaut.

Mundin tried everything. No Norma Lavin. Gone. After Ryan's phone call, the track was lost.

Mundin went first to the police, of course, and when he told them Norma Lavin was a Belly Raver they tried not to laugh right in his face.

"Look, mister," a kindly missing-persons sergeant explained. "People are one thing. Belly Ravers are something else. Are these people on the tax rolls? Do they have punch-card codes? Do they have employment-contract identification tattoos? No. No, they don't. So what can we do? We can find missing persons, sure, but this gal ain't a person. She's a Belly Raver." The sergeant shrugged philosophically. "Maybe she just took a notion to wander off. Maybe she's got her toes turned up in a vacant lot. Maybe not. We just wouldn't know, see?"

But he kindly took Charles Mundin's name, just in case.

However Mundin bought a gun and started his own inquiries in Belly Rave. Lots of people had seen Norma and her ancient Cadillac the day of the disappearance. But not afterward.

And that was that.

It took a week, during which Mundin found himself making regular trips to the Lavin Ryan home loaded down with groceries. He also found that Ryan was tapping him for cash to feed his habit.

Don Lavin was sinking into a kind of catatonia without his sister. Ryan, sometimes coldly confident with a bellyful of yen pox, other times devoured by the weeping shakes, begged Mundin to try something, anything. Mundin tried a doctor.

The doctor made one visit—during which Don Lavin, sparked by some flickering pride, rallied wonderfully and conversed good-humoredly with the doctor. The doctor left, with an indignant glare at Mundin, and Don lapsed back into his twilight gloom. "All right, Ryan," Mundin said bitterly, "now what?"

Ryan shook the last pill out of the tin, swallowed it, and told Mundin now what.

And Mundin found himself calling on William Choate IV.

Poor Willie's office was a little smaller than a landing field. He sprinted the length of it to embrace good old Charles.

"Gosh," he burbled, "I'm so glad you could come and see me! They just put me in here, after old Sterling died. It used to be his office, see? So when he died, they put——"

"I see," Mundin said gently. "They put you in here."

"Yep. Say, Charles, how about some lunch?"

"Maybe. Willie, I need a little help."

Willie said reproachfully, "Now, Charles, it *isn't* about a job, is it? Gee, that'd be an awful spot to put me in."

Well, Mundin thought, they had succeeded in beating one thing into his head, though not two. "No," he said. "I just want a little advice. I'd like to know when and where the annual stockholder's meeting of G.M.L. Homes comes off."

Willie said happily, "*I* don't know. Don't they have to publish it somewhere? In a newspaper?"

"Yes, they have to publish it in a newspaper, Willie. The trick is to find out what newspaper. There are maybe fifty thousand of them in the country, and the law just says that it has to be published in one—not necessarily English language."

Willie looked sorrowful. "I only speak English, Charles," he said.

"Yes, Willie. Why don't you ask your Periodical Search Department?"

Willie nodded vigorously. "Oh, sure, Charles. Anything to oblige. Anything at all!" Willie uncertainly asked his squawk box whether they had anything like a Periodical Research Department, and the squawk box said yes, sir, and connected him. Half an hour later, deep in the intricacies of the preliminary pre-hearing of the Group E Debenture Holder's Protective Committee, the squawk box coughed and announced that the G.M.L. Homes meeting was advertised in the Lompoc, California, *Picayune-Intelligencer*. Time, day after tomorrow. Place, Room 2003, Administration Building, Morristown, Long Island.

"Whew!" said Willie dubiously. "They won't get many people to come *there*, will they?"

The next morning Mundin was waiting at a two-dollar ticket window of the New York Stock Exchange when the opening bell rang.

He examined the crumpled instructions from Ryan nervously, as sweating and tense as any of the passionate throng of devotees pressing around him, but for other reasons.

Ryan's instructions were complete and precise, except for one thing: They didn't tell how to get the two thousand dollars to put them into effect. Mundin swore under his breath, shrugged, and swiftly punched Number 145. Anaconda Copper. He inserted his token, threw the lever and tore off his ticket. At 19,999 other windows in the gigantic hall, 19,999 other investors were doing the same. And outside, on the polychrome street, ten thousand late-comers milled and murmured, waiting for their turn inside.

The market moved.

The angular Big Board in the center of the hall flashed and twinkled—fast, then slow, then dead slow. It locked. The lights stopped. The pari-mutuel computers began to hum.

Mundin leveled his field glasses on 145, but it was hard to stay on it. His hands were trembling.

The gong rang, and the line he was watching flashed: 145, up 3.

The great hall trembled with noise, of which Mundin's obscene monosyllable was only the twenty-thousandth part. A lousy six cents profit, he groaned. Not worth taking to the cashier's window.

A passing broker, a grimy Member's button in his lapel, said intimately: "Hey, bud—watch metals."

"Beat it or I'll have you run in," Mundin snapped. He had no time to waste on phony touts. He swept his field glasses over the Big Board, trying to make some sense out of the first movement of the day.

Industrials were down an average of four, the helpful summary told him. "Rails"—meaning, mostly, factory-site land developments—were up three. Chemicals, up eight.

Mundin figured. That meant that the investors would lay off chemicals because they would figure everybody would be on chemicals because of the rise—except for the investors who would be on chemicals because they would figure everybody would lay off chemicals because they'd figure everybody would be on chemicals. Because of the rise.

Thirty-second warning bell!

"Bud," said the broker insistently, *"watch metals!"*

"Go to hell," Charles said hoarsely, his fingers shaking over the buttons. He punched Anaconda again, bought five tickets, cursed himself and waited.

When he heard the great groan at last he opened his eyes and swept the board with his glasses.

145, up 15

"Remember who told ya," the broker was saying.

Mundin gave him a dollar. He would, after all, need a pair of hands. . . . "Thanks, bud," the broker said. "You're doing a smart thing. Look, don't switch. Not yet. I'll tell ya when. This is a morning crowd—Tuesday morning at that. Not a crazy hysterical Monday-morning crowd that gets in fast and gets cleaned out fast. Look around and see for yaself. Little fellows taking a day off. The family men that play it smart—they think. Smart and small. I been watching them for twenny years. Don't switch."

Charles didn't switch.

He kept feeding a dribble of dollars to the broker, who was either lucky or a genius that day. By noon Charles had a well-diversified portfolio of metals with a cash-in value of four hundred and eighty dollars.

"Now," the broker said hoarsely. He had borrowed Charles's field glasses to scan the crowd. "See?" Some of them's leaving. Some of them breaking out sanniches. The handle's dropping. They're getting not-so-smart now, not-so-small. I been watching them twenny years. Now they start doing the stupid, obvious things, because they're gettin' hungry and a hungry man ain't smart. I feel it, mister, the way I never felt it before. Sell twenny points short. Jeez, I wish I had the nerve to say thirty!"

Two minutes later he was pounding Charles on the back and yelling, "We did it, bud! We made it! We made it!"

Metals had broken—thirty-eight points. Charles, by now icy-calm, gave him five dollars. Step One in Ryan's instructions; build up a stake. He'd done it.

He turned the dial to the five-hundred-dollar range. "Give me a winner," he told the tout.

The broker gasped and stuttered.

"I've got to," Charles said. "This is taking too long. I'm in a hurry."

The broker stammered: "Solid fuels ought to rise now—but—but—please, bud, make it two-fifty. One on solid fuels and one on—on——" He swept the board with his glasses. "Can's been sleepin' all day," he muttered. "A Tuesday crowd stays off Can, but after metals break——"

He said slowly, "Buy solid fuels and Can."

By two in the afternoon Charles had a cash-in value of $2,300 and the broker's pockets were bulging with small change. He was talking to himself in an undertone.

Charles said abruptly, "Okay. Now I want a share of G.M.L."

The broker blinked at him. "Old 333? No, you can't do that."

"Yes I can. I want it."

The broker shook his head. He said reasonably, "Bud, you don't understand. You're new here; I been around for twenny years. They have an investor, see? All day long he just punches 333. I know him well. That's him over there, third tier, second aisle. Like Steel and A&P—they don't take no chances on anybody claimin' no stock."

"I want it," said Mundin.

The broker, horrified, said, "Bud, ain't you made enough for one day? Come on, let's go get a drink; I'll buy. You fool around with the big boys, they *punish* you. Like G.M.L. You try to grab a share and you'll get hurt. Unlimited resources, see—un-lim-it-ed. They've got 'em. Every movement, all day long, he has a 'buy' bid in. He bids *ten thousand bucks*, way over real value. You get a wild idea and bid over ten thousand and you'll get it, sure. So next movement, what happens? He sells short, maybe. Maybe he waits. But sooner or later he does, and then you're squashed. You know what they say, bud—'Him who sells what isn't his'n must buy it back or go to prison.' And plenty have."

Mundin said coldly, "What's G.M.L. par?"

"Two thousand. But ya can't claim it, didn't I just tell you?

He's got a bid in every movement. So ya see?"

Charles set himself to persuade the broker to do the thing Ryan had planned. Two movements went by, while Charles pleaded and threatened and bribed.

At last the broker, shaking, stumbled off toward the third tier, second aisle. Mundin followed him with his field glasses.

It was working. Mundin, sweating, saw in miniature, through the glasses, the greeting, the silent shove, the wordless rejoinder, the growing heat of the quarrel. The G.M.L. investor was a small, elderly fat man. The broker was small too, but lean and wiry.

The fight broke out as the thirty-second warning bell rang. Charles took his eyes off the fighters and the for once untended investor's window, and steadily punched its two-hundred-and-fifty dollar tickets on Old 333.

One bid and no offerings did not constitute a transaction according to the electronic definitions of the New York Stock Exchange pari-mutuel machine. As it had all day, the Big Board said:

333, no change.

One bid, and no offerings. In a claiming movement, it meant a quick profit—the difference between the bid and the par value. An investor next to Charles, eyeing him respectfully, said, "What do ya like in Chemicals, bud?"

Mundin ignored him. He left his station, almost regretfully, and took the escalator up to the cashier's windows marked "Industrials—$1,000 and up."

"Two thousand dollars," said the bored clerk, inspecting the tickets, glancing at his miniature of the Big Board, noting the "no change." He began to count out hundred-dollar bills.

"I'm claiming," Mundin said through stiff lips.

"Okay, mister—uh." The clerk suddenly realized. "Jeez— Old 333! How'd you do it?"

"I'm claiming," Charles said stubbornly. "Two thousand dollars par value. Let's go."

The clerk shrugged and tapped out an order on his keyboard. Moments later, one share of G.M.L. Homes voting common stock fluttered from a slot in the desk. The clerk filled in Charles's name and home address and recorded them.

"You'll get that to the company's board of directors immediately?" the attorney asked.

"It's automatic," said the clerk. "It's in their files now. Say, mister, if you don't mind telling me how you pulled it off——"

He was being much too affable—and Charles saw, in his ear, the little plug of a personal receiver. Quite possibly he was being stalled.

He darted into the crowd and was lost to sight within seconds.

The two gambles had paid off, Mundin thought, heading for the street and Belly Rave. The dice had rolled, and he got the stake; the dice rolled again and he got his single share of stock in G.M.L. Homes, entitling him to a seat at the annual stockholders' meeting.

Now the real gambling would begin.

Mundin whistled for a cab. There was a commotion behind him, but the cab came before Mundin had time for more than a glimpse, not time enough to notice that the man who was being worked over, in broad daylight by three huskies, was a small, wiry man with a soiled Member's button in his lapel.

You fool around with the big boys, they *punish* you.

Chapter Thirteen

"GETTING ON FOR NOON," Shep said. "Let's find a restaurant."

"A restaurant?" Norvie Bligh giggled. He followed Shep down the littered, filthy street, wondering. In a week he had thought he had learned something about Belly Rave, under Shep's tutelage. But he had seen no neon-glittering, glass-fronted havens.

What Shep led him to was just another Belly Rave house. A wheezing old crone crept around the living room. There was a fire going in the fireplace, and water bubbling in a blackened kettle. Restaurant?

Shep took a couple of rations from his pocket. He never seemed to be without a dozen or so. They were easy enough to get from the R.C.; you could claim you had a dozen dependents and he would apathetically list you for 273 rations

71

a week. If you could lift them, they were yours. There was plenty of food.

And plenty of circuses.

Shep split the two-by-three-by-six plastic box with his thumbnail and Norvell clumsily followed suit. Things tumbled out. Shep tossed one of the "things"—an unappetizing little block of what looked like plastic-wrapped wood—to the crone.

She caught it and gobbled it down with desperate hunger, choking on crumbs.

"Business not so good?" Shep asked casually. In his voice there was an undertone of contempt.

She glared at him wordlessly. She bailed water out of the kettle with a rusted can and slopped it into his plastic ration box. Shep popped open a little envelope and sprinkled a dark powder on the water.

Coffee! The magic smell made Norvell suddenly ravenous. He handed the crone a similar block from his own ration, got his water, made his coffee, and greedily explored the other things that had come out of the box.

Biscuits. A tin of meat-paste. A chewy block of compressed vegetables. Candy. Cigarettes. The combination was one he hadn't encountered before; the meat-paste was highly spiced and salty, but good.

Shep watched as he gobbled. Shep sighed, at last, "When you've eaten each menu ten thousand times—well, I won't discourage you."

Outside, Norvell asked shyly what in the world the old woman thought she was doing for a living.

"It's simple," said Shep. "She gets her rations and trades them for firewood. She uses the wood to heat water—for coffee, or bouillon, or tea, or whatever. She trades the water for rations. She keeps hoping that some day she'll come out ahead on the deal. She never has."

"But *why?*"

Shep didn't speak for a long minute as they sauntered along in the afternoon sun. At last he said, "No offense. But it's easy to see you're a come-lately, Bligh. Why does she do it? Because it makes her feel like a human being."

"But——"

"But hell. It makes her feel as though she were master of her fate, captain of her soul. It's hard to starve to death in

72

Belly Rave, but in a bad week she comes close to it. She thinks she's a Rockefeller or a Weeks in miniature. Risking her capital in the hope of gain. Well, she is! What if she always loses? She's doing something—not just sitting and waiting for the ration day to roll around again. You've heard of hell?"

Norvell nodded. Like practically everybody else he was a member of the Reformed Rationalist Church of the Inchoate Principle, but hell had been mentioned in sermons now and then.

"Well, if a man who said that hell is a perpetual holiday was right, then this is it. Belly Rave, mister. Belly Rave."

Norvell nodded again. It made sense; he could see how it would make irresistible, unarguable sense, after the ten-thousandth sampling of each menu. The crone would try—anything. Being a crone; being an old woman with no talents and no hopes. Those who could do anything, anything at all, would try anything. Anything at all.

It gave him a clue to the enigma named Shep. He said comprehendingly, "So she has her restaurant, and you have your art, and——"

The giant turned on him, picked him up by the lapels and shook him like a kitten.

"You little louse," Shep growled shakily between the broken teeth. "You fool! What do *you* know? Listen to me, little louse! If you ever say, or hint, or *think* that I'm just piddling around to kill the time, I'll snap you in two!" He slammed Norvell down on the pavement so hard his arches ached; he stood glaring at Norvell, arms akimbo.

Strangely, Norvell was not frightened. In a clear, intuitive flash he realized that he had said the unspeakable, that the offense was terribly his.

He managed to say, very sincerely, "I'm sorry, Shep."

His knees were shaking and his heart was pounding, but it was only adrenalin. With an unclouded mind he knew what torment had driven this placid hulk to rage: Incessant, relentless, nagging self-doubt. Where leisure is compulsory, how do you tell the burning drive to create from its sterile twin, named "puttering?" You can't. Posterity can; but only posterity. And you won't be there to know. And the self-doubt must remain forever unresolved, forever choked down and forever rising again.

And when, unexpectedly, it leaps forth it burns like acid.

Norvell told the big man steadily, "I won't say that again. I won't even think it. Not because you scared me but because I know it isn't true." He hesitated. "I—I used to think I was a kind of artist myself. I know what you go through."

Shep grumbled, "Bligh, you're just beginning to find out what you go through—but I'm sorry I blew my top."

"Forget it." They walked on.

Shep said at last, "Here's where we get some more supplies." The place was one of the inevitable picture-window, fieldstone-chimney ruins, but with a fenced-in yard. The gate had a lock on it. Shep kicked the gate down, tearing out the hinges and the staples of the hasp.

Norvell said, "Hey!"

"We do this my way. Hey, Stearns!"

Stearns was a grim, gray man. He threaded his way to them around stacks of plastic fittings, guttering, and miscellaneous. "Hello, Shep," he said flatly. "What do you want?"

Shep said, "I don't have my notebook with me, but I guess I'll remember it all. You hijacked repair materials that a couple of friends of mine got through legitimate black-market channels. I want them back. With interest."

"Still on the protection kick, Shep?" the man asked. His voice was ugly. "If you had any sense you'd come in with me."

"I don't work for anybody, Stearns. I do favors for a few friends, they do favors for me. Trot out your team, Titan of Industry."

Shep, so lightning-fast to resent the slur himself, was insensitive enough to use it on others. With the same results.

Stearns's face went pasty with rage and Norvell knew what was coming next—unless he moved fast. "Stearns!" he yelled, and used the moment's delay to draw the pistol that Virginia had ordered him to carry. Stearns's hand stopped at his lapel and slowly, unwillingly, dropped to his side.

Shep gave Norvell a quick, approving glance. "Trot out your team, Stearns," he ordered.

Stearns didn't look away from the gun in Norvell's hand. "Chris! Willie!" he yelled. "Get the truck."

The truck was a two-wheeler stake job with one starved-looking teen-ager pulling between poles and another pushing against a canvas breast-band. Walking Stearns before him, Shep ordered him to pick up this or that article of building material and put it on the truck. He filled the truck, topped the load with a rusty pick and shovel from a tool shed, and told Chris and Willie, "Roll it, kids. It won't be far."

Norvell didn't pocket his gun until they had put three blocks between themselves and Stearns's final malevolent glare.

There were two stops before they headed for Norvell's home. At each of them a part of the supplies were unloaded, to the tearful thanks of sober-looking citizens who had thought them gone forever, and with them the months of accumulation, gambling, and wangling that had earned them in the first place.

Norvell, eyeing the heaving, panting teen-agers, suggested uneasily, "Let's give them a hand with the truck."

But Shep shook his head. "We might get jumped. Our job is convoying."

There was no trouble. The kids rolled the cart to the door of Norvell's house and unloaded the firewood and building materials, stacking them neatly on the shredded broadloom that covered the floor of the sunken living room.

Virginia cast an appraising eye over the neat heaps, weighing, planning. "No tar paper, linoleum, anything like that?"

Shep guffawed. "No diamonds, either," he told her. "You think your roof is the only one that leaks? You're lucky—you got two finished floors. Let the top one get soaked. You'll be all right down here."

"Cack," she said. Norvell winced. "If you can't get tar paper, see if you can find something else to make shingles out of. Sheet tin will do."

"So will the roof off a G.M.L," Shep said sourly, but he made a note. He tossed a couple of rations to the waiting kids, who took them and pushed their empty truck away. He said, "Anything else?"

Virginia, suddenly a hostess, said, "Oh, I suppose not. Care for a drink?"

Norvell, for politeness' sake, took a sip of the bottle Virginia produced—"Ration-jack," she called it; got by trading firewood with the evil-eyed octogenarian in the house next door. He didn't like it. The ration-jack tasted like the chewy fruit bars he had enjoyed until then, when he found them

75

in his ration pack; but the taste was overlaid with the bite of forty-proof alcohol. Beer was what he really liked. They didn't seem to have beer in Belly Rave.

Shep and Virginia were talking; Norvell let the conversation drift past him. He sat back, bone-weary. Physical weariness was a new thing to Norvie Bligh. He had never had it as a child, never had it at General Recreations.

Why was it that doing nothing involved physical labor, and doing actual creative, productive work—running a Field Day, for instance—involved only the work of the mind? Norvie admitted it to himself: Already he was taking on the coloration of Belly Rave. Like its other discouraged, hopeless inhabitants, he was living for the day and ignoring the morrow. Rations and a place to sleep. Perhaps it would not be long, he told himself wonderingly, before he would be one of the simians queueing up at Monmouth Stadium.

Unless he found something to do. But what was there to do? Work on the house? The essentials were done; the bars were up, the trash was carted out into the street, where by and by it would slump into a featureless heap like all the other middens along the road. The less urgent things to do couldn't be done. You couldn't fix the lesser roof leaks—no shingles. You couldn't fix the stairs—no materials; no tools. And no skill.

He said excitedly, oblivious of the fact that he was interrupting, "Virginia! How about starting a garden? A couple of fruit trees—orange, maybe. A few rows of——"

Virginia laughed and laughed, almost hysterically. Even Shep chuckled. Virginia said, "Orange trees don't grow around here, my dear husband. Nothing else does, either. You start digging out there and first you go through two feet of garbage and trash, then maybe six inches of cinder and fill. Then you hit the real pay-dirt. Sand."

Norvell sighed. "There must be something to do."

Shep offered, "You could paint your dump, if you're feeling ambitious. I know where there's some house paint."

Norvell sat up, interested. He accepted the bottle of ration-jack and took a small swallow. "Paint? Why not? No reason why we can't keep the place looking decent, is there?"

Shep shrugged. "Depends. If you want to start some kind of a business, paint's a good advertisement. If you want to just

76

drift, maybe you don't want to advertise. You make yourself too conspicuous, people get ideas."

Norvell said, dampened, "You mean robbers?"

Virginia reached for the bottle of ration-jack. "Cack," she said dispassionately, taking a long swallow. "We aren't painting."

There was a long pause. In the G.M.L. bubble-house, Norvell reminded himself, Virginia had never let it be in doubt who was boss, but she had seldom demonstrated her power in front of outsiders.

But they weren't in the bubble-house any more.

I want Arnie, Norvell cried to himself, suddenly miserable. It isn't working out right at all, not the way he said it would. He said it would be a chance to express myself, to make something of my marriage, to be on my own. And it's not that at all!

He reclaimed the bottle of ration-jack. It tasted by now quite disgusting; he fleetingly thought that he would never relish those fruit bars again; but he took a long pull.

Shep was saying, "—didn't do so badly today. Stearns gave me a little trouble, and if Norvie hadn't held a gun on him I might not have got the stuff so easy."

Virginia looked at her husband appraisingly. But all she said to Norvie was, "You better keep an eye on that gun. Alexandra tried to sneak out with my kitchen knife today."

"Eh?" said Norvie, jolted.

"That's right. Put on quite a scene," her mother said, almost admiringly. "She's getting in with the Goering Grenadiers and it seems they pack knives and guns. They look down on the Wabbits and their busted bottles."

Norvie took another pull at the ration-jack. He said vaguely, "Does she *have* to do that?"

Shep said grimly, "If she wants to stay alive she does. Get it straight, Norvie, will you? This is Belly Rave. Not a finishing school. It's a permanent Field Day, only without rules."

Now *there* was something he knew something about, Norvell thought, brightening. "You ever go in for a Field Day?" he asked eagerly.

"Nope. Just the weeklies."

"Oh, you ought to, Shep. That's where the real money is. And it's not very dangerous, if you play it smart. Take spear-carrying in Spillane's Inferno, for instance. Safe as houses.

And, from the artistic side, let me tell you from experience that——"

"Cack on spear-carrying, Bligh," Shep said, with a wire edge in his voice. "I don't do that any more. I've been there, sticking the poor slobs who fall off the high wire before they reach the blonde. I've been on the wire myself, too. Once." He reached for the ration-jack, his face blank. "She missed me with all eight shots. I fractured her femur with my first. And then I dropped the gun." He took a huge drink. "They booed me. I didn't get the killer's bonus. I didn't get the midriff bonus or the navel superbonus. I didn't want them. All I wanted was some brushes, some canvas, some graphite sticks and some colors. I got them, Bligh, and I found out I couldn't use them. For six god-damned months. Then for six months more I couldn't paint anything except her face when the slug hit her thigh and she fell off the perch."

Norvell said, "Oh." He contemplated the ration-jack bottle with distaste. He got to his feet, weaving slightly. "I—I think I want some air," he said. "Excuse me, folks."

"Certainly," said Virginia, not even looking at him. As Norvell went out the door he heard her ask Shep, "This blonde you shot—was she pretty?"

Chapter Fourteen

MUNDIN WAS NOT FOLLOWED from the Stock Exchange.

He got to Belly Rave by late afternoon, his share of G.M.L. Common securely tucked in a pocket. Ryan was coherent and jubilant.

"Ah," exclaimed Ryan. "One share voting. The meeting is tomorrow. And accessory before the fact to simple assault. A good day's, Counselor."

"I hope so," said Mundin, worn from the reaction of the morning's work and fretful. "I hope this share is going to be enough to get me in. What if it isn't entered, or they challenge it?"

Ryan said comfortably, "They can't. *Id certum est quid reddi potest, Counselor.*"

78

"Oh, of course, Counselor," glared Mundin. "But *affirmantis est probatio,* you know."

Ryan blinked and grinned. "Score one for your side," he said amiably. "Well, hell, Mundin, all you can do is go up there flat-footed and happy. The stock's your ticket of admission. If they won't let you in we'll have to think of something else, that's all."

Mundin said dubiously, "You've been right so far, I suppose." He stood up and took a turn around the dingy room, tripping over Don Lavin's feet. "Sorry," he said shortly to the sprawling youth, trying not to look at the staring, shining eyes. Don Lavin gave him the willies. And there was the excellent chance, he realized, that what had happened to Don Lavin might sooner or later happen to himself, if he persisted in sticking his nose into the corporate meatgrinders.

Mundin asked, "Nothing new about Norma, I suppose?"

Ryan shook his head. "They won't slip up, Mundin. You'll have to pry her loose from them tomorrow. Wish I could go with you ———"

"Oh, by all means do," Mundin said. "Love to have you. You'll like Morristown, it's so much like Belly Rave."

"I'd never stand the trip. You'll have to play it yourself, Counselor. I have confidence in you, boy. Just keep your head, and remember the essential nature of a great private utility corporation."

"A legal entity," guessed Mundin. "A fictive person."

"No, boy." The old eyes were gleaming in the ruined face. "Forget that. Think of an oriental court. A battlefield; a government; a poker game that never ends. The essence of a corporation is the subtle flux of power, now thrusting this man up, now smiting this group low. You can't resist power, boy, but you can guide it." He reached shakily for the battered tin of pills. "Oh, you'll manage," he said. "The thing for you to do now is to vanish. Get lost. Don't be seen anywhere until you turn up at the meeting. I wouldn't go to my office or my apartment if I were you." He glanced at Don Lavin, and Mundin cringed.

"What then," Mundin demanded. "You want me to stay here?"

"Anywhere. Anywhere out of sight."

Mundin looked at his watch. If he could sleep——if he

could go to bed now, and wake up just in time to start for the meeting. But it was far too early for that; and besides, he would scarcely be able to sleep. He had nearly twenty-four hours to kill. Twenty-four hours in which to think and get nervous and lose the sharp edge of his determination.

"I'm going out," he said. "I don't know if I'll see you before the meeting or not."

Mundin said good-by to Don Lavin, who never noticed him, and wandered through the growing dusk of Belly Rave. It was relatively safe until dark; he changed direction a couple of times when he caught sight of what looked like purposeful groups of men or children ahead, but there was actually small chance of attack before the sun went down.

He found himself nearing the General Recreations recruiting station, and felt somewhat more secure in the shelter of the inviting, pink-spun-candy-looking structure. General Recreations policed its area with its own guards; it was a good place to get a cab to go into Monmouth City.

But there was no hurry. Mundin studied the gaudy posters and the shuffling, gossiping men and women. It was the first time he had got really close to the raw material that Stadium shows were made of, and he felt a little like an intruder. He had seen the shows themselves, of course. Plenty of them, in his time. He had gone religiously to the Kiddies' Days back in Texas. As an adolescent, he had been a rootin', tootin' red-hot fan, as able as any to spout the logbook records on hours in combat, percentage kills, survival quotients and so on. Naturally, his enthusiasm had quieted down when the Scholarship people approved his application and he started law school, and he had never quite picked it up again. It didn't seem to go too well with membership at the bar—nothing against the games, of course; but an attorney was expected to go in for more cerebral forms of amusement.

Like dodging creditors, he told himself bitterly.

Somebody called from the shuffling mob, "Mr. Mundin! Hey, Mr. Mundin!"

He started, half ready to run.

But it was only whatsisname—Norvell Bligh, that was it. The client Dworcas had sent. But so shabby!

Then Mundin remembered: Bligh had quit on his contract.

80

A contract with General Recreations, ironically enough—and then to find him here!

The little man panted up to Mundin and wrung his hands. There was moisture in his eyes. "Mr. Mundin, my God it's good to see a friendly face! Were you—were you looking for me, maybe?"

"No, Mr. Bligh."

Bligh's face fell. Almost inaudibly he said, "Oh. I—uh—thought perhaps you might have a message for me—as my attorney, you know—maybe the company. . . . But they wouldn't, of course."

"No, they wouldn't," Mundin said gently. He looked around; he couldn't stand the little man's misery, nor could he wound him by walking away cold. He said, "Is there any place we can have a drink around here?"

"*Is* there!" Mundin thought he was going to cry. "My God, Mr. Mundin, the things I've seen in the week I've been here——"

He looked around to get his bearings and led off, Mundin following. It was only half a block to the nearest blind pig. Bligh knocked on an unlit door. "Shep sent me," he told a bitter-faced woman through a peephole.

Inside, the place reeked of alcohol. They sat at plank tables in the wretched living room, and through the careless curtains Mundin saw the gleam of copper tubing and shiny pots. They were the only customers at that hour.

The woman asked tonelessly, "Raisin-jack? Ration-jack? Majun? Reefers? Gin?"

"Gin, please," Mundin said hastily.

It came in a quart bottle. Mundin gasped when she said, "Fifty cents."

"Competition," Bligh explained when she had gone. "If it was just me she would've sold it for twenty-five, but of course she could tell you were just slumming."

"Not exactly," Mundin said. "Health!"

They drank. At first Mundin thought that somebody had smashed him on the back of the head with a padded mallet. Then he realized it was the gin.

Hoarsely, he asked Bligh, "How have you been getting along?"

Bligh shook his head, tears hanging in his eyes. "Don't ask

me," he said bitterly. "It's been hell, one day of hell after another, and no end to it. How have I been doing? It couldn't be worse, Mr. Mundin. I wish to heaven I——" he stopped himself, on the verge of breakdown. He sat up straighter. "Sorry," he said. "Been drinking all afternoon. Not used to it."

"That's all right," said Mundin.

Bligh said, "Sure." He eyed Mundin with a curiously familiar expression; Mundin, trying to place it, heard the words come tumbling out as Bligh abruptly clutched his sleeve and said, "Look, Mr. Mundin, you can help me. Please! You must have something. A big lawyer like you—working for the County Committee and everything—you've *got* to have *something!* I don't expect a contract and a G.M.L. I had them; I was a fool; I threw them away. But there must be some kind of a job, any kind, enough so I can get out of Belly Rave before I split right down the middle and——"

Mundin, holding back the recollection of himself and silly Willie Choate, said sharply, "No! I can't, Bligh. I don't have a job to give."

"Nothing?" Norvell cried. "Nothing I can do for you here, Mr. Mundin? Ask me. I know the ropes; *ask* me!"

It was a new thought. Mundin said uncertainly, "Why— why, as a matter of fact, there just might be something, at that. I've been trying to locate—ah—a friend here in Belly Rave. A girl named Norma Lavin. If you think you could help me find her——"

Bligh looked at him expressionlessly. "You want me to find you a girl?"

"A client, Bligh."

Bligh shrugged. "Sure, Mr. Mundin." Eagerly. "I can do it, I bet. I've got friends—contacts—you just leave it to me. You want to come along? I can get to work on it right now. I've learned a lot in a week; I can show you the ropes."

Mundin hesitated. Why not? His job was to stay out of sight. Until the stockholders' meeting, at least. . . .

"Certainly," he told Bligh. "Lead the way."

Mundin thought at first that the little man had taken leave of his senses.

Bligh led him through the growing dusk to a vacant lot—the burned-out site of one of Belle Reve's finest 40-by-60-foot estates. And then the little man cupped his hands to his mouth and hooted mournfully into the twilight: "Wa-wa-wa-wa-wab-bit twacks!"

Mundin, stupefied, began: "What——?"

Bligh put his finger to his lips. "Wait."

They waited. Two minutes; five. Then a small figure oozed from the dusk.

It asked suspiciously, "Who wants a wabbit?"

Bligh proudly introduced Mundin. "This gentleman is look-ing for a young lady——"

"Cack, buster! Us Wabbits don't——"

"No, no! A *particular* young lady. She has disappeared."

Mundin added, "Norma Lavin is her name. Disappeared a week ago. Lived at 37598 Willowdale Crescent. Drove an old Caddy."

"Um. Gee-Gee territory, that is," the shrill young voice in-formed them. "We got a Grenadier POW, though. What's in it for the Wabbits?"

Bligh whispered to Mundin, "Ten dollars."

Mundin said promptly, "Ten dollars."

"For a starter?"

"Sure."

"Come on." The Wabbit led them a desperate pace through a mile of Belly Rave. Once a thick-set brute lunged at them from a doorway, mumbling. The child snarled, "Lay off. Wab-bits!" The man slunk back; there had been a flash of jagged bottle glass from the fist of the Wabbit.

They moved on. Then, a mounting chorus down a street, rhythmic and menacing: "Gah-*damn!* Gah-*damn!* Gah-*damn.* . . ."

"In here!" the Wabbitt said shrilly, darting into a darkened house. A startled old man and woman, huddled before the cold fireplace, looked once and then didn't look at the in-truders again, having seen the busted-bottle insigne. The Wab-bit said meagerly to Mundin, "Patrol. This is Goddam ter-ritory."

They watched through cracks in the warped boards that covered the splintered picture window. The Goddams, still chanting, came swinging past, perhaps fifty of them, expertly twirling improvised maces. Some carried torches; one gangling boy in front bore a tall pole decorated with—with——

83

Mundin covered his eyes with a cry.

He was ignored. The Wabbit, frowning, muttered, "That's no patrol. War party, heading west."

Mundin said tightly, "My God, kid, he was carrying——"

The kid moved fast. The jagged bottle-edge was at Mundin's throat, which closed tight as a submarine hatch. "No noise, friend," the Wabbit murmured. "There'll be a rear guard."

There was.

You could barely see them. They were black-clad; their faces and hands were darkened.

"All right," the Wabbit said at last, and they slipped out. The old man and woman, still ignoring them, were munching rations and bickering feebly about who should chop up the chair to start a fire.

They dived into a house like any other house, except that it was full of pale, snake-eyed kids from eight to perhaps thirteen.

"Who're these?" a girl asked their Wabbit.

"Hello, Lana," Norvie Bligh said tentatively. She shriveled him with a glance and turned again to their guide.

"Customers," he said shrilly. "Missing persons. Ten bucks. And something important: War party of Goddams heading west on Livonia Boulevard, the 453-hundred block, at 7:50. Fifty of them with those hatchets of theirs. Advance guard and rear guard."

"Good," she said calmly. "Not our pigeon; looks like a cribhouse raid. Who's the missing person?"

Mundin told her.

As the Wabbit guide had said before her, she said, "Um. Goering Grenadier territory. Well, we have one in the attic. Want us to ask him, mister—for fifty bucks?"

Mundin paid.

The Goering Grenadier in the attic was an eight-year-old scooped up in a raid on the headquarters of the Grenadiers itself. At first he would only swear and spit at them. Then Lana took over the interrogation. Charles left abruptly.

The Grenadier was still crying when Lana joined him downstairs and said, "He talked."

"Where?"

"Fifty bucks more."

Mundin swore and searched his pockets. He had thirty-seven dollars and eighty-five cents. Lana shrugged and accepted twenty-five with good grace. She said:

"Seems there's a Mr. Martinson. He has jobs for the Gee-Gees now and then. He told the Grosse Hermann, that's their boss, that he wanted this Lavin dame picked up and doped. They were supposed to deliver her to some place on Long Island. The kid didn't go along; he doesn't remember just where. Says if he heard it he'd——"

Mundin was tearing upstairs. To the weeping child he barked: "Room 2003, Administration Building, Morristown, Long Island!"

"That's it, mister," said the kid, sniffling. "I *told* her I'd remember if——"

Mundin went back into the living room and leaned against a wall, brooding. So Norma was being kept on tap for the stockholders' meeting. Why? More conditioning? A forced transfer of her stock? No—not *her* stock, she didn't have any. Don Lavin's stock. She was the legatee; her brother had the stock——

So they would knock off her brother, and they would have the owner.

As simple as that.

Mundin said to Lana, "Listen. You saw that I have no more dough, not right now. But I need help. This thing is big— bigger than you might think. There are—well, thousands involved." What a fool he would have been to tell the truth and say billions! "It's big and it's complicated. First, can you throw a guard around 37598 Willowdale? I think your friends the Grenadiers are overdue to kill a young man named Don Lavin." He didn't wait for an answer but went right on: "Second, can you get me to the Administration Building in Morristown? I swear you'll be taken care of if this thing breaks right."

Lana measured him with her eyes. Then she said: "Can do. We won't haggle right now."

She barked orders; a silent group of children collected their broken bottles from the mantel over the wood-burning fireplace and slipped out.

Lana said definitely: "The Gee-Gees won't get to your friend. As for Morristown—well, if the Gee-Gees can make a delivery there I guess I can. Frankly, I don't like it. Morristown's tough. But we have an arrangement with the Itty-Bitties there. They're rats; they use guns; but——"

She shrugged helplessly. You gotta go along, her shrug said.

Mundin found himself escorted to the door. "Wait a minute," he said. "I want to hole up somewhere for the night. I'll meet you here in the morning, but what about right now?"

Bligh volunteered, "How about my place, Mr. Mundin? It isn't much, but we've got bars."

Lana nodded. "That'll do. In the morning—what now?"

One of the Wabbits slipped in the door and reported to her. "Gee-Gee scouts," he said. "We got one of them but there's a couple more around. Might be a raid."

"We'll fix them," Lana said grimly. "Guess they want their boy back. Come on, you two; I'll have to convoy you out of here."

She led the way. The street was black and silent; before they had taken three steps Lana was invisible. Mundin followed Bligh's confident stride with some qualms.

Lana melted back out of the darkness and said, "Hold it! There's one of the Gee-Gees under that fence. I'll get her——"

Her bottle glimmered. Bligh choked and tackled her from behind as she was about to slice into a pudgy ten-year-old face. Lana floundered on the ground swearing while Bligh addressed his stepdaughter, "Sandy, get the hell out of here. These are friends of mine. I'll see you at home!"

Alexandra, wriggling as he clutched her arm, said philosophically, "Sorry, Norvell. That's the way the little ball bounces." She threw back her head in a barking, strangling yell: "Sieg—heil! Sieg——"

Norvell held off Lana with one hand and with the other measured the distance to Alexandra's jaw. He knocked her out, heaved her over his shoulder and panted, "Let's go, Mundin. You tag along, Lana."

In ten minutes Mundin had to relieve the little man of Alexandra's weight. By the time Mundin's knees were buckling, the girl was coming to.

Bligh addressed her quietly and seriously, rubbing his knuckles the while. After that she trailed sulkily along with them.

Mrs. Bligh tried to raise hell when the four of them came

in. "And," she screamed at Norvie, "where have *you* been? Out of here without a word—gone for hours—we could have——"

Norvell said it was none of her business. He said it in such a way that Alexandra gasped with indignation, Lana with admiration. Mundin blushed at the language, but reflected that Belly Rave was doing things for little Mr. Bligh. And the things were not necessarily bad.

"And," Norvell concluded, "if I see any more monkey-business between that hairy ape Shep and you, there is going to be trouble. I'm warning you!"

"Hah!" sneered Virgina Bligh. "I suppose you'll beat him up."

"Don't be silly," Bligh said. "He could break me in two. I'd wait until he went away, and then I'd beat *you* up."

Lana said sweetly, "I'm going now. What about this little stinker?" She jerked a thumb at the sullen Alexandra.

"I'll take care of her," Bligh promised. "She didn't know any better, that's all."

Lana gauged him. "Okay," she said. "Be back in the morning." She was gone, as Virginia Bligh, regaining her breath, started in for the second round.

Mundin said, "Please. I've got a hard day tomorrow—can I get some sleep?"

Chapter Fifteen

THEY SPENT THE MORNING in Old Monmouth, Mundin and Lana and Norvie Bligh, who tagged along in a sort of vague secretarial capacity.

First they stopped by Mundin's bank, where he plugged in his key, punched "Close Out Account," and scooped up the bills that rolled out.

He counted morosely. Two hundred thirty-four dollars, plus eighty-five cents in change. Lana looked hungry, and Mundin recalled that he owed her twenty-five dollars balance from the night before. He gave it to her reluctantly.

They ate in Hussein's. Over coffee Lana brooded. "I guess

the big shots'll ride out to Morristown in armored cars. Too bad we ain't rich. Well, let's get to the jumping-off place."

A taxi took them through the Bay tunnel to the Long Island Railroad terminus in Old Brooklyn. Just for the record, they tried the ticket window.

"Nossir," the man said positively. "One train a day, armored. For officials only. What the hell do you want in Morristown, anyway?"

They canvassed the bus companies by phone, without luck. Outside the railroad station, at the head of the cab rank, Lana began to cry.

"There, little girl," one of the hackies soothed glaring at Mundin and Bligh. A fatherly type. "What's the matter?"

"It's my daddy," Lana bawled heartrendingly. "He's in that terrible place an' he's lost an' my mommy said we should go help him. Honest, mister, just take us to the edge, please? Please? An' Uncle Norvie and Uncle Charlie won't let anything bad happen if those bas—if those bad men in Morristown try anything. Honest!"

He broke down and agreed to take them to the edge. It was a two-hour drive over bad roads.

The hackie let Lana ride next to him in the front. Swinging her little handbag gaily, with the volatility of a child, she chattered, all smiles, all the way. Uncle Norvie and Uncle Charlie exchanged looks. They knew what was in the little handbag.

Morristown, being older, was better organized than Belly Rave. The driver stopped a couple of weed-grown blocks from the customs barrier.

"Here we are, little girl," he said tenderly.

The little girl reached into her handbag. She took out her busted bottle and conversed earnestly with the driver. He cursed, whined, and then drove on.

At the gate, a couple of men looked genially in. Lana whispered something—Mundin caught the words "Wabbits" and "Itty-Bitties"—and the men waved them on. A block past the gate, on Lana's orders, the driver stopped at another checkpoint, manned by a pair of dirty-faced nine-year-olds with carbines.

They got a guide; an Itty-Bitty with a carbine. On their way through the busy, brawling streets to the Administration Building, not a few grown-ups turned white and got out of sight when they saw him clinging to the cab.

At the Ad Building Lana said curtly to the driver, "Wait."

Mundin shook his head. "No," he told her, pointing to the rank of steel-plated wheeled and tracked vehicles drawn up in the building's parking lot. "We get out of here in one of those or not at all."

Lana shrugged. "I don't get it, but all right." She told the Itty-Bitty, "Pass the cab out, will you? And whenever you guys need something in Belly Rave, you know who to come to."

It was one o'clock; the meeting was scheduled for one-thirty.

The check-point in the lobby passed Mundin and Bligh on the strength of Mundin's stock certificate. Lana was to wait in the visitors' room.

Room 2003 was a suite—perhaps the whole floor, Mundin suspected. He told the receptionist, "Stockholders' meeting. G.M.L. Homes." The receptionist passed them on, with a thoughtful stare.

Some twenty men filled the meeting room. Quite obviously, they were Titans. Beside these richly, quietly dressed folk, Mundin and Bligh were shabby interlopers. They were also ridiculously young and awkward.

From here on it gets hard, Mundin told himself. Corporate law!

The vision blinded him with its brightness.

Another new arrival was greeted cheerfully by the Titans. "Bliss, old man! Never thought you'd turn up for this nonsense. Old Arnold's just going to tramp all over you again, as usual."

Bliss was thin and younger than most of them. "If a couple of you gutless wonders would back me up we'd stop him," he said cheerfully. "Anyway, what else have I got to do with my time?"

Archly: "I *did* hear something or other about a Miss Laverne——" It broke up in laughter.

Mundin dove into the breach. "How do you do, Mr. Bliss," he said breathlessly, taking the man's hand. "I'm Charles Mundin, former Regular Republican candidate in the 27th District—and a small stockholder here."

The thin man gently disengaged his hand. "It's Hubble, Mr.

89

Urmurm, Bliss Hubble. How do you do." He turned to one of the Titans and demanded with mock belligerence, "Didn't you get my wire, Job? Then why haven't I got your proxy for the contract thing?"

Job seemed to be a cautious cuss. "Because," he said slowly, "I like old Arnold's policies so far. You'll rock the boat, one of these days, Bliss. Unless we kick you out of it first."

"Mr. Hubble," Mundin said insistently.

Hubble said absently, "Mr. Urmurm, I assure you I'd vote for you if I lived in the 27th District, which thank God I don't." His eyes were wandering; he headed across the room to buttonhole another Titan. Mundin followed him in time to hear, "—all very idealistic, I'm sure, my dear Bliss. But many an idealistic young man has turned out to be a hard taskmaster. I mean no offense."

Bliss Hubble was off again. Mundin judged that this last Titan was angry enough to talk to him; a vein was throbbing nicely in his reddened temple. Mundin asked in tones of deep disapproval, "Same old scheme, eh?"

The Titan said angrily, "Of course. The fool! When young Hubble's seen as many raids on management as I have, he'll think twice before he tries to pull wool over *my* eyes. The contract thing! Indeed! He's trying to shake the faith of all us in the present management, stampede a board election, bribe— oh, bribe in a gentlemanly way, of course—bribe himself onto the board and then do as much damage as he can. But by Godfrey it won't work! We're keeping a solid front against him——" His eyes focused. "I don't believe I know you, sir. I'm Wilcox."

"Delighted. Mundin. Attorney."

"Oh—proxies, eh? Whom do you represent? Most of the chaps seem to be here."

"Excuse me, Mr. Wilcox." Mundin followed Bliss Hubble, who had thrown himself into a chair after another rebuff. He handed him the power of attorney from Don Lavin that Ryan had prepared.

"Hey? What's this?"

"I suggest you read it," Mundin said shortly.

There was a patter of applause as half a dozen men came in. One of them—Arnold?—said, "Good afternoon, gentlemen. I suggest we all be seated and proceed."

Mundin sat beside Hubble, who was mechanically reading. One of the new arrivals began to drone out the minutes of the last meeting. Nobody was paying a great deal of attention.

Hubble finished reading, handed the document back to Mundin and asked with an amused smile, "Just what am I supposed to do about it?"

Mundin said sharply, "Looks foolish, doesn't it?"

The tactic worked. Disconcerted, Hubble said, "I didn't say that. And—well, there have been rumors. Rumors to which you might have just as much access as I."

Mundin looked knowing. "We're not going to be greedy, Mr. Hubble," he said, wondering what he was talking about. "Assuming that I'm not a swindler and that this isn't forged, how would you like to be on the board?"

"Very much," Hubble said simply.

"We can put you there." Mundin measured him. "That should be obvious, Mr. Hubble. Our twenty-five per cent voting stock plus your——?"

"It's a matter of record. Five and a half per cent."

"As much as that?"

"As much as that. I vote the family holdings."

Mundin did sums in his head. Thirty and a half per cent. If they could take Hubble into camp, and then swing twenty per cent more——

He faced front. Let Hubble think it over for a while.

The minutes were accepted as read, in a bored mumble. One of the new arrivals grinned. "Now, gentlemen, to business. Election of a board member to replace Mr. Fenelly, to begin with."

Somebody proposed Mr. Harry S. Wilcox, the gentleman with the throbbing vein in his temple. Somebody else proposed a Mr. Benyon and nominations were closed. Secretaries moved among the stockholders with ballots, which they filled out after an inspection—brief and with deferential smiles—of the stockholders' proxies and share certificates. Mundin blandly presented his one share to a secretary's horrified gaze; the man gave him his ballot as if he were passing alms to a leper.

Wilcox won, and there was a social round of applause and back-patting. From certain broad smiles Mundin suspected the result of the balloting was as fixed as the morrow's rising of the sun. He grinned at Hubble, who didn't seem to think it was at all funny.

"Coming in with us?" Mundin asked.

Hubble scowled.

The chairman passed on to the matter of compensation of officers. Mundin gathered from the reading of a long, involved statement of capital gains and tax depreciation that the corporation officers didn't think they were making enough money. They wanted more.

During the reading stockholders chattered sociably. Mundin began to wonder why they had bothered to come, as the pay-raise was lackadaisically approved by a unanimous voice vote.

At the next order of business he found out why.

It was called "Diversification of Raw Material Sources, with Special Reference to Alumina and Silicates." Mundin couldn't make head or tail of the dull technicalities, but he noticed that the sociable conversations tapered to a halt. One group, not more than four or five men, were putting their heads together with much figuring on the backs of envelopes and checking of records. Secretaries were running in and out with books and sheaves of documents as the reading droned on.

At last, the chairman said genially, "Well, gentlemen, the question. Shall we save time by asking for a unanimous vote of 'Aye?'"

A thin, gray old man rose and said: "I call for a record vote." He looked daggers at an elaborately unconcerned man in the first row and quavered menacingly, "And let me say to you gentlemen that I'm going to keep a copy of the record. And I will be guided by it in reaching future decisions, particularly during the last week of the coming quarter. I trust I have made myself entirely clear."

The chairman harumphed and the record vote was taken.

The proposition was defeated by a narrow margin, in an atmosphere of restrained passions. Mundin sensed dimly that there had just been a pitched battle—a corporate Gettysburg, a trial of strength between two mighty groups, with millions a year as the least part of the stakes. Beyond that he couldn't see.

Hubble, beside him, was growing restless. Mundin leaned over and whispered, "You could hold the balance of power in a matter like that if you came in with us."

"I know," Hubble said. "I know." And then, after a long while, "Let me see that paper again."

That was how Mundin knew he had him.

The meeting continued.

There were three other clashes—Union Representation; Petition for Lowered Haulage Rates; and Committee to Study Design Improvements. Between votes Hubble read the spots off the power of attorney and fished for information. Mundin was noncommittal. "Yes, they're clients of mine. No, sorry, can't tell you just where Mr. Lavin is staying at present, I'm afraid. Yes, there is a sister. Mr. Arnold up there can probably give you more information than I."

"*Arnold* is in it?"

"Up to his eye-teeth. Arnold will probably attempt before long to—why, here it comes now!"

One of the colorless secretaries was reading, just above a mumble: "Proposal to rectify an anomalous distribution of voting stock. Proposal is to empower board to acquire at par dormant stock, dormant to mean stock unvoted since issue, provided time in question be not less than ten years, stock to be deposited in company treasury." It sailed through the air of the room without raising a ripple.

Mundin whispered, "Ask him how much stock is involved. That'll be your answer."

Hubble hesitated, then firmly swallowed the hook. He rose, looking grim, and put the question.

Arnold smiled. "I'm afraid we haven't got the exact figures. It's more of a contingency measure, Mr. Hubble."

Hubble said, "I'd be satisfied with an estimate, Mr. Arnold."

"No doubt. But as I said, we haven't got the figures. Now to proceed——"

Hubble began to look mulish. "Is the amount by any chance twenty-five per cent?" Throughout the room people sat up and conversations broke off short.

Arnold tried to laugh. Hubble snapped: "I repeat my question. Is or is not the amount of stock which you are asking us to empower you to buy and deposit in the company treasury, under your control, twenty-five per cent?"

As it soaked in there was a mild uproar. Hubble ignored it. "Is it or is it not, Mr. Arnold?" he demanded. "A very simple question, I should think! And if the answer is 'no,' I shall ask to see records!"

Arnold grimaced. "Please, gentlemen! Please, Mr. Hubble! I can hardly hear myself think. Mr. Hubble, since you have objections to the proposal, we'll withdraw it. I presume I have the consent of all present for this agenda change. To pass on——"

Hubble clamored, "You do *not* have my consent to this agenda change, Mr. Arnold. I am still requesting information on the proposal."

Somebody slid into a seat beside Mundin. A big, handsome, well-preserved old man. "I'm Harry Coett," he muttered. "What's all this about? I see you talking to Bliss and then all hell breaks loose. Say, weren't you with Green, Charlesworth? No? Thought I knew you. Well, what's up? Arnold's scared. You've got something. What is is?"

Mundin smugly asked, "What's in it for me?"

The man stared. "Hell, boy! I'm *Harry Coett.* Where are you from, anyway?"

And a third party joined them as the debate between Hubble and the chairman raged and spread. "You seem to have put Hubble onto something, young man," the newcomer whispered. "I like that. Spirit. Somebody told me you were an attorney, and it happens there's a vacancy on our law staff. Quite a nice vacancy. I'm Roadways, you know. Nelson's the name——"

Coett snapped: "I was here first, George!"

By then the floor debate had escaped from Hubble's hands. Scenting blood or gold, half the stockholders present were fighting for the chance to question Arnold, who was sweating and grimly managing not to say a thing—at great length. The other half of the stockholders seemed to be clawing their way into the group around Mundin, the odd young man who seemed to know things. Mundin, smiling politely and meeting no one's eye, heard the whispers and conjectures: "—an attorney, from the S.E.C., I guess, going to throw the book at old Arnold for——" "—into camp, but how do you know it isn't Green, Charlesworth or——" "No, you ass! Proxies! They've been quietly——"

He judged the time was ripe. He said politely, "Excuse me, gentlemen," and stood up.

"Mr. Chairman," he called. Arnold pointedly avoided his eye and recognized somebody else—who was at once the goal of a ten-yard dash by Harry Coett. Coett whispered urgently in the man's ear and he said: "I yield to Mr. Mundin."

"Thank you," said Mundin. "Perhaps I can clarify this confused situation. However, Mr. Arnold, first I should like to talk to one of my principals, the young lady."

"Principals?" Arnold asked distractedly. A secretary murmured something to him. "Oh. Miss Lav—oh, certainly. She'll —uh—be free to talk to you immediately after the meeting concludes. Is that satisfactory, Mr. Urmurm?"

"Quite satisfactory."

And that was that, and more, far more, than he had dared hope for. Not only had he thrown an egg into the corporate fan, so that half the stockholders in G.M.L. were swarming around him, but Arnold was returning Norma as his price for not "clarifying the situation." Arnold's raid had blown up in his face; far less than getting the Lavin stock to vote, he would be lucky to hold his domination of the board.

Mundin sat down comfortably—and silently, acknowledging leading questions and offers from the Titans with polite nothings.

The stockholders' rebellion began visibly to peter out. With Mundin quieted, angry and uncertain men perceived that some sort of deal had been made under their noses. They didn't like it; they had done it themselves too often to enjoy feeling the spur on their own flesh. One of them called for unseating Arnold, but cooler heads prevailed. Wait until this thing is a little more settled. Wait until this Mundin tell what he knows.

The rest of the meeting went at breakneck speed.

Hubble spent much of it railing, "Damn it, Mundin, you made me the first offer! The hell with these vultures. They'll use you and throw you away. I'm the only heavy stockholder in the company with an open mind and——"

"Nonsense!" Harry Coett said decisively. "I don't know what you're up to, Mundin, but whatever it is it'll need financing. And I'm *Harry Coett*. Let me handle——"

George Nelson said, "Tell him what you did to old Crowther, why don't you? *He* needed financing too."

Mundin never did find out what Harry Coett had done to

old Crowther. As the meeting was adjourned he buttonholed Arnold, who gave him a wan smile. "Come and see me, Mr. Mundin," he urged. "I'm sure we can get together. Don't we know each other? Weren't you with Green, Charlesworth?"

"The girl, Arnold," Mundin said shortly.

Arnold said, "Miss Lavin is waiting for you in the reception room."

Trailing tycoons, Mundin raced to the reception room.

Norma Lavin was indeed there, pale and angry. "Hello, Mundin," she said, not so crisply, not so mannishly. "You took your time about it, I must say." And then she was weeping on his chest, sobbing. "I didn't sign it. I knew Don wasn't dead, I didn't sign, I——"

"Shut up, superwoman," Mundin snapped. "Stop giving things away to the eavesdroppers. Your every word is golden." But he found that he was shaking himself—from the reaction to the hours of strain. And from—Norma.

He got a grip on himself as Coett, behind him mused, "So this is the young lady Arnold horse-traded you, eh? Your principal, Counselor?"

"Maybe," said Mundin.

"Oh, come off it, Mundin," Coett said shrewdly. He turned to Norma. "My dear," he offered expansively, "can I drop you anyplace? You too, of course, Counselor."

"Listen, Mundin," Nelson urged, "get him to tell you about old Crowther——"

"Damn it," raged Hubble, "if you vultures will step aside——"

Mundin said, "I'll lay it on the line, gentlemen. Miss Lavin and I have to stop in the waiting room to pick up an—uh—a young lady. In five minutes we will be at the front entrance. We'll go along with all three of you, or with any two of you. You fight it out among yourselves."

He swept Norma out to the visitors' room. Lana was perched on the receptionist's desk, looking hostile, but not as hostile as the receptionist. Mundin asked her, "What happened to Bligh?"

"Outside," Lana said. "He said he'd already had a bellyful of Field Days, whatever he meant by that. This your girl?"

"Yes," said Mundin, "this is my girl." The three of them collared Norvie Bligh, sitting in the sun outside, and started

96

toward the ranks of parked cars and half-tracks. They were met by an amicable committee of three.

"All settled, Mundin," Hubble said happily. "Coett and Nelson are coming with us."

"Good," Mundin said. "Where do we go to talk?"

Hubble said joyously, "Oh, my place. It's all settled. You'll like it—simple, quiet, but comfortable."

They made quite a procession: Two cars and a half-track. They didn't stop for anything, neither the Itty-Bitty checkpoint nor the customs shed.

"We'll go through Fifth Avenue," Hubble said.

"Oh, no!" Coett and Nelson groaned.

"I like it," the younger man said.

They rolled slowly through the condemned Old City, empty and dead. Mundin gasped at the sight of a car other than theirs; it buzzed across their path at 34th and Fifth, under the towering shadow of the Empire State Building. He craned his neck after they passed it and exclaimed, "There's somebody getting out. Going into the Empire State!"

"Why not?" grunted Hubble over the intercom. He was riding with Nelson and Coett, because none of the three trusted any of the others alone with Mundin and Norma for the ride.

"I'd always understand it was as empty as the rest of the Old City," the lawyer said with dignity.

"They keep it lit up at night, don't they? Well, that calls for maintenance. The man was an electrician."

Mundin was not a very good lawyer, but he was good enough to be quite sure that Hubble was lying to him.

Chapter Sixteen

LANA WAS TUGGING at Mundin's shoulder. "I want to go home," she said.

Mundin said peevishly, "Sure, sure." Norma, exhausted, had fallen asleep on his arm, and his circulation had been cut off ten miles back. The girl was a solid, chunky weight—but, he was thinking, curiously pleasant.

"I mean now." Lana insisted. "I got a duty to the Wabbits."

"I'd kind of like to go home too," Norvie Bligh chimed in.

Mundin flexed his arms, considering. Lana and Bligh had done what they had bargained for. He said:

"All right. If I have the driver let you off at the bus depot in Old Yonkers, can you make it from there?" They nodded, and he leaned forward to tap on the window.

At Old Yonkers their car stopped outside an Inter-City depot. The car behind skidded to a stop beside them. Hubble, Nelson, and Coett peered out anxiously. "Anything wrong?" Hubble yelled through a window.

Mundin shook his head, let Lana and Norvie out, and permitted his driver to start up again.

And twenty minutes later they reached Hubble's home.

Quiet and comfortable it was. Simple it was not. It was a Charles Addams monster in a fabulous private park in Westchester. They rolled up its driveway and parked next to what appeared to be a 1928 Rolls-Royce limousine.

Bliss Hubble was already at the door of their car, holding it open for them. "My wife," he explained, indicating the limousine. "She makes a fetish of period decoration. Today it's Hoover, I see; last week it was Neo-Roman. Can't say I care for it, but one has one's obligations."

"And one has one's wife," said Norma Lavin, who appeared to be back to her normal self.

"Oh, it's very nice," soothed Mundin. "So stately."

Mrs. Hubble greeted them with an unbelieving look. She turned to her husband with an "explain-*this*-if-you-can" air.

Hubble said hastily, "My dear, may I present Miss Lavin——"

"Just Lavin," Norma said coldly.

"Of course. Lavin. And this is Mr. Mundin; I believe you know Harry and George. Mr. Mundin was good enough to compliment the way you've fixed up the house."

"Indeed," said Mrs. Hubble, ice forming on her gaze. "Please thank Mr. Mundin, and inform him that his taste is quite in agreement with that of our housekeeper—who is no longer with us, since I woke up this morning and found she had set the house for this unsightly, trashy piece of construction. Please mention to Mr. Mundin, too, that when she left—rapidly—she took with her all the key settings, and as a consequence I have been condemned to roam through these revolting rooms until my husband chose to come home with his keys so that I might change them into something more closely resembling a human habitation." Hubble stiffened, thrust a hand into a pocket, brought out a set of keys. With them his wife swept off through the vast, bare rooms.

"Sensitive," Hubble muttered to his guests.

Coett said eagerly, "We got a couple of things straight on the way over, Mundin. Now——"

Hubble said severely, "Harry, I insist! I'm the host. Not another word until we've had dinner."

He led the way through a majestic corridor, keeping carefully to the middle. At some unnoticed sign he said sharply, "Watch it!"

The others obediently stood clear of the walls, which were coming into curious, shimmering motion. "My wife," Hubble explained with a glassy smile. "You'd think a regular bubble-house wall would be enough, but no! Nothing will do but full three-D illusion throughout. The expense! The stumbling home in the dark! The waking up in the middle of the night because the four-poster is changing into a Hollywood bed! She's a light sleeper, you see——"

The walls had firmed up now; the old furniture was fully retracted, and new pieces had formed. Mrs. Hubble's present preference seemed to be Early Wardroom—a satisfactory enough style for the flying bridge of a cruiser, but not really Mundin's idea of how to decorate a home. He withheld comment.

The table talk was not sparkling; everyone was hungry. "Am I to understand," Hubble probed gently, "that Miss— that Lavin, I mean, was actually abducted by Mr. Arnold?"

"Doubt it very much," said Norma, chewing. "He probably just looked unhappy and said something like, 'Dear me, I wish something could be done about that stock.' Some foot-kisser standing by set the wheels in motion. Arnold's hands would be clean. Not *his* fault if people insist on exceeding their authority."

She took another forkful of wild rice. "They had me for about a week. My God, what confusion! I could go and I couldn't go. I was free to leave any time I cared to, but temporarily they thought it would be better to keep the door

99

locked. Sign your residuary legatee's share of the stock to us and we'll pay you a cool million. But we don't *want* the stock, of course. It has only a certain small nuisance value. Now, lady, are you going to be reasonable or do we have to get tough? My dear girl, we wouldn't dream of harming you!"

She scowled. "Arnold came to see me once. He kept pretending that *I* was trying to sell to *him*. I don't know, maybe that's what somebody told him. All I know is, I feel as though someone hit me over the head with a lighthouse."

A butler shambled in. "Are you at home to Mr. Arnold, sir?" he whispered.

"No!" crowed Hubble delightedly. "You hear that, Coett?"

Nelson cut in, "Hold it a minute, Bliss. Are you sure you're doing the right thing? Maybe if the three of us got together——" he looked quickly at Mundin. "That is, perhaps *all* of us could freeze out the Toledo bunch."

Coett said, "Tell him to go to blazes. Tell the butler to tell him, so we can all hear it. First we settle things among ourselves—then we figure who else we have to cut in, if anybody. But I don't think we need anybody else."

"Tell him," Hubble said gleefully to the butler. "Fellows, if you knew how long I'd waited—— Well, all right. Harry's right, George. Figure it out. You've got eleven per cent under your thumb, counting proxies for the voting trust. I've got five and a half, solid. Harry has three of his own, and he influences—how many, Harry?"

"Nine," said Coett shortly.

"You see?" said Hubble. "That's plenty. With these people's twenty-five per cent, we——"

Mundin came down heavily on Norma's foot just as she was opening her mouth to ask how they had located the stock. He said rapidly, "Don't you think we should save this till dinner's over?"

Hubble cast an eye around the table. "Why, dinner's over now," he said mildly. "Let's have our coffee in the library."

Hubble stopped at the entrance to the library and did something with a switchbox before permitting the others to enter. "Have my own controls here," he said pridefully. "Wife has most of the house, hah-hah, she can't begrudge me one little nook of my own! Let's see if we can't get something more cheerful." The "library"—there wasn't a book or microfilm in sight—shimmered and flowed, and turned into something like a restoration of a nineteenth-century London club.

Mundin tested one of the wing-back chairs suspiciously, but it was good. Norma was still staring at him thoughtfully; but she kept her mouth shut and he said cheerily, "Now, gentlemen, to work."

"Right," said Harry Coett. "Before we get too deep, I want to know how we stand on one thing. I'm sure it's just one of those crazy things that get started, but I heard somebody say something at the meeting. They mentioned Green, Charlesworth. Just for the record, have you got anything to do with them?"

Green, Charlesworth. Ryan had mentioned them, Mundin recalled; they seemed to be something to worry about. Mundin said definitely, "We are *not* from Green, Charlesworth. We are from ourselves. Miss Lavin and her brother are the direct heirs of one of the founders of G.M.L. I—uh—happen to have a trifling amount of stock myself—besides being their attorney."

Coett nodded briskly. "Okay. Then it's a plain and simple raid; and we've got the muscle to do it. I take it we are all agreed, then, that the first step is to throw the corporation into bankruptcy?"

Mundin said in a strangled voice, "Hey!"

Coett grinned. "I thought you were no expert," he said amiably. "What did you expect, Mundin?"

"Why," Mundin floundered, "there's—ah—your stock, and our stock, and—well, it seems clear-cut to me. Majority rules, doesn't it?"

He stopped. All hands were enjoying a good, though polite, laugh. Coett said, "Mr. Mundin, you have a lot to learn. Do you seriously think we could vote our stock *outright* under the existing rules?"

"I don't know," Mundin said honestly.

"You don't," Coett agreed. "You can't rock the boat. The proxies won't stand for it; a raid, yes, but handled *right*."

Norma Lavin commented, "I suppose he's right, Mundin. They've stopped us so far, one way and another. The only real change is that now these people know we're alive and think they can take us to the cleaners."

101

"Please," said Hubble and Nelson unhappily.

Coett, grinning, assured her "You are absolutely correct. For the first time I begin to doubt that we can do it."

Mundin interrupted, "Why bankruptcy?"

They all stared at him. Finally Hubble asked diffidently, "Ah—how would you do it, Mr. Mundin?"

Mundin said, "Well, I'm no corporation lawyer, gentlemen —I leave that aspect of it to my colleague, Mr. Ryan, who is a member of the Big Bar. But it seems to me that our first step is, obviously, to form a stockholder's committee and request an accounting from the present board. We can back it up, if you think it necessary, with a notification to the S.E.C. I know, naturally, that Arnold's group will stall and attempt to compromise, probably offer us some kind of board representation far less than our holdings entitle us to. But that's simple enough to handle; we simply enter protest and file suit in——"

Hubble and Nelson said, "Risky."

Coett said, "It'll never work. Look, youngster, that won't get us to first base. I remember when the Memphis crowd tried——"

Mundin interrupted, "The who?"

"The Memphis crowd. Arnold's group. They took G.M.L. away from the Toledo bunch eighteen years ago through due process, the way you're talking about. But it took six years to do it, and if the Toledo bunch hadn't been caught short in Rails they never would have made it. And they're still strong; you saw how Arnold had to put Wilcox on the board to placate them."

Mundin, who did not know what in hell the man was talking about, said desperately, "Can't we at least try?"

"Waste of time! When Arnold took over, G.M.L. had assets of less than ten billion. We have before us an immensely larger mass of capital. It has inertia, Mundin. Inertia. You can't move it with a feather; you need dynamite. It's going to take time and it's going to take money and it's going to take hard work and brains to budge it. I'll tell you how."

And he did. Mundin listened in growing bewilderment and something that came close to horror. Bankruptcy! How did you put a corporation worth fourteen billion dollars, eminently solvent, unbelievably prosperous, into bankruptcy?

He didn't like the answers when he heard them. But, he

told himself, you can't make an omelette without breaking a few golden eggs.

Coett, enjoying himself, was planning in broad, bright strokes: "All right, Bliss, you get your chaps on the petition for composition and arrangement; we'll spring that one ourselves, before they think of it, and we'll want it ready. Then——" Mundin, grimly taking notes, stuck through it to the end. But he wasn't enjoying the practice of corporate law nearly as much as he had always thought he would. He wished urgently for the presence of old Ryan. And a nice full tin of yen pox.

It was nearly midnight. Mundin had never felt so bone-weary in his life; even Norma Lavin was slumped in her chair. Coett, Hubble and Nelson were bright-eyed and eager, skilled technicians doing the work they best knew how to do.

But the work was done. Mundin, yawning, dragged himself to his feet. He said tiredly, "So the first thing for me to do is set up offices, eh?"

There was a pause.

Harry Coett sighed. He said, "Not quite the first thing, Mundin."

"What then?" Mundin peered at him.

Coett said crisply, "Call it a matter of personal satisfaction. We've all heard rumors about young Lavin. I don't say they're true; I don't know if they're true or not. But *if* they're true we don't get off the ground."

Mundin blazed, not quite quickly enough: "See here, Coett——"

Coett said quietly, "Hold it. We've all had a look at that paper of yours. It's a power of attorney, all right, and I've no doubt that it's as valid as it can be. But it isn't a stock proxy, Mundin. It doesn't mention G.M.L. stock in it anywhere, except in the affidavit at the end, and Don Lavin didn't sign that himself."

"What do you want?" Mundin asked sullenly.

Coett said, "Let me tell a fantastic story. Mind you, I don't say it's true. But it's interesting. There are two young people, like a brother and sister, for instance. One of them has some stock, but can't use it. The other is—ah—temporarily out of circulation. Let's suppose that a smart young lawyer gets hold of them. First thing he does, he walks in on a meeting and lets it be known that the stock exists. With that as a wedge, he pries the girl loose from wherever she is. With the girl, he sucks in three good, dumb Joes—like Hubble, Nelson, and me, for instance. With the dumb Joes in the palm of his hand, he squeezes recognition of the stock out of, for instance, Arnold. That's pretty good work: He has the girl, and he has the stock. The question is, what do the dumb Joes have then?"

God, thought Mundin, and I never believed in mind-reading. He said, "Am I supposed to take this fantasy seriously?"

Coett shook his head. "Of course not, Mundin. Just, for the sake of the record, before we get too far involved in any of this, let's see the stock. Tomorrow morning be time enough?"

"Tomorrow morning will be fine," Mundin said hollowly.

Chapter Seventeen

TAKE THE Port of New York.

Not the slagged-out, cinder-crusted waters that lap at the fringe of Belly Rave, but *Old* New York, when Belle Reve was fresh and the plaster had not yet cracked. The harbor is filled with ocean-going ships. (Remember ships?) Between Manhattan and the Jersey shore ferries ply. There are many of them in the mid-twentieth-century bustle, half a dozen lines and more; some old, some new, some fast, some slow. . . .

There are two ferry lines owned by railroads. (Remember railroads?)

One is a proud green fleet. Half a dozen thousand-tonners, steel-hulled, Newport-built. Radar charts their crossings, and the pilings in their slips stand straight and tall.

The second fleet: Three rust-colored midgets, shambling blindly back and forth between snaggle-toothed berths.

Consider the paradox: The weary red ferries belong to a rich and solvent railroad. The radar-eyed giants are chattels of a corporation which has been in the hands of the receivers for four decades and two years.

It is a matter of recorded fact that, in the middle of the

twentieth century, the only ferries in New York Harbor which could afford to install the expensive blessings of science belonged to a line in bankruptcy.

Let us rewrite the dictionary:

> **bank'-rupt-cy** (n) the state of having affairs managed by disinterested parties, not owners; *therefore*, the natural and preferred state of Big Business.

Mundin said stubbornly:

"All right, all right, all *right!* You don't have to go through it again, Ryan. Finance is Coett's business, not mine; and corporate law is your business, not mine; and if you all say that G.M.L. has to go into bankruptcy I'm not going to stand in your way. But I don't like their methods."

Ryan shifted achingly on the lumpy couch. Mundin was getting worried about him; his skin was pale yellow, his eyes black circles. Obviously the old fool had given up food almost entirely for the past weeks. But he could still make sense when he talked. He said, "If you go to a doctor to save your life, do you complain about the taste of the medicine?"

Mundin didn't answer. He shook his head worriedly and paced the room.

Norma came back from putting Don Lavin to bed. She sat down wearily and poured herself a drink. "Mud," she growled. She made a face as she swallowed it. "I've poured better liquor off laboratory specimens. Mundin, what about the stock?"

Mundin said: "Lavin—Norma—if you ask me that one more time, I swear I pick up and walk out of here. I don't *know* what about the stock. Maybe we can't deliver it. If we can't, we can't; I've had a rough day and I'm just not up to any more miracles right now. Maybe we can talk Coett and the others out of it tomorrow morning."

"Maybe not," said Norma; but she looked at Mundin's rebellious expression and that was all she said.

It was after midnight; but Ryan needed to hear everything that had happened, and they all needed to plan for the next day. Mundin gave the old man a blow-by-blow account of the stockholders' meeting and the later discussion at Hubble's house; the three of them picked apart every word and hint of the whole exhausting day, checking and rechecking their progress.

Norvell Bligh joined them at about one. Mundin let him in, astonished to see the little man there.

"Just wanted to know if you need us any more tonight," Norvell said. His voice was eager; he was enjoying this, Mundin thought, with a faint prick of irritation—not realizing what *a job*, any kind of job for whatever sort of pay, meant to a Belly Raver.

"Who's 'us,' Bligh?" Norma Lavin demanded.

"Me and the Wabbits," he grinned. "Lana stopped me on the way in. She said to tell you the Gee-Gees had a patrol near here about ten o'clock, but the Wabbits took care of them; didn't know if they were trying to knock off your brother or not."

Ryan's sallow face was abruptly pale; but he didn't speak. Norma said suspiciously, "I didn't see any Wabbits when we came in."

Bligh looked at her. "You wouldn't," he said.

Mundin said dubiously, "I guess you might as well go home, Bligh. There's nothing more you can do for us tonight."

"Meaning I should mind my business?" Bligh inquired. "Okay. If you need anything, all you gotta do is ask, that's all." He grinned amiably and headed toward the door.

Surprisingly, Harry Ryan stopped him. "Wait a minute, Bligh. Mundin—Norma—will you come here a moment?"

Mundin and the girl, in response to his gestures, leaned close to him. He said in an undertone, "What about seeing if he can get some, well, medical attention for Don?"

Mundin said sharply, "Ryan, you told *me* we couldn't do that! G.M.L. won't let us, remember? Unauthorized use of conditioning techniques; fourteen billion dollars; if we break the law, G.M.L. will——"

"Shut up, Mundin," said Norma. "Ryan's right. The situation has changed now. We've got backing from Coett, Hubble, and Nelson."

They battled in whispers for minutes while Bligh leaned cheerfully against the doorframe, out of earshot, watching them. It was Mundin, flushed and angry, against the other two; Mundin who objected and refused and shook his head. He said tightly, "If we *did* try to get Don deconditioned, this isn't the way to do it. If we're going to break the law, let's at least do it privately, not by taking every derelict in Belly

Rave into our confidence. I've said it before, Ryan, *I don't like dirty methods.* Surely we can get Don fixed up legally some way or other—we've got some strength now, we'll try for a court order, or at least an inquiry, and——"

"And we'll have the stock by tomorrow morning," Ryan finished. "Good work, Counselor. Go ahead and do it."

Mundin said furiously, "How do you know Bligh can help us? Suppose we ask him and draw a blank? Then we've advertised our troubles, and we're no farther ahead than before."

From the doorway Norvell Bligh called, "Let me try, Mr. Mundin; that's all I ask."

Mundin glared at him incredulously. Bligh said apologetically, "Lip-reading, Mr. Mundin, remember? I haven't been deaf for thirty years without learning a little bit. Anyway, Lana can find you a doctor, I'm sure of it. All you have to do is ask her."

Mundin slumped into a chair and groaned. "That's the end," he said bitterly. "One accomplice after another; one more loose mouth."

Norvell looked alarmed. "I wouldn't say anything against Lana, Mr. Mundin."

"Who's saying anything against her? But she's only a thirteen-year-old kid. She's *bound* to talk. I won't deny that she was pretty helpful in locating Miss Lavin, but that doesn't mean she's a superwoman. No, I absolutely decline to have anything to do with letting her know that we're even *thinking* of going to an illegal doctor." He stopped short; Bligh had made a noise that sounded suspiciously like a choked-off laugh. "What's the matter now?" he demanded.

Norvie Bligh controlled himself. "Well, nothing, Mr. Mundin," he apologized. "It's just that you—uh—kind of underrate Lana."

"She's only thirteen, Bligh!"

"Oh, sure." He coughed diffidently. In an ordinary conversational tone he said, "Lana, come on in."

The trapdoor at the head of the stairs creaked and opened; Lana, with an eight-year-old in attendance, came placidly down. Bligh explained, "You see, Mr. Mundin, the Wabbits are pretty thorough. What about it, Lana—can you find a doctor to fix the kid up?"

It took a little time—while the eight-year-old aide-de-camp

ran courier duty to Crib Row. "It's a bag named Two-Ton Tessie," Lana explained while he was gone. "She had a special gentleman friend, a doctor. And when she got picked up and conditioned he couldn't get along with any of the other girls. So——"

So the doctor found another doctor, a diagnostician; and the diagnostician, as a professional courtesy, found a surgeon. . . .

It took a long phone call to Coett, and quite a lot of Coett's money.

Mundin made a disgusted noise in his throat. But they had a lead.

Don Lavin had himself a brain tumor—just as, once upon a time, a young lady who had made a mistake could have it rectified by means of an expensive attack of appendicitis—and there would be even a skin-deep MacBurney's incision to prove it . . . which would bewilder, in the case of real appendicitis attack, a subsequent surgeon.

The highly reputable diagnostician whose name had been given them described Don's "tumor" as a spongioblastoma, the commonest and most malignant of the intracranial gliomas. He recommended immediate surgery . . . and then bought himself a new Cadillac copter with power doors, windows, ramp, and steering.

The surgeon was even more reputable—and expensive. He extirpated the spongioblastoma in his own private hospital—or at least the hospital Tissue Committee examined what he said he had removed from Don Lavin's skull, and this indisputably was spongioblastoma multiforma, consisting of round, elongated, and piriform cells, characteristically recalling the varied cytological picture in osteogenic sarcoma of bone. The surgeon then built a new wing on his hospital. . . .

But that's getting a litle ahead. . . .

Chronically suspicious, Norma scowled down at her brother, mumbling under the last of the anesthesia. She said to Mundin, "He could have left Don an idiot. What better way to cover his tracks?"

Mundin sighed. They had watched the surgery: The lights, the sterilizer, the hole saw. The wisp of scorched smell from the bone; the nerve-wrenching moment when the disk of skull lifted out. Insertion of anode and cathode needles, minute electroshocks that smashed this pattern, blurred that memory, shattered this reflex into jangling neuronic rubble. The three days and their fifty hours of endless tests and questions, the strobe flickers in Don's eyes, the miles of EEG tape, the mapping of Don's brain and its workings.

Norvell Bligh, handy little man, looked in. "Doctor's coming," he said. And, faithful little man, resumed his post outside the door.

Dr. Niessen, F.A.C.S., asked them, "Anything yet?"

On cue, Don chose that moment to open his eyes and smile at Norma. "Hello, sis. It feels better now."

Norma burst into tears and Dr. Niessen looked mightily relieved. "Check the block?" the doctor suggested to Mundin; but Don broke in:

"The stock, you mean? That's all right. Safe deposit box 27,993 Coshocton First National. No key. Identification is a picture of me, my fingerprints. And a code phrase: 'Gray, my friend, is all theory and green life's golden tree.' Goethe," he went on chattily. "Pop used to say that one a lot after they put the boots to him. It cheered him up a little."

Dr. Niessen nodded and looked at the others. Norma choked, "Have you got it all back, Don? All?"

Her brother winced. "Oy, have I! Fifty hours they worked on me. That part I don't *want* to remember."

The doctor muttered, "Barbarous. We're all lawbreakers here, but I'm glad you came to me. Mr. Kozloff——" That was Don. "Mr. Kozloff, are you able to verify my conjecture that flicker-feedback was the principal means employed?"

"Yep, I guess so. If flicker-feedback is them shining a light in your eyes and you go into convulsions. And there were those guys in the bottles."

"Bottles?" the doctor demanded sharply.

"Yeah. Bottles. Or did I dream that one?"

The doctor looked professionally concerned. "If it happened," he said gravely, "you should remember. Perhaps a further series——"

"The hell with that!" yelled Don Lavin, and it took three of them to push him down on the bed again.

"Stow it, Don," Norma ordered. "Doctor, what do you think?"

Dr. Niessen shrugged. "You tell me that the main block is gone. Are there any others? I don't know. Fifty hours is a lot of time, and I haven't got their working charts, I can't see what they planted down deep."

"That's not very satisfactory, Doctor," Norma said.

"Shall I put him through a new series of tests?" They subdued Don again, and the doctor went on, unruffled, "I thought not. If there's any trouble, bring him back; that's all I can say."

Norma snapped, "And you'll put up another wing, I suppose."

The doctor looked at her gravely. "I might," he said. "I don't suppose I mentioned to you that the wing I contemplate building with your kind donation is a free ward."

She had nothing to say.

"Very well. Mr. Kozloff, I think you've recovered from your—ah—tumor. One of the staff physicians will check you for traveling. Come back if there's anything new; in these spongioblastomas there is always a possibility that some malignant tissue was overlooked. And if you can possibly arrange it, Mr. Kozloff, don't bring your sister."

Bligh closed the door for him. Don looked fondly at Norma. "You and your big mouth haven't changed, have they?"

Mundin went into the corridor for a smoke and refuge from the touching scene of reconciliation which followed. But he could hear it even out there. . . .

The manager of Brinks-Fargo looked skeptical. "Naturally we're for hire," he said. "Now, have I got this straight? Armored copter to Coshocton First National, guarded pickup of securities from there and immediate hop to Monmouth, you four riding all the way, right?"

"Right," said Mundin.

"Twelve thousand five hundred dollars," the manager said after some scribbling. "Our biggest and best, with six guards."

It was paid.

The pickup went off smooth as silk. A conditioned clerk handed over the little box in which were certificates of Don Lavin's fantastic claim to twenty-five per cent of G.M.L., and Mundin examined them wonderingly as the armored whirlybird bumped off the streets of Coshocton. Three and one-half billion dollars at par, he kept saying to himself.

They didn't talk much, all the way back to Monmouth.

Hubble demanded: "Did it work, Don?"

Coett said, "If that sawbones didn't deliver after the way we strung along——"

Nelson said, "How much did it cost?"

"I'm all right, thanks," said Don Lavin politely.

"And," Mundin added casually, "we came back by way of Coshocton. No need to horse around with duplicate certificates, gentlemen."

They examined the originals with awe, gloating. "We're in," Coett exulted. "As of the next stockholders' meeting. Three months—plenty of time to shake up the firm and pick up what we need for a majority. My God, a majority! The hell with the proxies and the voting trusts!"

There was a long hassle about pooled stock and irrevocable joint agreements; and suddenly Mundin, looking at the three titans of finance, saw predacious jungle animals. He blinked, and the illusion was gone; but he couldn't help thinking of G.M.L., rapacious as it was, as some huge and helpless vegetarian beast, harried by sharp-toothed little carnivores. Even Norma felt something; because she burst out:

"Daddy never meant——" She choked herself off, and looked wildly at the conspirators for a moment. Then she said wearily, "Ah, the hell with it. Excuse me. I don't vote, anyhow." And she was gone out of the room.

"Now," said Coett, hardly noticing her departure, "it is possible that while we are throwing G.M.L. into bankruptcy, Green, Charlesworth may take an interest. I don't suppose it will happen. But if they *should* show up, Charles, don't attempt to handle it yourself. Buck it to us. Understand?"

"Understand," said Mundin. Green, Charlesworth. Insurance and bankers' bankers; odd how their name kept coming up. "Is that all we have to worry about now—Green, Charlesworth?"

"No," Coett said honestly. "It's a long, tough row, Mundin. Bankruptcy's tricky, even when the corporate mass is relatively small."

"And you're determined to go through with the bankruptcy?
111

We can't just try to vote our stock, or manipulate it on the market?"

"If anything," Coett said shakily, "would bring Green, Charlesworth down on us, that's it. No, no, Mundin. Simple blackmail and bribe, bankruptcy and ruin—let's not upset the applecart." His face was actually white. But Mundin put it out of his mind and said worriedly to Don, "What was the matter with Norma?"

"Forget it," said Don. "Daddy wanted this, and Daddy gave his life to that—forget it. She has the idea Pop's invention is a sacred trust, and it's up to us to use it for the common good." He grinned easily, but his eyes were as hooded as ever before Dr. Niessen carved into his brain. "Who do you like in the Field Day?" he asked opaquely.

Chapter Eighteen

MUNDIN SAID, "You have to be careful. Don't *say* that you represent G.M.L. You're just acting for a business associate."

"I understand, Mr. Mundin," said Norvie Bligh.

Mundin brooded. "If we could only come out in the open instead of this cloak-and-dagger business. Well, things are looking up. You're sure you've got it straight?"

"Positive, Mr. Mundin," said Norvie. He met the lawyer's doubtful eye and, surprisingly, winked. "We'll give 'em hell, pal," he said, and left.

Later on, outside Candella's private office at General Recreations, Norvie wasn't quite so confident. This was the office in which he had had so many difficult days; these were the rooms where young Stimmens had cut his throat; that was the door through which Candella had booted him out.

But the electronic secretary summoned Candella, and Norvie was all right again.

Candella came bustling through the door with a huge, friendly smile plastered on his face. "Norvie, boy!" he yelled. "Damn, but it's good to see you! How the hell have you been?"

Norvell said curtly, "Morning, Candella." He allowed Candella one limp touch of his hand and withdrew it.

"Well," said Candella heartily. "Uh—well!"

Norvie said, "I'll be brief. You got my message."

"Oh, yes, Norvie. Yes, indeed. you're here about——" he looked around him rapidly and said in a lowered tone "—G.M.L."

"Speak up, Candella," Norvell said sharply. "Yes, I'm here about G.M.L. Not officially, mind you. Not at *all* officially."

"Of course not, Norvie!"

Norvell nodded. "And I have your promise that you'll keep what I say in strict confidence?"

"Oh, certainly, Norv——"

"Not a word to anyone?"

"Of *course* n——"

"Good. In a word, Candella, we have had complaints."

Candella kept his smile, but it was like the rictus of a loathsome disease. "Complaints?"

"Oh, not about you. I have no idea how well or badly you are doing your job now, and in any case," Norvie said severely, "that would have nothing to do with G.M.L. My associates would never dream of interfering in another corporation's affairs."

Of course not!" Candella agreed.

"The complaints are about the bubble-houses, Candella. One of my associates is a rather substantial holder in G.M.L. We've heard—well, reports. I'll be frank with you; we haven't been able to track them down. But they are alarming, Candella; very alarming. So alarming that I can't repeat them, or even hint at what they concern. You understand that, don't you?"

"Certainly, Mr.—certainly, Norvie!"

Norvell nodded. "I can only ask you a couple of questions, without giving you any clue as to *why* I ask them. The twenty-eight thousand bubble-houses General Recreations leases are devoted almost entirely to married couples, I believe. How many of these marriages are sterile? Of those where children have been born while living in a bubble-house, what percentage of the children are malformed?"

Candella's eyes were cesspools of curiosity. "I—I don't know off-hand," he said, "but——"

"Of course not," Norvell said impatiently. "I don't want you asking any direct questions, either. No sense starting any rumors. But if you can find out—*quietly*—I'd appreciate your giving me a ring." He produced the most splashily engraved calling card Mundin's printer had been able to turn out overnight. "Here's my number. Remember, I'm not offering you any inducement—that would be unethical. But it would be very much appreciated by me and my associates. We show our appreciation, Candella. Good-by."

He nodded curtly. Candella cried, "Hey, Norvie! Don't—don't run off like that! Can't you stay a little while and have some lunch, or a drink or something?"

"Sorry. Afraid not."

Candella rushed on, "But gee, Norvie, everybody's been looking forward to seeing you again. Stimmens particularly—I don't know what to say if you won't have lunch with us."

Norvell frowned. "Stimmens," he said thoughtfully. "Oh, *Stimmens*. Sorry, Candella. But do give Stimmens my regards, and tell her that I think of her often."

He left.

Norvell had a busy day. His schedule was General Recreations, Hussein's, and an even dozen bars in Monmouth City. By evening he was tired, happy, and about seventy-five per cent drunk. He approached his last call with a mixture of sadness, anger, and nostalgia.

Arnie Dworcas let him in.

Norvell tried none of the tricks he'd used on Candella with Arnie Dworcas; he was the old Norvell, the true friend, the shy acolyte. Sitting there with Arnie, listening to Arnie's explanations of the world's affairs, it seemed to Norvie that Belly Rave was a nightmare and Mundin a figure from a dream; nothing had changed; nothing would ever change, as long as he could sit and drink Arnie's beer.

But there were changes. . . .

Arnie drained his glass of beer, wiped his mouth and dialed another. "No, Norvell," he said meditatively, "I wouldn't say that you have succeeded. Not as We Engineers understand success. To Us Engineers, a mechanism—and all of us are mechanisms, Norvell, I, you, everybody—a mechanism is a success when it is functioning at maximum efficiency. Frank-

114

ly, in my little experiment of suggesting that you try Belly Rave I was attempting to perform what we call 'destructive testing'—the only way in which maximum efficiency can be determined. But what happened? You didn't rise through your own efforts, Norvell. By pure fortuitousness you made a connection and are now a *really* able man's secretary." He sipped his beer sorrowfully. "To use an analogy," he said, "it's as if my slipstick were to take credit for the computations I make on it."

"I'm sorry, Arnie," Norvell said. It was very difficult to decide whether he wanted more to laugh in Arnie's face or take out some of his front teeth with a beer glass. "Mr. Mundin thinks a great deal of you and your brother too, you know."

"Naturally," Arnie said severely. "That's one of the things you'll have to learn. Like seeks like, in human relations as well as electrostatics."

"I thought in electrostatics like *repelled*—"

"There you go!" yelled Arnie violently. "The layman! The quibbler! It's people like you that——"

"I'm sorry, Arnie!"

"All *right*. Don't get so excited. Really able people never lose control of themselves, Norvell! That was a stupid thing for you to get all upset about."

"I'm sorry, Arnie. That's what I was telling Mr. Mundin."

Arnie, raising his glass irritatedly, stopped it in mid-air. "*What* were you telling Mr. Mundin?" he asked suspiciously.

"Why, that you never lost control in an emergency. That you would be a damned good man to put in charge of—oh, God, Arnie, I shouldn't have said anything!" Norvell covered his mouth with both hands.

Arnie Dworcas said sternly, "Norvell, stop stammering and come out with it! In charge of *what?*"

Norvie, who had been fighting back a tendency to retch, removed his hands from his mouth. He said, "Well—well, it isn't as if I couldn't trust *you*, Arnie. It's—it's G.M.L."

"What *about* G.M.L.?"

Norvie said rapidly, "It's too soon to say anything definite and, *please*, Arnie, don't let a word of it get out. But you've heard the rumors about G.M.L., naturally."

"Naturally!" Arnie said, though his eyes were vacant.

115

"Mr. Mundin is associated with the—uh—the Coshocton bunch, Arnie. And he's looking around, quietly, you know, for key men to replace some of the old duffers. An l I took the liberty of mentioning you to him, Arnie. The only thing is, Mr. Mundin doesn't know much about the technical end, you see, and he wasn't sure just how much experience you had had."

"My record is in the professional journals, Norvell. Not that I would feel free to discuss it in this informal manner in any case, of course."

"Oh, of course! But what Mr. Mundin asked me was just what G.M.L. Homes models you had worked on—serial numbers and locations and so on. And I had to tell him that all that information was locked up, and you couldn't possibly get your hands on it."

Arnie shook his head wonderingly. "Laymen," he said. "Norvell, there is no reason in the world why I can't get microfilms of all that information. It's only corporate fiddle-faddle that causes all the secrecy; We Engineers are accustomed to cutting right through the red tape."

Norvell looked worshipful. "You mean you *can?*" he cried.

"I have already said so, have I not? It's just a matter of going through the records and picking out the units I've worked on myself, then making microfilms——"

"Better microfilm *everything*, Arnie," Norvell suggested. "It'll help Mr. Mundin understand the Broad Picture."

Arnie shrugged humorously. "Why not?"

"Don't forget the serial numbers," Norvell said.

Norvell met Mundin at Hussein's late that night, by arrangement, and made his report.

Mundin's expression began to relax. "So far," he said, "so good. And I've done my rounds too; and I imagine Hubble and Coett and Nelson are right on schedule. Let's have a drink."

"Thanks, no," said Norvell Bligh. "It's a long way to Belly Rave and my wife's all alone, except for the kid."

Mundin said, "Look, Bligh, why do you stick to Belly Rave? If it's money——"

Norvie shook his head. "You're paying me plenty for right now. Tell you the truth, I'm getting so I kind of like Belly Rave. As long as I don't *have* to stay there, you know, there's a lot to be said for it."

"There is?" Mundin asked.

Norvie laughed. "Maybe not a lot. Anyway, I'll stick a while; and I better get along. The Wabbits are supposed to be watch-dogging the house, but they don't think much of Sandy—that's my little girl—and I don't feel right without a man in the house at night."

A vagrant memory stirred in Mundin's mind. "I thought you had a kind of bodyguard?"

"Who? You mean Shep? He doesn't work for me any more." Norvie's expression was unreadable. "He had an accident with a lead pipe."

Chapter Nineteen

THE SIGN ON THE DOOR SAID:
RYAN & MUNDIN, ATTORNEYS-AT-LAW

The office occupied a solid floor-through of a very good building.

Del Dworcas had to take several long, deep breaths before he pushed the door open and announced himself to a ripely curved blonde receptionist. One of Mundin's minor pleasures these days, when he could spare time for it, was telling salesmen of automatic office equipment just what they could do with their merchandise.

"Pleased be seated, Mr. Dworcas," the girl cooed. "Mr. Mundin asked me to tell you that you'll be the *very* next person he sees."

The dozen or so other individuals in the waiting room glared at Del Dworcas. However, being a professional politician, he had no difficulty in striking up a conversation with the fellows nearest him. One was a petrochemist who understood there were consultant jobs opening up at Ryan & Mundin. Another was a publisher's bright young man who thought there must be a whale of a story in old man Ryan's sensational comeback, and stood ready to sign it up. The others were easy enough to tag—a couple of crack-pots, two attorneys obviously seeking affiliation with the new firm, a handful of persons who seemed to be in the market for lawyers, and had suddenly come to think that it might be a good idea to retain

Ryan & Mundin. Nobody in the waiting room seemed to have any idea what, if anything, was going on in the remainder of the enormous suite.

Dworcas—being a professional politician—was able to absorb information, pump for more, evaluate what he had heard and speculate on its meaning. But the answers were slight and cloudy. All he could make out for sure was: Ryan & Mundin were rising like a rocket; and plenty of shrewd operators were trying to hitch a ride.

At last he got the nod from the receptionist. A hard-faced young man with a badge that said *Guide* took him in tow.

Ryan & Mundin operated the damnedest law offices that Dworcas, in a full life, had ever seen. Law offices . . . complete with such eccentricities as chemistry labs and kitchens, living quarters and a TV studio, rooms locked off from his view, and open rooms that he could make no sense of.

Dworcas said tentatively, "You must be proud to be working for Mr. Mundin. Of course you know his record with our Party in the 27th—right down the line for Arab rights."

"That's nice," the guide said. "Right in here, mister." He guided Dworcas into a bay; it lit up with a shimmering violet light; the guide scanned a fluoroscope screen. "You're clean," he said. "In that door."

"You searched me!" Dworcas gasped. "Me! Mr. Mundin's oldest friend!"

"That's nice," the Ay-rab said. "In that door."

Dworcas went through the door.

"Hello, Del," Mundin said abstractedly. "What do you want?" He was checking off items on a list; he said, "Excuse me," and picked up an interoffice phone. Five minutes later he put it down, glanced at Dworcas, and turned to another list.

Dworcas, in 'cello tones, said, "Charlee. . . ."

And waited.

Mundin looked at him, with annoyance on his face. "Well?"

Dworcas waved a finger at him, smiling. "Charlie, you're not treating me right," he said. "You really aren't."

"Oh, the hell I'm not," said Mundin tiredly. "Look, Del. Business has picked up. I'm busy. What do you want?"

Dworcas said, "Nice office you've got. G.M.L. fix it for you?"

"What do you think?"

Dworcas retained his smile. "Remember who got you in with G.M.L.?"

"Oh, hell, you've got a point," Mundin conceded unwillingly. "It isn't going to do you much good, though. I haven't got time for favors. Some other time I'll listen closer."

"I want you to listen now, Charlie. I want to retain you for the County Committee."

Mundin stared. "Work for the County Committee?"

"I know it sounds like small potatoes. But it can lead to big ones, Charlie. You can make something out of it. And what about us, Charlie? You owe me—the Party—all of us something for putting you on to the Lavins. Is this the time to let us down? I'm not too proud to beg if I have to. Stick with the Party, boy!"

It wasn't going over. "Sorry, Del," Mundin said.

"Charlie!"

Mundin looked exasperated. "Del, you old crook," he said, "just what are you up to now? I've got nothing to sell you —even if you could outbid my other clients. Which you can't."

Dworcas leaned forward, his face completely changed. "I underestimated you, Charlie," he admitted. "I'll tell you the God's truth. No, haven't anything to sell, right now. But— something's on the fire. I smell it, Charlie. I never miss on something like this. I feel it through the soles of my feet."

He had Mundin's full attention now. "What do you feel?"

Dworcas shrugged. "Little things. Jimmy Lyons, for instance. Remember him, the captain's man at the precinct?"

"Sure."

"He isn't, any more. Captain Kowalik transferred him out to Belly Rave. He's been knifed twice. Why? I don't know why, Charlie. Jimmy was a bastard, sure; he had it coming to him. But why did it happen? And what's happening to Kowalik? He's losing weight. He can't sleep nights. I asked him why, and he wouldn't tell me. So I asked somebody else, and I found out. Kowalik's trouble is that Commissioner Sabbatino doesn't talk to him any more."

"And what's the matter with Sabbatino?" Mundin was playing with a pencil.

"Don't kid me, Charlie. Sabbatino's trouble is a man named Wheeler, who had a long, long talk with him one day. I don't know what about. But I know something, Charlie. I know Wheeler works for Hubble, and Hubble is one of your clients."

Mundin put the pencil down. "So what else is new?" he asked.

"Don't joke, Charlie. I never used to kid you—well, I mean, not much, you know. Don't you kid me. The folks in the 27th are all upset. There's a crazy rumor they're all going to be moved into G.M.L. Homes. They don't like the idea, the old folks don't. Some of the young folks do, so there's family fights. Every day, all day, all night, yelling and screaming, sometimes knives. A dozen riot calls a day in the 27th. So I asked my brother Arnie, the mechanic with G.M.L. You met him, you know what a fathead he is. But even he feels something in the organization. What?"

A secretary-ish person—with a start, Dworcas saw it was his brother's friend, Bligh—put his head in the door. "Excuse me, but they phoned from the landing stage, they're holding the D.C. copter for you."

"Hell," said Mundin. "Look, Norvie, thank them and ask them if they can give me five more minutes. I'll be free shortly." He glanced at Del Dworcas.

Dworcas stood up. "You're pretty busy. Just one more thing. What did you want with my brother Arnie?"

Mundin stood, thoughtful and relaxed, the very model of a man who is trying to remember the answer to an unimportant question for courtesy's sake.

"Never mind," said Dworcas. "I'll ask you some other time. I just want you to remember, I'm leveling with you."

"Good-by, Del," Mundin said cordially.

"Thanks, Norvie," he said a moment later. "You were very smooth. I wonder what the hell he meant by that business about Arnie."

"I guess Arnie mentioned I'd been to see him."

Mundin nodded thoughtfully. "Well, the hell. Let's walk over to Ryan's office. We'd better hurry; the copter really does leave in twenty minutes."

Ryan, as usual, was snoozing with great dignity at his desk. He looked good, considering. His opium was diluted and rationed to him these days; and he took it with good grace. "As long as you know you can get it, you can say 'no' to it most of the time," he said. As a consequence his very able brain had cleared and he was able to work as much as an hour at a time. He personally had evolved most of the seventy-eight steps in wobbling G.M.L.

Mundin reported Del's conversation carefully. Ryan rubbed his hands. "In effect, steps one through twenty-four are clicking nicely, hey?" he beamed. "The absolutely trustworthy G.M.L. begins to look a little shoddy at the seams for the first time; we begin to feel the unrest that will bring the whole structure down."

Mundin flicked a teletype message. "It ties in with the story from Princeton Junction, I suppose," he said without enthusiasm. "The little piece about the doctorate thesis on *Homeostasis in Housing: An Investigation into Potential Drawbacks of Controlled-Climate Dwellings.*"

Ryan nodded. "The first effects," he said. "People are questioning what has never been questioned before. But Dworcas is more significant. There is no public-opinion poll as sensitive as the judgment of a practical politician." He chuckled. "A very pleasant miasma of doubt and confusion. The spreading rumors about the possibility of sterility in G.M.L. homes—a wonderful touch. Yours, my boy, I am gratified."

Mundin said glumly, "Wonderful. Doubt and confusion. Knifings every night in the twenty-seventh ward." He felt regret as he saw the old man's face droop. "Excuse me, Mr. Ryan——"

"No, no." Ryan hesitated. "You remember the state I was in when we first met?" Mundin did. "It was partly Green, Charlesworth that brought me to it—partly them, and partly conscience. Don't strain yours too far, Charles. . . ."

They flew in the whirring copter to Washington, Mundin and Bligh. Mundin said fretfully, "We ought to have a couple of executive ships of our own. There's going to be more and more ground to cover. Put some one on it, will you, Norvie?"

Bligh made a note.

Mundin asked, "What about Del's brother? We can't stall on it. We've got to have those serial numbers, or today's work —and this whole buildup—is down the drain."

"Tomorrow all right?"

"Fine, fine," said Mundin dispiritedly. He took a briefcase

out, shuffled through reports he ought to read, memoranda he ought to sign, notes he ought to expand. Irritably he stuffed them back into the case.

Bligh said, incredibly, "Conscience, Charles." And winked.

Mundin said glumly, "Don't try to kid me out of it, Norvie. You don't know what it's like. You don't have the responsibility." He tossed the briefcase down. "Let's just talk; I don't have to be a louse again until we get to the museum. How've things been with you?"

Bligh considered. "Well," he said, "Virginia's pregnant."

Mundin was genuinely shocked. "Norvie, I *am* sorry!" he exclaimed. "I hope you're not going to do anything foolish——"

Bligh grinned. "Oh, no, nothing like that," he said cheerfully. "The kid's mine. First thing I did was drag her to an immunochemist and get that settled. Good thing; I would've broken her back. And how's *your* girl?"

"Huh?"

"Norma. Or Lavin."

"Oh, no, Norvie. You're dead wrong there. We can't stand each other and——"

"Sure, boss," said Bligh soothingly. "Say, Charles, can we raise the allowance for the Wabbits? Lana's been hinting. And my kid says they've really been working."

"Why not? How is your foster-daughter, by the way?"

Bligh grinned. "I'm almost proud of her. Came home five days running, beaten to a pulp. Sixth day, not a mark on her. She's a Burrow Leader in the Wabbits now. And she closes her mouth when she chews, and she calls me 'sir.' "

Mundin felt a sudden flash of insight. "That's why you're still living in Belly Rave, isn't it?"

Bligh got defensive. "Well, now, maybe that's part of it. But actually there's something to be said for Belly Rave. When you can install a water tank and a generating system and fix your place up—it's kind of lively." His voice rang with civic pride. "I'm looked on as a kind of community leader, Charles. We've organized a real volunteer police force in our block—not one of those shakedown squads. And——"

Mundin, grinning, said, "Who knows? One day it may be Norvell Bligh, first mayor of New Belly Rave!"

The little man was suddenly gray. He fiddled defensively

122

with the earpiece of his hearing aid. "Well, make a joke out of it if you want to," he said slowly. "The fact is they like me, I'm doing something for them, in a small way, sure, but something. And something has got to be done for these millions of outcasts. From the inside, Charles! I'm a funny-looking little man and I'm deaf and you automatically thought Virginia put the horns on me when I said she was pregnant. So what are you doing for Belly Rave, big man?"

Mundin choked and started to apologize; but Bligh waved him to silence. "Doesn't matter," he said. "Here's Washington."

The Museum of the National Association of the Builders of the American Dream was the by-blow of a long forgotten public-relations campaign with an added dash of non-profit-foundation tax evasion. The slickers who had sold the campaign to the businessmen were dust; the inspirational ads forgotten; but what can you do with a granite building full of junk and professors and janitors? You can ignore it and go your sensible business way. Of all this Mundin was reminded as he entered the shabby anteroom of the director's office.

His withered secretary said to the gentlemen from Monmouth, "Dr. Proctor is a *very* busy man. You must go away and telephone for an appointment."

Mundin said gently, "Please tell the director that it is in connection with a rather substantial donation. We *don't* expect to be in the city long. . . ."

The director came flying out of his office, beaming.

The attorney introduced himself. "Of the law firm of Ryan and Mundin," he explained.

"Yes, indeed, Mr. Munsen! Even here, even in our remote and dedicated corner of the world, we have heard of your firm! Might one ask the name of——?"

"Sorry."

"Oh, I quite understand, Mr. Munchkin! And the, ah, amount——?"

"Flexible," Mundin said firmly. "My client has commissioned me to inspect the museum and report to him on which departments seem most deserving of additional support."

"Ah! Pray allow me to guide you, sir. Just through here is the Collection of Coelenterates——"

Mundin said blandly, "I think we would prefer to see the Hall of Basics first."

Dr. Proctor very nearly frowned. At the last minute he changed and merely looked confidential. "For the general public," he said, nudging Mundin. "Mere engineering. Gimmicks and gadgets, eh? Not *important*, though perhaps of some limited interest to the engineer, the sociologist, that sort of quasi-scientist. Now, our Collection of Coelenterates, just through——"

"The Hall of Basics, please?"

"Mr. Monkton! A tourist trap, I assure you. On the other hand, the Coelenterata—which happen to be my specialty, I might add——"

Mundin said sadly, "Norvell, I'm afraid Dr. Proctor isn't really interested in our client's bequest."

Bligh said, "Too bad. Well, luckily the copter's waiting."

Dr. Proctor sputtered and led them to the Hall of Basics. They gravely studied the spinning jenny, the first sewing machine, the first telegraph, the first telephone, the first airplane, the first Model T, the first atomic pile, the first G.M.L., the first segment of Belt Transport.

They stopped before the G.M.L. bubble-house, beaming approvingly—except for Dr. Proctor. Tourists were ambling through it. It was a minute or so before they could get close enough to read the plaque.

#342371
The First G.M.L. Home Ever Erected
Donated by Mr. Hamilton Moffatt, "Father of the Bubble-House."

> This G.M.L. Home, moved to the Institution from its original site in Coshocton, Ohio, was fabricated in the plastics factory of Donald Lavin. Electrical circuitry and mechanisms are designed and installed by Bernard Gorman. It has stood for more than five decades without a scar or a malfunction. Chemists and Engineers estimate that, without any sort of maintenance, it will last at least 1,000 more years, standing virtually forever as a tribute to the immortal genius of—
> MR. HAMILTON MOFFATT

"Do tell," murmured the attorney. The crowds of tourists began to thin out and the director glumly started to lead them through the bubble-house.

"Hell with it," said Mundin. "Let's go back to your place."

In Dr. Proctor's private office Mundin looked at the small, dusty, and dubious bottle the director exhumed from an umbrella rack, and shuddered. He said decisively, "No, nothing to drink. Dr. Proctor, I think I can definitely state that my client would be interested in donating one hundred thousand dollars as a fund to be divided at your discretion between the Hall of Basics and the Coelenterata."

"Dear me!" Dr. Proctor leaned back in his chair, fondling the bottle, his face wreathed in smiles. "Dear me! Are you sure you wouldn't care to—just a very small—no? Perhaps, do you know, perhaps I will, just to celebrate. A *very* wise decision, sir! It is, believe me, *most* unusual to find a layman who, like yourself, can at once perceive the ecological significance and *thrilling* morphology of the humble coelenterate!" He tipped the bottle into a dusty water tumbler and raised it in toast. "The Coelenterata!" he cried.

Mundin was fumbling in his briefcase. He produced a check, already made out, a typed document in duplicate and a flat can that gurgled. "Now," he said matter-of-factly, "pay close attention, doctor. You, personally, are to dilute the contents of this can with one quart of ordinary tap water. Fill an ordinary garden sprayer with the solution and spray the G.M.L. Home in the Hall of Basics with it, covering all plastic parts from the outside. It shouldn't take ten minutes, if you have a good sprayer. Naturally, you will make sure nobody sees you doing it. That should be easy enough, in your position; but make sure of it. And that will be that."

Dr. Proctor, eyes bulging, coughed and spluttered four ounces of tinted grain neutral spirits over his desk. Choking and wheezing, at last he got out, "My dear sir! What on *earth* are you talking about? What is in that container? Why should I do any such preposterous thing?"

Mundin said calmly, "I'll take your questions in order. I am talking about one hundred thousand dollars. What is in that container is something worth one hundred thousand dollars. You should do it because of one hundred thousand dollars."

Dr. Proctor wiped his mouth with the back of his hand, almost speechless. "But—but—if you assured me that the fluid would be entirely harmless——"

"I'll do no such thing! Where I come from you can get away with doing quite a lot of harm for one hundred thousand dollars." Mundin smiled frostily. "Come now, doctor. Think of one hundred thousand dollars! Think of the ecological significance and the thrilling morphology. And then sign this receipt, and *then* take the check."

Dr. Proctor looked at the check. "It's post-dated a month," he said tremulously.

Mundin shrugged and began to repack his briefcase. "Well, if you're going to *quibble*——"

Dr. Proctor snatched the check. He scribbled his name on the receipt and, with a quick, furtive movement, dropped the flat can of fluid into his desk.

In the copter Mundin and Bligh looked at each other. "Right on schedule, Charles," Norvie Bligh said gravely.

The attorney shook his head, marveling. "Yes, Norvie. Right on schedule."

They were back in the offices of Mundin & Ryan, Attorneys-at-Law, before close of business. And Norvie Bligh had not yet sat down when Mishal came hunting him with news that he had a visitor. "Bring him in, Mike," Norvie ordered the Ay-rab. "No, wait a minute. I'll get him."

Norvie flustered out to the waiting room. "Arnie!" he said eagerly. "Come in, come in, come in!" He piloted Arnie by the elbow down the halls, around the corners, through the labs and recreation rooms, chattering and ignoring Arnie's bulging eyes. There was a shorter way; but it didn't lead past the labs and recreation rooms.

"Beer, Arnie?" Norvell asked, in his own office. He pushed a button; Miss Prawn came in and dialed the beer for them. "Not those chairs, please; something more comfortable." Miss Prawn dialed two enormous armchairs.

Arnie said, swallowing his beer with some difficulty: "I imagine you realize that I've gone pretty far out on a limb for you."

"Oh, no, Arnie! Please! How do you mean?"

Arnie shrugged, covertly looking around the enormous

room. "Oh, nothing I begrudge you," he said. "After all, friendship is what really counts. As We Engineers say, 'You brace my buttress, and I'll brace yours.' " He set his glass down. "And when you asked me, as a friend, to get you the file numbers and locations of the G.M.L. units, why naturally I did it. Though I confess I never expected," he went on moodily, "to stir up such a ridiculous fuss about perfectly trivial records. Corporate secrecy that hampers an able technological man is inefficiency, and inefficiency is a crime. Still, anything to oblige you and Charles Mundin."

"I never expected you'd have any difficulty!" Norvie lied. "But you got them?"

Arnie raised his eyebrows. "Naturally, Norvell. And microfilmed them. I have them right here. But——"

"Let's see them," Norvell said bluntly.

He finally got his hands on the microfilm and riffled through the index tables. All there, on film—lots of it. Serial numbers. Dates. Locations. Maintenance histories. "Arnie," he said gently, "stand up, will you, please?"

The engineer frowned, "What's the matter?" He stood up.

Norvell Bligh put the microfilm in his desk. He said, "Arnie, you didn't get those as a favor to me. You got them because you thought it would get you a better job."

Arnie flushed and said severely, "Norvell, a friend doesn't——"

"Shut up, Arnie. Remember what you said about 'destructive testing' the other day?" Bligh demanded. "Well, let's try some."

He swung. In the next three minutes he took quite a clobbering about the head and ears, but when the three minutes were up Arnie was on the floor, trying to stanch a nose that ran with blood, and Norvell was still on his feet.

"Good-by, Arnie," he said, happily, ringing for the guide. "Mishal will show you the way out."

He made his way to the chem lab that operated behind locked doors and tossed the film onto the desk where Mundin was sitting, watching the flow of golden fluid into enamel-lined cans. Mundin snatched it up testily. "Keep it away from *that* stuff, for God's sake!" he cried.

Norvell grinned. "I guess we better," he agreed. "If this get ruined we'll have trouble getting any more out of Arnie. I beat him to a pulp."

Which was a considerable exaggeration; but pardonable under the circumstances.

Mundin, holding tight to the arms of the seat, said, "Norvell, are you *sure* you can fly this thing? After all, it's a lot bigger than the ones General Recreations——"

Norvie Bligh said briefly, "Don't worry about a thing." The helicopter zoomed straight up from the landing stage into the night. Apparently from sheer joy of living, Norvie buzzed the tallest nearby building before locking the course for Coshocton, Ohio.

He turned around casually in the pilot's seat. "Well, that's that. Play a game of cards? It's a long trip."

Mundin shook his head. "I'm a little jumpy," he admitted.

"Oh, everything's going to go off all right," Norvie said reassuringly.

The little man had changed more than somewhat in a few weeks. Now all Mundin hoped was that The New Norvell Bligh really could fly a copter as advertised, well enough, at least, to get the night's dirty work out of the way.

Bligh cheerfully switched on a dome light and began reading a magazine. Mundin leaned back and tried to relax, thinking about the things that had happened in one crowded, tense week.

Everything seemed to be running smoothly. Ryan, packed to the eyebrows with new and expensive drugs, walked and talked like a man, though collapse would come, sooner or later. Still, he was happy; and, more important, he was keeping the Lavins under control. Norma Lavin was even helping, to some small extent; and Don was catching up on his months of quiescence with a protracted bout of hell-raising. Still, he was always on hand when needed; Norma made sure of that.

And the three silent partners—Hubble, Coett, and Nelson—had complimented Mundin on the way he was spending their money. At the last meeting Hubble had been worried by only one thing, he said.

"Speak up, Bliss," Mundin smiled. "We'll certainly try to straighten it out."

"Oh, it's not your end of it, Charles," Hubble said slowly. "Actually, it's ours. We can't get through to Green, Charlesworth."

Coett scowled; Hubble turned on him warningly. "Now, Harry, don't start that again. How can Charles run things intelligently unless we level with him?"

Green, Charlesworth, thought Mundin. Again. "Level with me about what, Bliss?" he asked.

Hubble shrugged. "It's just some kind of an abnormal situation, Charles, that's all. The three of us just don't seem to be getting through to Green, Charlesworth. Oh, we're doing business with them. But not, you know, any kind of real communication."

Mundin thought of Captain Kowalik, unnerved and jittery because Commissioner Sabbatino didn't talk to him any more. He said: "Do I run into Green, Charlesworth anywhere along the line?"

They smiled politely and said no, that wouldn't be likely. Green, Charlesworth did nothing on the operating or manufacturing end. They were money men. "But," Bliss Hubble said, trying to appear unconcerned, "if they *should* show up, Charles, don't try to handle it yourself. Get in touch with us."

Nelson nodded worriedly. "Frankly," he said, "we don't know where they stand on this thing, Charles. Bliss and I rather think they wouldn't give a damn one way or the other. Harry thinks they'd be all for us, not that they vote any G.M.L. stock, you know, but they have, well, moral influence." He swallowed. "But we can't get through to them."

Mundin asked, "Want me to go calling on them?"

They smiled ghastlily and shook their heads. Hubble said abruptly, "My guess is that they're onto us. That they know every move we make and just haven't committed themselves. Yet."

Mundin looked around at the three Titans, wonderingly. He asked, "When you say 'they,' who do you mean, exactly?"

A three-cornered wrangle developed. Coett believed that Green, Charlesworth was essentially the top men in the Memphis crowd plus the organic solvents crowd and the New England utilities. He himself was, actually, most of the Southwest crowd and practically all of the inorganic chemicals crowd.

Nelson, who was New England and nonferrous metals, believed that Green, Charlesworth was, essentially, California, coal-oil-steel and mass media.

Hubble, who was mass media and New York, said that couldn't be. He thought that Green, Charlesworth was essentially money.

On that everybody agreed. Worriedly.

"Look," said Mundin, "I just want to get this straight in my mind. Would we scuttle this whole project if Green, Charlesworth came out against it?"

They looked at him as though he were a two-year-old. "If we could, boy," Harry Coett said grimly. "Don't even talk about it. I doubt it could be done; unscrambling eggs is child's play compared to stopping a thing like this. At the very least, we'd lose really serious amounts of money. . . . But I'm confident that it's simply a matter of getting in touch with them. After all, we're taking a step forward. And Green, Charlesworth has always been on the side of progress."

"Reaction," said Nelson.

"Middle-of the-roaders," Hubble insisted.

Mundin demanded, "But who *are* they? Where are they? Is there a real man named Green and a real man named Charlesworth?"

Hubble said, "Their offices are in the Empire State Building —the whole building." He coughed. "I fibbed to you that time we passed the Empire State Building. I apologize. I didn't know you very well in those days."

Mundin's eyebrows climbed. "But *in New York?* I thought the whole city was condemned after the bombing."

Hubble shook his head. "I suppose that's what they want one to think, Charles. They're there, all right. You can see the lights in the building at night—the only one in the city. It isn't a beacon as most people suppose. And as for a real Mr. Green and a real Mr. Charlesworth—no. Or I should say, probably no. The firm name is a couple of hundred years old, so—— But I admit I'm not sure. When you go there you never see anyone important. Clerks, junior executives, department heads. You do business with them; and there are long waits, weeks sometimes, while they're 'deciding policy questions.' I suppose that means while they're getting their instructions. Well—congratulations, Charles. Now you know as much about Green, Charlesworth as anybody else. Just remember, if they turn up anywhere, or you encounter anything, well, anomalous that makes you *suspect* they're turning up, blow the whistle. We'll handle it."

Harry Coett said, "But this is just a precaution. There won't be any trouble, I'm confident. They'll go along with us when the chips are down. Fundamentally, after all, they're progressive."

"Reactionary!" said Nelson.

"Middle-of-the-roaders!" Hubble insisted.

Norvie Bligh sang out: "Coshocton! End of the line!"

Mundin jumped in his seat, and looked around dazedly. The copter was turning and swooping low.

He peered out. There below lay Coshocton, the most average city in the most average state in the union. Fifty years before, Hamilton Moffatt, "father of the bubble-house," had signed the first of the industrial-lease G.M.L. contracts with the Federated Casket Company of Coshocton.

Mundin asked, "Can you find the bubble-city?"

"We're over it now. Get out your squirt gun."

It wasn't a squirt gun; it was a belly tank pressurized with freon. Mundin pushed on a bowden wire to open the nozzle; the needle on the gauge before his eyes quivered to show that the "squirt gun" was squirting.

"Make your first pass," Mundin ordered.

The coptor fluttered over the bubble-city at a thousand feet, trailing a falling plume of golden fluid. The drops partly vaporized; but the fluid was heavy, and the liquid reached the bubble-houses in quantity large enough to film them.

Four times Norvell Bligh quartered the bubble-city, until all of the fluid was gone. Then he set course for the long trip home, leaving behind the glittering domes which had been leased to Federated Casket for its contract employees; which had been duly absorbed by General Foundries when Federated Casket went under in the big switch to cremation; which had been duly swallowed by National Nonferrous; which was Mundin's friend Mr. Nelson, who was at home gritting his teeth as he counted the cost of the night's work that Mundin and Bligh were putting in.

Chapter Twenty

BLIGH WAS PASSING OUT CIGARS. "It's a boy," he proudly told anybody in the office who would listen. "I looked through the foetoscope myself. Doctor says it's the finest forty-day embryo he's ever seen, and that wasn't just a snow-job. By God, when that kid gets born he's going to have every advantage I——"

Charles Mundin emerged from his office.

"Morning!" Norvie Bligh bellowed. "It's a boy, boss! The doctor raved about him. Have a cigar."

"Congratulations," Mundin said sourly. "Norvie, can we get to work now? This is the big day, after all!"

Norvie, sobered, said, "Yessir." They entered Ryan's office.

A clerk had overheard. Norma Lavin, following half a minute behind Mundin and Bligh, saw the girl pick up a vase of flowers and hold it to her lips. Thirsty? Norma wondered. But the girl did not appear to be drinking the water; her lips were moving. Getting rid of her gum, Norma thought. Or—talking? But then Bliss Hubble hailed her and she forgot it.

Which was a pity, in a way, for the girl had not been getting rid of her gum. Norma Lavin vaguely heard the clerk's low-pitched murmur, but by then Norma was slapping Bliss Hubble's hand off her arm and no one was looking at the clerk.

The girl put the vase back and returned briskly to work.

The Big Seven—the two Lavins, Mundin, Ryan, Hubble, Nelson, and Coett—and Norvell Bligh were assembled in Ryan's office.

Norma was saying with fire, "I trust I do not impose on the biological fact that I am a woman, and I don't expect anyone to impose on *me*. If Mr. Hubble can't keep his damned hands to himself I at least expect him to leave me alone during working hours. After hours I can manage to avoid him."

Bliss Hubble grinned. "Sorry, Norma, but——"

"Lavin!"

"Sorry, Lavin, but I guess I was off-base. I don't mind admitting I'm a little jumpy today; this is make-or-break, you know."

"We're all a little tense, young lady," soothed Harry Coett. "I must admit that I, for one, am a little tired of sitting here. You're sure, Mundin, that your friend—uh—did what he was supposed to?"

Mundin shrugged. After a moment he said, "Anybody want coffee or anything?"

Nobody did. Nobody wanted anything except an end to their vigil. Except for Norma, whose fires were still raging internally, and Don Lavin, who was in a state of chronic joy after his long torpor, every face in the room was showing signs of worry.

And then——

Norvie Bligh, huddling over a muted radio in the corner, yelled, "Here it is!" He dived for the video and volume knobs.

"—AT FIRST BLAMED ON VIBRATION," bellowed the newscaster; then Norvie got the sound where he wanted it. "Experts from G.M.L., however, said that at first glance this appears unlikely. A team of G.M.L. engineers is being dispatched to Washington to study the wreckage. We bring you now a picture from our library of the First Bubble-House. As it was——"

The slide flashed on; there stood G.M.L. Unit One, dwarfed by the vast Hall of Basics.

"—and as it is——"

A live shot this time: Same site, same hall—but instead of the gleaming bubble-house a tangle of rubbish, with antlike uniformed men crawling about the wreckage.

Norma Lavin blubbered, "Da-da-daddy's first house!" and burst into tears. The others gave her swift, incredulous looks, and went right back to staring in fascination and fear at the screen.

"Our Washington editor now brings you Dr. Henry Proctor, Director of the Museum. Dr. Proctor?" The rabbit-face flashed on, squirming, scared.

"Dr. Proctor," asked the mellow tones, "what, in your opinion, might be the cause of the collapse?"

"I—really—I—I really have no opinion. I'm—uh—completely in the—uh—dark. It's a puzzle to me. I'm afraid I can't—uh—be of the slightest—— I have no opinion. Really."

"Thank you, Dr. Proctor!" To Mundin it seemed that all was lost; any fool could read guilt, guilt, guilt plastered on the director's quivering face and at once infer that Proctor had sprayed the bubble-house with a solvent supplied by someone else; and it would be only moments until "someone else" was identified as Charles Mundin, LL.B. But the newscaster was babbling on; the rabbit face flickered off the screen. The newscaster said, "Ah, I have a statement just handed to me from G.M.L. Homes. Mr. Haskell Arnold, Chairman of the Board of G.M.L. Homes, announced today that the engineering staff of the firm has reached tentative conclusions regarding the partial malfunction——" Even the newscaster stumbled over that. The listening men, recalling the pile of rubble, roared and slapped their knees in a burst of released tension. "The—uh—partial malfunction of G.M.L. Unit One. They state that highly abnormal conditions of vibration and chemical environment present in the Museum are obviously to blame. Mr. Arnold said, and I quote, 'There is no possibility whatsoever that this thing will happen again.' End of quote." The announcer smiled and discarded a sheet from the papers in his hand. Now chummy, he went on, "Well, ladies and gentlemen, I'm certainly glad to hear that, and so, I'm sure, are all of you who also live in bubble-houses.

"And now, for you sports fans, the morning line on Grosse Pointe Field Day. It's going to be a bang-up show produced by the veteran impresario Jim, 'Blood and Guts,' Hanrahan. Plenty of solid, traditional entertainment. First spectacle——"

"Turn that thing off," someone ordered Norvell. Wistfully, he did, straining to catch the last words. Remembering.

Harry Coett broke the silence. Brutally, "Well, that's that. We're committed. Is everybody here as terrified as I am?"

"I guess so," Hubble said slowly. "You know, Mundin, we still haven't been able to get a line on Green, Charlesworth."

The offices of *Alive*, flagship of the *Alive-Space-Chance* publishing squadron, were rocking. Hot on the heels of the disaster in Washington, a new cataclysm had just flashed in from their stringer in Coshocton, Ohio.

"Keep talking it!" yelled the editor to the stringer, switching him to a rewrite man. He yelled at the picture editor, "Standby squad to Coshocton, Ohio. Whole goddam bubble-city fell apart!" The picture editor acknowledged and spoke a few quiet words into a phone. Overhead on the landing stage, a transport plane that stood with its engines just ticking over, quickened to a roar and took off, its paunch laden with six photographers and their gear. A klaxon screamed in the ready room next the landing stage; another standby squad put down their poker hands and climbed into a second plane, which taxied to the take-off line and stood waiting.

The editor snapped, "Morgue! Send up the file on G.M.L. Home failures, collapses, service guarantees, and so on. Science! Put two writers on to whip it into a sidebar. Photoroom! Hold everything; stand by to remake the issue. Transmitter! Hold everything; stand by to remake; three pages of four-color transmission upcoming. Midwest! *Midwest*—what the hell held you up? Get a squad to Coshocton, Ohio; G.M.L. Bubble-City collapse. Art! Stand by for visualization—scene of collapsing bubble-houses——"

And so on. Until ——

The editor quite suddenly stopped what he was doing and softly said to his assistant, "Oh, Jesus. Take over, Manning. Policy."

He got up, fixed his cravat, and walked up a flight of carpeted stairs. When he got past the publisher's secretary, he said delicately:

"Of course, sir, it looks like big news to us. But we'd like the benefit of your judgment in a, well, sensitive area like this. I understand you hold some G.M.L. stock, sir, so naturally you'd have an insider's slant. What I want to know is, do you consider it—uh—in the best public interest to splash the story?"

"Splash it," the publisher said nobly, in the best tradition of no-fear-nor-favor journalism.

The editor, grateful but wondering, said, "Thank you, Mr. Hubble."

He almost backed out of The Presence.

He said to his assistant, marveling, "Sometimes I think the old boy isn't such a selfish louse after all." He shrugged, and shook his head, and turned to his desk panel, yelling:

"Hasn't anybody got through to G.M.L. yet?"

Chapter Twenty-One

NORMA LAVIN'S OFFICE was more than comfortable; it was luxurious.

But Norma was not particularly happy in. it. Ryan thought it would be better if she didn't venture out of the suite. Her brother Donald, over his spree, was busily engaged in office-managing the hundred employees of Ryan & Mundin. Mundin was *busy*. There wasn't much for Norma to do but sit and think.

She sat. And she thought.

She thought: G.M.L. Bankruptcy. Melt down the bubble-houses. Destroy Daddy's memorial, tear everything apart. Does it *have* to be that way? Does everything *have* to be ripped to pieces and slimed up and all the goodness taken out of it?

She thought rebelliously, They treat me like some sort of degenerate because I'm a woman. Hubble with his crawly, girl-clutching hands. Coett with his fatherly, superior, shut-your-yap-little-girl look. Mundin with his—with his——

She thought wonderingly, Mundin, with his infuriating, aggravating way of treating me as if I were *not* a woman. . . .

She thought about that a great deal; after all, she hadn't much to do but sit and think.

Until she saw the beat-cop in the lobby talking to his nightstick.

At first, Norma's reaction was what anybody's reaction would be if they saw someone talking into a nightstick. She thought he was nuts.

But he wasn't being flamboyant about it; he was off in a corner, hidden from sight—except the sight of someone who happened to be staring idly out of a window directly above him, like Norma. Just a few murmured, unselfconscious words.

She decided the cop was being whimsical, of course. Or absent-mindedly rehearsing a speech to the desk sergeant.

Or else he really was nuts. There was some perfectly reasonable explanation; so she forgot about it and went back to sitting and thinking. She thought about the old days, with a touch of wistfulness—not the *old* old days, but the Belly Rave old days, when she and Mundin had had work to do together. When she was bankrupt and he was a pauper—instead of the way things were now, when she was well-to-do on the verge of billions, and he was *busy*.

Damn Mundin, she thought. Wonderingly . . . for she had never damned a man for failing to pay attention to her before.

It was three days before Norma's boredom overbalanced the common-sense view about people talking into nightsticks; and it might not have done it then if Miss Elbers hadn't had to take a day off with periodic functional disturba..ces.

Miss Elbers was the clerk whom Norma had observed talking into a flowerpot.

The vase was on Miss Elbers's desk still; Norma made several trips through the room, peering at it inconspicuously. It looked very much like any other vase with flowers in it.

But she was bored. During the coffee break she photographed it from several angles; a Chinesey thing some eight inches tall. Even then, it took another three days before she got around to taking the photographs to a bric-a-brac dealer with Chinesey things in his window.

He said promptly, "I don't want it, lady. It's a copy, and they copied it wrong."

She handed him money. He looked surprised, but he explained, "It's a copy of a very well-known piece, a Chinese funerary jar. If memory serves——" and it obviously, pridefully did "—from the Fairy Kiln of Wu Chang, near Soo Chou. The proportions of this copy are good, and so are the colors. But the characters on the four medallions and on the band around the shoulder are wrong. Funerary jars always have the characters for 'never,' 'mountain,' 'aging,' and 'green.' I don't know what these characters on the copy are, but they aren't the right ones. I guess you got stuck."

"Thanks," she said thoughtfully.

Further inquiry turned up the name of a man who could translate the characters for her. A professor at Columbia.

She caught the man wiping his television makeup off in his office. He gallantly assured her it would be a pleasure. He wrinkled his brows over the photographs and finally said:

"It's gibberish. Not Chinese of any period, I'll swear to that. Here and there a piece of a character looks like something or other, but that's as far as the resemblance goes. One can easily imagine the layman being fooled, of course. Does it matter? After all, somebody simply faked a vase, and did a poor job of decorating it. Though why he didn't copy authentic characters I don't understand."

"I do," Norma Lavin whispered, her face bloodless.

Ryan and Mundin and her brother shifted impatiently as she tried to explain:

"They must be printed circuits. Maybe the crackle in the glaze is metallic—an antenna. There must be transistors and little silver-acid batteries and God knows what in the body of the thing. We could X-ray it—but anybody who'd make a communicator like that would probably have it booby-trapped."

Mundin asked slowly, "Have you handled the thing?"

"No!"

"Norma's right," Ryan said. "Work through the clerk. The gadget's dynamite. Don, find out who she is."

Don Lavin went to his files. Mundin exploded, "Damn it, I'm not convinced. This thing coming right in the middle of our whole campaign—are Haskell Arnold and his crowd that smart?"

"No," Ryan said gravely. "Not Haskell Arnold and his crowd."

"Here it is." Don Lavin produced a card. "The clerk's name is Harriet Elbers. Single, twenty-six, B.B.A. from Columbia, corporate-case researcher for Choate Brothers three years, discharged in staff reduction on closing a case. Um, efficiency rating high, yes, contract status standard—uh—nothing much else about her. Lives with widowed mother."

"Fine-sounding girl," Ryan said dispiritedly.

"Ryan, if it isn't Arnold——"

Ryan looked at Mundin and shrugged. "Who? Who but Green, Charlesworth? Arnold wouldn't play it this way. He's a slugger, nothing else. Green, Charlesworth—they're judo experts. They wait until we're charging full speed ahead and then they stick one foot out and we go crashing and break our necks. Or—they don't. As they think appropriate. I tangled with them once. You may recall my recent career."

Mundin said, "One thing's for certain. We've got to buzz Hubble, Nelson, and Coett on this. That's orders; and they've been putting up the cash."

"Sure," said Ryan absently. He was staring at the flower vase on his own desk.

The three money-men weren't scared; they were petrified.

Coett said in a rage, "By God, those bastards! Letting us run along like idiots, spending money like water!"

Nelson wailed, "My Coshocton employees! And this damn law-suit against G.M.L.—it's already on the calendar! My God, Mundin, can't there be some mistake?"

Hubble was almost philosophical, as he could afford to be. He had spent least; if anything, he had picked up some change on increased circulation of his publications. "Better lose some than all," he said consolingly. "Anyway, I'm still going to take some convincing that a screwy-looking vase and our— ah—breakdown of communications with Green, Charlesworth means that they're against us. Naturally, when I *am* convinced, that's that."

Norma Lavin looked thunderstruck. "You'd quit?" she gasped.

They looked at her. "My dear," Harry Coett said, "we remember what happened to your father. Don't you?"

Mundin said furiously, "Damn it, Coett, this is crazy! They're just *people*. They've got nothing but *money*. We're people and we've got money too, plenty of it. All right, maybe they've got more, but they're not God Almighty! We can lick them if we have to!" He stopped; Hubble, Nelson, and Coett were wincing at every word.

Hubble opened his eyes. "Mundin," he remonstrated faintly. That was all he could manage to say.

Ryan said shakily, the jerks in his hands more visible than Mundin had seen them in weeks, "Maybe if one of us went to see them, Coett. Maybe——" his whole body was shaking, but he said, "I'll do it myself. At the worst they'll refuse to see me. That's happened before, God knows, but I can't see how we'll be any worse off——"

Coett said, "Shut your face, you old fool."

Hubble, more kindly, said, "You know how it is, Ryan. If we sent anyone but a very top man—God!"

"I'm not going," said Nelson very positively.

"*I'm* not," said Harry Coett.

And Nelson said, "So you see? There's just too much to lose. Sorry."

Norma Lavin, pale and quivering, stood up. "My Daddy invented the bubble-house for——" she began tremblingly, then caught herself. "No! The hell with that. Leaving my Daddy out of this, one-quarter of G.M.L. Homes belongs to Don and myself. It's *ours*, understand? Ours! Not yours or Green, Charlesworth's. If you yellow bastards want out, you can have out. We're sticking, and I can tell you right now we're sticking until we drop dead, or hell freezes over, or we win—in descending order of probability. It isn't just money, you know. We got along fine on no money. We can do it again. It's *people*, Coett! It's making life worth living for the poor slobs who buy their bubble-houses with their life's blood! Slavery's against the law. G.M.L.'s been breaking the law, but *we* are taking over, and *we* are going to make some changes. You hear me?"

They heard her, and that was the ball game. Seven people were shouting at once, even old Ryan: "—no better than a Republican, young lady!" Nelson was howling; and "For God's sake, let her talk!" screamed Mundin; and Coett was spouting endless obscenities.

And the door opened. Mishal, the guide, stared in, looking upset. "Visitor," he got out, and disappeared.

"Oh, hell," said Mundin in the sudden silence, starting toward the door, "I *told* those idiots—oh, it's you!" He looked irritatedly at the figure of William Choate IV, now entering. "Hello, Willie. Look, I'm awfully busy right now."

Willie Choate's lower lip was trembling. "Hello, old man," he said dismally. "I have a—uh—message for you."

"Later, Willie. Please." Mundin made pushing motions.

Willie stood his ground. "Here."

He handed Mundin a square white envelope. Mundin, torn between annoyance and hysteria, opened it and glanced absently at the little white card inside.

Then he glanced at it again.

Then he stared at it until Coett came to life and leaped

140

forward to take it out of his hand. It said in crabbed handwriting:

> *Messrs. Green, Charlesworth*
> *request the appearance*
> *of Mr. Charles Mundin*
> *and Miss Norma Lavin*
> *when convenient*

It was a long ride.

Willie apologetically took out a magazine as soon as they settled down in the car. "You know what Great-Great-Granddaddy Rufus said, Charles. 'Happy is he who has laid up in his youth, and held fast in all fortune, a genuine and passionate love for reading.' I always like to———"

"Sure, Willie," said Mundin. "Look, what's all this?"

Willie smiled regretfully. "Of course," he explained, "he wasn't my *real* Great-Great-Granddaddy; Granpap just kind of took that name when he bought into the firm. It's just a way of———"

Mundin said urgently, "Willie, *please*. Remember how it was in law school?"

Willie seemed about to cry. "Gee, Charles! What can I say?"

"You can tell me what this is all about!"

Willie looked at Mundin. Then he looked all around him, at Norma, at the fittings of the car. Then he looked at Mundin again. The implication was unmistakable.

"At least tell me what your connection is," Mundin begged.

"*Gee*, Charles!" But the answer to that one, at least, was plain, written in those soft cow's eyes, spelled out in that trembling lip. Willie was what God had made him to be: an errand boy, and doubtless knew little more than Mundin about what, why, or wherefore. Mundin gave up and let Willie read his magazine, while he stared morosely at the crumbled city they were driving through.

The building *smelled* old. Mundin and Norma and Willie stepped into a creaking elevator and slowly went up fifty floors. A long walk, and then another elevator, even smaller, even creakier.

Then a small room with a hard bench. Willie left them there; all he said was "See you."

Then—waiting. An hour, then several hours. They didn't talk.

Mundin thought he was going to flip.

Then he thought that that was what Green, Charlesworth wanted him to think, and got a grip on himself.

And by and by a small, quiet man came and led them into another room.

There was no place to sit, and no place for Mundin to hang his coat. Mundin draped his coat over his arm, and stood, staring back into the unblinking eyes of the man seated at the desk. He was an imposing figure of a man, lean-featured, dark-haired, temples shot with silver. He leaned forward, comfortably appraising; his chin was in one cupped hand, the fingers covering his lips. His eyes followed Mundin, and his chest rhythmically rose and fell; otherwise he was stock-still.

Mundin cleared his throat. "Mr.—ah—Green?" he inquired.

The man said emotionlessly, "We despise you, Mr. Mundin. We are going to destroy you."

Mundin cried, "Why?"

"You are Rocking the Boat, Mundin," the man said through his fingers, the piercing eyes locked with Mundin's own.

Mundin cleared his throat. "Look, Mr. Green—you are Mr. Green?"

"You are Our Enemy, Mundin."

"Now, wait a minute!" Mundin took a deep breath. *Please,* he silently begged his adrenal gland. *Gently!* he ordered the pounding sensation in his skull. He said temperately, "I'm sure we can get together, Mr.—sir. After all, we're not greedy."

The figure said steadily, "Men Like You would Ruin the World if we let them. We won't."

Mundin swept his eyes hopelessly around the room. This man was obviously mad; someone else, *anyone* else—— But there was no one. Barring the desk and the man, there was nothing in the room but a pair of milky, glassy cabinets and Mundin and the girl. He said, "Look, did you call me down here just to insult me?"

"You put your Fingers in the Buzz-Saw, Mundin. They will be Lopped Off."

142

"Insane," Norma murmured faintly.

"Dammittohell!" Mundin yelled. He hurled his coat violently to the floor, but it did nothing to calm him. "If you're crazy say so and let me get out of here! I never came across such blithering idiocy in my life!"

He stopped in the middle of a beginning tirade; stopped short.

The man wasn't looking at him any more. The same unblinking and unwavering gaze that had been on Mundin was now piercingly directed at the coat on the floor. To the coat the motionless man said, "We brought you here, Mundin, to See Infamy with Our Own Eyes. Now we have seen it and we will Blot It Out." And then, startlingly, shrilly, "Hee!"

Mundin swallowed and stepped gingerly forward. Three paces and he was at the desk, leaning over, looking at what should be the neatly tailored trousers of the man's modest suit.

The personnel of Green, Charlesworth were not wearing trousers this year. The personnel of Green, Charlesworth were wearing bronze pedestals with thick black cables snaking out of them, and brass nameplates that read:

WESTERN ELECTRIC SLEEPLESS RECEPTIONIST
115 Volt A.C. Only

"Hee!" shrilled the motionless lips, just by Mundin's ear. "That's far enough, Mundin. You were right, I suppose, Mrs. Green."

Mundin leaped back as though the 115 volts of A.C. had passed through his tonsils. A flicker of light caught his eye; the two milky glass cabinets had lighted up. He looked, peripherally aware that Norma had crumpled beside him.

He wished he hadn't.

The contents of the cabinets were: Green and Charlesworth. Green, an incredibly, impossibly ancient dumpy-looking, hairless female. Charlesworth, an incredibly, impossibly ancient string-bean-looking, hairless male. Mercifully, the lights flickered out.

Another voice said, but from the same motionless lips, "Can we kill him, Mr. Charlesworth?"

"I think not, Mrs. Green," the Sleepless Receptionist answered itself in the first voice.

143

Mundin said forcefully, "Now, wait a minute." It was pure reflex. He came to the end of the sentence, and stopped.

The female voice said sadly, "Perhaps he will commit suicide, Mr. Charlesworth. Tell him what he is up against."

"He knows what he is up against, Mrs. Green. Don't you, Mundin?"

Mundin nodded. He was obsessed by the Sleepless Receptionist's eyes, now piercingly aimed at him again—attracted, perhaps, by the movement.

"Tell him!" shrieked Mrs. Green. "Tell him about that *girl!* Tell him what we'll do to her!"

"A Daughter of Evil," the voice said mechanically. "She wants to take G.M.L. away from us."

Mundin was galvanized. "Oh, no!" he cried. "Not you! Just Arnold and his crowd!"

"Are Our Fingers Us?" the voice demanded. "Are Our Arms and Legs Us? Arnold is Us!"

The female voice piped, "The girl, Mr. Charlesworth. The *girl!*"

"Painted courtesan," observed the male voice. "She wants to free the slaves, she says. Talks about Mr. Lincoln!"

"We Fixed Mr. Lincoln's Wagon, Mr. Charlesworth," chortled the female voice.

"We did, Mrs. Green. And we will Fix Her Wagon too."

Mundin, thinking dazedly that he should have been more careful where he put Ryan's yen pox, it was stupid of him to get it mixed up with his vitamin pills, said feebly, "Are you *that* old?"

"Are we that old, Mrs. Green?" asked the male voice.

"Are we!" shrilled the female. "Tell him! Tell him about the *girl!*"

"Perhaps not now, Mrs. Green. Perhaps later. When we have softened them up. You must go now, Mundin."

Mundin automatically picked up his coat and helped Norma to her feet. He turned dazedly to the door. Halfway he stopped, staring at the milky glass. Glass, he thought. Glass, and quivering, moving corpses inside, that a breath of air might——

"Try it, Mundin," challenged the voice. "We wanted to see if you would try it."

Mundin thought, and decided against it.

144

"Too bad," said the voice of Charlesworth. "We hate you, Mundin. You said we were not God Almighty."

"Atheist!" hissed the voice of Mrs. Green.

Chapter Twenty-Two

BACK IN RYAN'S OFFICE Mundin said, lying, "It wasn't so bad."

Ryan had taken advantage of their absence to get coked to the eyebrows. He said dreamily, "Think of them. Hundreds of years old. You know what H. G. Wells said around 1940? 'A frightful queerness is coming into life.' Nothing went right, no matter what you did. Green, Charlesworth must have been hitting their stride about then. You know what Jonathan Swift called Green, Charlesworth? Struldbrugs. Only people were on to them, then. Gulliver said they had a law, no Struldbrug could keep his money after he was a hundred. Think of them. Hundreds and hundreds of years old, hundreds and hundreds and hun——"

Don Lavin touched his shoulder and he stopped. Harry Coett was smiling affably at his thumbnail. He started and said gently, "How about a drink?"

Mundin poured it for him, pretending not to notice that the big man was weeping.

"We must proceed to an orderly liquidation," said Nelson, his eyes roving from one corner to another. "Naturally any further action along our previous lines is out of the question."

Norma appeared at the door. Mundin had left her with the company nurse; but she had obviously pulled herself completely together. "Is it all settled by now?" she demanded grimly.

Mundin said, "Everybody seems to be in agreement." He felt weighted down by a tremendous apathy. Green, Charlesworth. They spoke, and the Titans lay down to die. Four men who aggregated eight times his age, thirty times his experience—you couldn't buck it.

"An orderly liquidation," nodded Nelson. "We'll take our licking. Of course. Under the circumstances——"

Norma cut in, "Do you want to fold?"

Coett rubbed his face. "Is there any question?" he asked.

"You mean you do. All right. Who else?"

Nelson said stiffly, "Norma, are you out of your mind?"

"Maybe," she said. "Maybe I am. You tell me. I'll tell you what I'm thinking, and you let me know if it's crazy. I'm thinking that Green, Charlesworth are a couple of old imbeciles. I don't know if they've lived a hundred years or a thousand. I don't care. I suppose there's no reason a man can't live a long time, if he's got plenty of money to spend on medicine; and I suppose that a man who pays the doctors to keep him going, no matter what, has plenty of chances to line up money. . . . I don't care. It doesn't matter. They're human. I saw them, and, believe me, they're human—old; feeble; half insane. At least half. What have they got?"

Ryan, nodding his head to an inner music, chirped, "Money." He smiled.

"Money. So they've got it. As Mundin pointed out, so have we. Maybe they'll lick us, but by God they can't *bluff* us. I'm speaking just for me—I won't deny they can do anything they like to me, but they'll have to *do* it before I give up. Hear?"

Mundin said quickly, "Me too!"

Coett said reasonably, "Good-by."

He stood up, bowed, and headed for the door. Norma, suddenly shaking, said, "Damn you!" She pushed blindly past him.

Coett paused and shook his head. "Crazy," he said.

And in a moment she was back, holding a small celadon vase with blue shoulder-band and medallions. A couple of roses and small ferns were dangling limply from its neck.

Norma dumped the flowers and yelled to the vase, "I don't give a damn what you do, Green, Charlesworth! The bubblehouse is going to be used the way my father planned it! If you people get in the way you're going out the window—and so are any of my yellow-bellied colleagues who don't back me up!"

The vase hummed and shattered in her hands. A flying chip of glass plowed a shallow, bloody furrow in her cheek. Among

146

the shards on the carpet were tiny lumps of metal and crystal that glowed white-hot, fused and were gone. Mundin stamped out the dozen tiny fires on the rug, conscious of screams in the offices outside.

There was pandemonium for ten minutes. The damnedest things were exploding—a pen in Coett's jacket, the stockroom air-conditioner switch, a polarimeter in the lab, the 'in' basket on Ryan's desk. But, except for hysteria among the women, there was no damage. The small fires were easily extinguished.

Coett, dabbing at the scorched mess that was left of his jacket, bellowed at Norma, "You and your screwball schemes. Upset the contract-rental plan, will you? We're slave-drivers, are we? You cheap——"

He was hardly making sense. Mundin and Don started for him at the same time. Mundin was closer; he won the honor of knocking him down.

Nelson picked Coett up and dusted off the carbon from the charred rug. "Blood-pressure, Harry," he advised the older man. "Don't worry. We'll get these skunks."

Hubble was gnawing his nails. He said slowly, "You know, I was brought up to be a sensible, dollar-fearing young man, and Green, Charlesworth have more dollars than anybody else around. . . . You know—for God's sake, don't laugh at me. But I'm sticking, as long as my nerve holds out."

Norma flung her arms around him and kissed him. Charles said, "Hey, cut that——" and then stopped, as he realized he had no right to the sense of outrage which had suddenly overwhelmed him. The other two financiers looked scandalized.

"Traitor," Nelson said incredulously. "Well, all right. Get the hell out of this office—all of you lunatics. If I'd ever *dreamed*——"

"Suppose," Ryan told them gently, "you get out. Think it over. If you leave, you're in the clear—on paper at least. But we hold the lease; and you will kindly blow before we call the cops."

"Blood-pressure, Harry!" Nelson said sharply to Coett.

They left, reducing the Big Seven to a Big Five—and Norvell Bligh, who truculently demanded to be filled in.

When he had been, he looked around at the glum faces and

147

laughed. "Cheer up," he said. "Worse things happen in Belly Rave."

"We'll find out, no doubt," Mundin said numbly.

Norvell patted him on the shoulder. "Exactly," he nodded. "Exactly, Charles; that's the worst that can happen to you. And I've been there, folks. Oh, it's hell, no doubt about it. But—what isn't?"

Norma said imploringly, "Charles, listen to him. He's right. The world's in jail, Charles, and my father put it there, trying to make things nice. I'm almost glad he's dead, just so he can't see what his bubble-house did to the world. Nero never had a weapon like the bubble-house! And think of it in the hands of people like Mrs. Green and Mr. Charlesworth!"

Mundin said, breathing heavily, "Am I to understand that all you ask of an attorney is that he turn the world upside-down for you?"

Norvie Bligh snapped, "Come off it, Charlie!" He advanced almost menacingly on the lawyer, staring up into the bigger man's eyes. He said, "I've got a kid coming. I want him to have a chance at real life—*not* contract slavery. Oh, if it's money you want, we'll make money. G.M.L. is worth lots of money, and as I see it our first move is to take over G.M.L. But that's only the beginning!"

His cocksure confidence made something in the bridge of Mundin's nose tickle; he called it a beginning laugh, and suppressed it. But—Norvie Bligh, five-feet-four and without two nickels in his pocket, saying, "Let's take over G.M.L.—fourteen billion dollars and a nation of resources. . . ."

Mundin swallowed and grinned. "Well, as you say, what have we got to lose? Except you, Hubble."

"Call me Bliss," said the financier, wryly. "It's so descriptive of my entire life." He hesitated. "Oh, hell," he said after a moment. "Might as well show my credentials in the club. What you said, Bligh—'What isn't hell?' A good question. You think Belly Rave is tough, you ought to spend some time at a directors' meeting! You've met my wife—fine woman," he added hastily. "Or was once. But—corruption spreads. Disease spreads. Things are bad at the bottom, they've got to get bad at the top."

He shook his head, staring like a trapped animal at the

scorched rug. "All my life, looking for something, trying to do something, trying to take over and change things—I didn't know how. And I don't know how now, but maybe you people do. Anyway, I'll help you try."

Norma, for once compassionate, said, "And even all that money doesn't help?"

Hubble laughed. "You ask me that. That's a good one. You've got more than I'll ever see, free and clear. Sell your stock on the Big Board if you want to find out for yourself." He shook his head and said abruptly, "Hell with it. What do we do now?"

Mundin, looking around the room, was astonished to find that everyone was looking at him. And then he saw why—*Norma* was looking to him; and Don was looking where Norma looked; and the others followed the Lavins.

He cleared his throat; and then he heard, with his mind, what his ears had heard moments before. "The Big Board!" he cried.

They looked at him. "Don't you see?" he demanded. "The Big Board, what Hubble said. If we can—what's that?"

"That" was a clear, ringing note that came, startlingly, from nowhere. They all looked up; Don Lavin shook himself and got to his feet, staring around. He started to walk toward the door; Mundin said:

"Hey, wait a minute! Where are you going?"

Don called something over his shoulder that sounded like "high wire"; but Mundin didn't catch it. For just then there was another little explosion in the room, the base of a lamp next to where Don had been sitting; and he had a couple more little fires to put out.

But there was, as before, no serious damage. "Hope they haven't got any more of these on a time fuse," Mundin commented. "Well, where were we?"

"You started to tell us what to do," Norvie Bligh said helpfully.

"Well, not exactly. I was just going to say that we may not be quite licked yet. We've got resources. For one, we owe money—maybe a million dollars, I guess; when you get into that kind of red ink, you're an important firm. For another, our campaign against G.M.L. isn't going to dry up just because a couple of men walked out on it. They're going to be in

149

trouble for a while, come hell or high water; maybe we can fish in the troubled waters. For a third, we still have our biggest resource of all—Don and his stock. Where'd Don go?"

"He went out just before that thing blew up," Norvie said uneasily. "I thought he said something about 'the high wire,' but I guess I heard him wrong."

"That's the way I heard it," puzzled Mundin. "Funny. Excuse me." He phoned the reception desk, and slowly hung up the receiver. "They say he went out. They asked when he'd be back, and he said he wouldn't be. Said he was going to the Stadium."

There was a dense silence. "Does anybody," Hubble demanded, "know anything about what a 'high wire' may be? There could be some perfectly simple explanation——"

Norvie Bligh said faintly, "I know quite a lot about high-wire work. It's the most dangerous turn at the Field Day." He coughed. "It's kind of late to mention it. But, Charles, did you get the impression Don's eyes were *shining?*"

Norma and Mundin gasped at once. "The doctor," said Norma.

"The doctor!" echoed Mundin. "He *said* it might not all be out. There might be something deep, planted and left there——"

Ping.

A raucous cackle filled the room. Two voices chanted:
"Absolutely, Mr. Charlesworth?"
"Positively, Mrs. Green!"

Chapter Twenty-Three

THEY WORKED through the night—hard—and they found the cabby they were looking for by dawn.

"Sure, mister. The kid with the con? I hacked him. Right to the artists' entrance at Monmouth Stadium. Friend of yours? Some kind of a dare?"

They tried to bribe their way into the arena, and they almost made it. The furtive gatekeeper was on the verge of swallowing their cock-and-bull story and palming their money when the night supervisory custodian showed up. He was a giant. His eyes shone.

He said politely, "I'm sorry, folks. Unauthorized access is prohibited. However, lineup for bleacher seats begins in a couple of hours, so—— Hello, Mr. Bligh. I haven't seen you around lately."

"Hello, Barnes," Norvie said. "Look, can you possibly let us through? There's a fool kid we know who signed up on a dare. It's all a silly mistake, and he was muggled up."

The giant sighed regretfully. "Unauthorized access is prohibited. If you had a pass——"

The hackie said, "I don't mind waiting, folks, but don't you have better sense than to argue with a con?"

"He's right," said Norvie. "Let's try Candella. He used to be my boss, the louse."

The taxi whizzed them to General Recreations's bubble-city and Candella's particular pleasure dome. Ryan snoozed. Norma and Mundin held hands—scared, without erotic overtones. Bligh looked brightly interested, like a fox terrier. Hubble, hunched on a jump seat, mumbled to himself.

Candella awakened and came to the interviewer after five solid minutes of chiming his bell. Obviously he couldn't believe his eyes.

"Bligh?" he sputtered. "Bligh?" This time, no fawning on Bligh of G.M.L. The word had been passed.

"Yes, Mr. Candella. I'm sorry to wake you, but it's urgent. Can you let us in?"

"Certainly not!" The interviewer blinked off. Norvell leaned on the chime plate and Candella reappeared. "Damn it, Bligh, you must be drunk. Go away or I'll call the police!"

Mundin elbowed Norvell away from the scanner eye. "Mr. Candella——" in his best hostile-witness voice "—I'm Charles Mundin, attorney-at-law. I represent Mr. Donald Lavin. I have reason to believe that Mr. Lavin took a release and is now in the artists' quarters at Monmouth Stadium, due to appear in tomorrow's—today's, that is—Field Day. I advise you that my client is mentally incompetent to sign a release and that therefore your organization will be subject to heavy damages should he be harmed. I suggest that this contretemps can be most quickly adjusted by your filling out the necessary

151

papers canceling your contract with him. Naturally, we're prepared to pay any indemnity, or service fee, that may be called for." He lowered his voice. "In small bills. Plenty of them."

"Come in," said Candella blandly.

The door opened. As they entered he muttered, "My God, an army!"

The house intercom said in a female voice, "What is it, Poopsie?"

Candella flushed and said, "Business. Switch off, please, Panther-Girl. I mean Prudence." There was a giggle and a click. "Now, gentlemen and miss—no, I don't care what your names are—let me show you one of our release forms. You, you said you were a lawyer, have a look."

Mundin studied it for ten minutes. Iron-clad? Water-tight? No. Call it tungsten-carbide-coated. Braced, buttressed, riveted, welded, and fire-polished. Airtight, hard-vacuum-proof, guaranteed not to wilt, shrink, sag, wrinkle, tear, or bag at the clauses under any conceivable legal assault.

Candella was enjoying his face as he read.

"Think you're the first?" He snickered. "If there's been one, there's been ten thousand. And each one that got away with it at first caused an overhaul job on this release. But there hasn't been a successful suit for thirty years, Mr. Attorney-at-Law."

Mundin pleaded, "The hell with the law, Mr. Candella. The hell with the bribe too, if you don't want it. Think of the kid. It's a humanitarian matter. The kid's got no business in there."

Candella was being righteous. "I'm protecting my company and its stockholders, Mr. Whoever-you-are. As a policy matter we can allow no exceptions. Our Field Days would be a chaos if every drunken bum——"

Mundin was about to clobber him when Norvell unexpectedly caught his arm. "No use," the little man said. "I never saw it before, Charles. He's a sadist. Of course. Who else would hold his job and enjoy it? You're interfering with his love life when you try to take one of his victims away. We'll have to go higher."

Candella snorted and showed them pointedly to the door. In the taxi again, Mundin said meditatively, "We *could*

152

hook them for damages, of course. But they don't care about that. Bliss, I guess this is where you take over."

The financier flipped through a notecase and reached for the phone as they rolled back toward the Stadium. He snapped, "Sam? Mr. Hubble here. Good morning to *you*. Sam, who's in charge of General Recreations—the outfit that puts on the Monmouth Field Days? I'll wait." He waited, and then said, "Oh. Thanks, Sam." He hung up the phone and told them, looking out the window, "Trustee stock. Held by the Choate firm. And we know who they run errands for, don't we?"

He drummed his fingers and snapped, "Bligh, you must know *some* way for us to get in. You worked there, after all."

Norvell said, "The only way in is with a release."

Norma Lavin said with dry hysteria, "Then let's sign releases." They started. "No, I'm not crazy. We want to find Don, don't we? And when we find him we restrain him—with a club if we have to. We can sign for crowd extras or something like that—can't we, Norvie? Something not too dangerous. It's all volunteer, isn't it?"

Norvell swallowed and said, "Remember, I wasn't a pit boss. I was on the planning end. From the planning end it was all supposed to be volunteer all right." He looked sick; but he said brightly, "Maybe it's not such a bad idea. I'll tell you what, I'll go in alone. I know the ropes, and——"

"Like hell," said Mundin shortly. "He won't *want* to be found, is my guess. He'll fight. I'll go."

They would all go, even Hubble and old Ryan. And then Norvell had a bright idea and it took a lot more small bills to get the hackie to take them to Belly Rave and an hour to find Lana of the Wabbits.

"We'll be there," she said grimly.

The briefing room beneath the stands was huge and it was crowded. About a quarter of the occupants were obvious rumdumbs, another quarter were professionals, another quarter swashbuckling youngsters in for a one-shot that they could brag about for the remainder of their lives. The rest seemed to be—just people. It was twelve-thirty and everybody had been given an excellent hot lunch in the Stadium cafeteria. One professional noticed Mundin greedily wolfing down his meal and

153

said casually, "Better not, stranger. Belly wounds." And Mundin stopped, suddenly thoughtful.

There was no sign so far of Don Lavin, which was not odd. Easy enough to lose yourself in that crowd, even if you didn't try. And Don, under the compulsion implanted in him, would be trying. They looked, as thoroughly as they could; but it was no use. They gathered together when time grew short and looked at each other searchingly, but no one had seen Don. "The Wabbits," Norvie said hopefully. "They'll spot him from the stands and signal us. Then——"

Then it might be too late. The whole thing depended on getting to him at once, which meant being in the same event; and they couldn't be sure of that. It had been a job keeping even the Wabbits in the stands; Lana had held out for signing up for the Kiddie Kut-Ups number, until Norvell had threatened to leave her out entirely, on the grounds that that was one number they could be sure Don wouldn't be in.

Mundin looked up, startled. Norvell was saying coldly, "Get the hell away, damn it! I thought you learned your lesson after I bent the pipe over your head."

A big, shaggy man was backing away from the little game-cock. "No, no," he said pleadingly. "Shep had it coming, he shouldn't have been fooling around with——Never mind. Shep's sorry. Damn, damn inpounding debt worry; I got to pay you back. I want to help."

Mundin caught Norvell's eye. "Where'd he come from?"

Norvell said blackly, "That Lana. She brought him along. He used to be a kind of bodyguard till I—fired him. My wife's idea."

Mundin said, "We can use another man."

Norvell shrugged. All he said was, "Watch yourself."

The big man fawned on Norvell gratefully, and Mundin looked on wonderingly.

Someone on the rostrum said, "May I have your attention, please? Will you all God-damn-it shut your yaps, please? You stumblebums in the corner there, that means you too. Shut up, you bastards! Thanks, all." He was a distraught young man who ran his fingers through his hair. Norvell muttered to Mundin:

"Willkie. He'll have a nervous breakdown by tonight. Every year. But——" wistfully "—but he's a good M.C."

154

Willkie snapped, "You know this is the big one, the show of the year, ladies and gentlemen. Double fees and survivor's insurance for this one. And in return, ladies and gentlemen, we expect you all to do your damnedest for the Stadium."

He measured the crowd. "Now, let's get on with the casting. First, a comedy number. We need some old gentlemen and ladies—nothing violent; padded clubs in a battle-royal to the finish. The last surviving lady gets five hundred dollars; the surviving gentlemen gets one thousand. Let's see some hands there! No, not you, buster—you can't be a day past sixty."

"Take it," Bligh urged Ryan. "Go with them and keep your eyes open for Don."

Ryan got the nod, and tottered away with the other old ladies and gentlemen.

"Now, are there two good men who fancy themselves as knife-fighters? Scandinavian style? It'll be naked, so don't waste my time if you have a potbelly." Scandinavian style was fastened together by a belt with two feet of slack. "One thousand? Anybody at one thousand? All right, damn it, I'll make it twelve fifty, and if there isn't a rising ovation we drop the number, you yellow skunks!" Perhaps a dozen pros hopped up, grinning. "Fine response! Let's make it six matches simultaneous. Take 'em away, boys!"

The casting went on. Spillane's Inferno; Lions and Tigers and Bears; High-Pressure Chug-a-Lug. Lana shot Mundin a despairing glance. No Don Lavin—but the crowd was thining. "We must have missed him," croaked Hubble.

"Roller Derby!" Willkie called. "Spiked elbows, no armor. Five hundred a point to contestants. Twenty flat to audience, a hundred if a contestant lands on you and draws blood."

Norvell gathered the eyes of Mundin, Norma, and Hubble. Shep trailed along as they rose, were accepted for "audience" and were hustled out of the briefing room, still vainly peering about for Don.

And then, of course, they saw him—only after the glass door closed irrevocably behind them. He was rising—with glazed eyes—for High Wire with Piranha. Price, ten thousand dollars.

And he was the only volunteer, even at that price.

Norma struggled with the immovable door until two matrons peeled her away and shoved her in the direction of the ready room.

"I'll think of something," Norvell kept saying. "I'll think of something."

Chapter Twenty-Four

NORVELL TRIED the chummy approach with the ready-room manager. He was brushed off. Norvell tried entreaties, and then threats. He was brushed off. The ready-room manager droned, "You made yer bed, now lay in it. Alluva sudden you an' yer frenns get yella, it's no skin offa my checks. Derby audience ya stood up for, derby audience yer gonna be."

"What's the trouble, Kemp?" A fussy and familiar voice suddenly demanded.

It was Stimmens, strolling through the pits like an Elizabethan fop through Bedlam. Norvie's ex-assistant, Norvie's Judas of an ex-assistant who had quietly and competently betrayed his boss into Belly Rave.

It would have been delicious to jump him, but the stakes were too high.

"Mr. Stimmens," Norvell said humbly.

"Why, Mr. Bluh—why, Norvie! What are you doing here?"

Norvie brutishly wiped his nose on his sleeve. "Trying to make a buck, Mr. Stimmens," he whined. "You know how it is in Belly Rave. I stood up for the Roller Derby audience, but—but Mr. Kemp here says I got yellow. Maybe I did, but I want a switch. From Derby Audience to High-Wire Heckler. I know it's only ten bucks, but you don't get one of those spiked-elbow girls in your lap. Can you do it for me, Mr. Stimmens? And a couple of friends of mine?"

Stimmens basked. "It's unusual, Norvie. It makes trouble. It creates confusion."

Norvell knew what he was waiting for. *"Please!"* he wept.

Stimmens said tolerantly, "We can bend some rules for an old employee, eh, Kemp? See that he's switched."

"And my friends, please, Mr. Stimmens?"

Stimmens shrugged. "And his friends, Kemp." He sauntered on, glowing with the consciousness of a good deed done that humiliated his ex-boss and caused him no trouble at all.

"You heard him," Norvell snarled. "Switch!"

Kemp growled and reached for his cards.

Back on the bench, Norvell told the others briefly, "We're in. It ups his chances plenty. We might even fish him out, if—"

"Nah," said Shep. "Excuse me. But nah. Tell you what, though. Any of you got money on you, real folding money? Pass some around to the other High-Wire Hecklers when we go on. Tell them to lay off."

"Or else," seconded Norvell, after a momentary resentment. "That's all right, Shep. Reward 'em if they lay off, into the drink if they don't. Hubble, you've got money?"

Hubble had. And then there was nothing to do but watch through the glass wall. Norvell inconspicuously pointed out the Wabbits, spotted throughout the ringside seats—trust Lana's gang to worm their way to the front. "Zip guns," he whispered. "She promised. The idea was, knock off the hecklers if necessary."

The Old Timer's Battle Royal was on. They saw Ryan laid out by a vicious swipe to the groin by a lady of eighty or more. The clubs were padded, but there was a lot in knowing how to use them. He was carried past the wall, groaning, to the infirmary. Mundin and Norma glanced at each other with masked eyes; there simply was no time for sympathy.

It was a responsive audience, Norvell noted with dull technical interest, laughing, howling, and throwing things at the right time. He heard the familiar chant of the vendors, "Gitcha rocks, gitcha brickbats, ya ca-a-an't hit the artists without a brickbat——"

It would be a good show, all of it, even if they had to louse up the feature spectacle a little. Norvell shivered and took his mind away from the feature spectacle. He glanced at the others. He felt queerly alert, as though he were ready for something big and new——

157

But he wasn't, precisely, happy. Because he knew what he very probably might have to do.

Click, click, and the Scandinavian knife-fighters were on, and snip-snap, the knives flashed and the blood flowed; there were two double-kills out of the six pairs and the band blared from Grieg to Gershwin for the Roller Derby, which would last a good ten minutes. . . .

It was gory. Time after time, the skaters shot off the banked boards into the "audience" of old stew-bums and thrill seekers rather than get a razor-sharp elbow spike. And their own spikes worked havoc. Almost us, Norvell thought numbly. At a hundred bucks a lapful, almost us.

For the first time in his life, he found himself wondering when and where it all had started. Bone-crushing football? Those hockey games featured by concussions? Impatient sidewalk crowds that roared "Go-go-go" to a poor crazed ledge-sitter? Those somewhat partisan Chicago fans who flipped lighted firecrackers at the visiting team outfielders as they raced for a fly? "We don't take no prisoners in this outfit, kid"? White phosphorus grenades? Buchenwald? Napalm?

And then before he knew it Kemp was shaking his shoulder and growling, "All right, ya yella punk. You an' yer frenns, yer on. Take yer basket." Numbly he took the basket and looked at the noisemakers and the "gravel"—three-inch rocks, some of them. He followed the section as it moved out onto the field. He became aware that Hubble and Mundin were half-carrying him. Shep was staring open-mouthed.

"Don't flake out on us, damn it," Mundin was begging. "We need every man, Norvie!"

He gave Mundin a pale grin and thought, Maybe I won't have to, anyway. Maybe I won't have to. That's the thing to stick with. Maybe I won't have to. . . . But if I do——

"Ladies and gentlemen!" the M.C. was roaring as they assumed their places around the tank, as the riggers hastily finished setting up the two towers and stringing the wire. "Ladies and gentlemen, Monmouth Stadium is proud and happy to present to you for the first time in this arena's distinguished history a novel and breath-taking feat of courage and dexterity. This young man——"

Don had been hustled atop one of the towers. Norma was

weeping uncontrollably. Hubble and Mundin were passing among the hecklers handing out bills, Shep looming ominously behind. "No heckling, understand? Shut your lip. I said *no heckling*. Just keep quiet. You'll get this much more after it's over—if the kid makes it. Anybody crosses us up, we'll throw him to the fish. Understand? It's your life if he goes. No heckling, understand?"

"—this young man, utterly without previous experience in the gymnastic art, will essay to cross the fifteen feet from tower to tower against the simultaneous opposition of these sixteen energetic hecklers. They will be permitted to jeer, threaten, sound horns, and cast gravel but not to shake the towers——"

Audience identification, thought Norvell. The sixteen "opponents" would be there to do exactly what the audience wanted to do but was too far away to do. Still, a good strong arm with a favoring wind and a brick—or a zip gun, if someone besides the Wabbits had smuggled one in——

"The special feature, ladies and gentlemen, of this performance lies now in the tank above which this young daredevil will essay to cross. At enormous expense, Monmouth Stadium has imported from the headquarters of the Amazon River in far South America a school of the deadliest killers, the most vicious fish known to man, the piranha. Your binoculars, ladies and gentlemen! Don't miss a single second of this! I am about to drop a fifty-pound sheep into the tank alive, and what will ensue you shall see!"

In went the bleating, terrified animal—shaved and with a few nicks in its side for the scent of blood. Then they pulled on the rope and hauled out—bloody bones. There were still ghastly little things flopping and wriggling, dangling remorselessly from the skeleton. The stagehands beat them off into the water as the crowd shrieked in delight.

Just like you, you bastards, Norvell thought. But maybe I won't have to do it——

Shep was looking at him curiously again, and Norvell instinctively moved away. He glanced up at Don Lavin, waiting immobile for the signal, unmoved—at least outwardly unmoved—by the spectacle below. Twenty-two years old, thought Norvell. A moment of absent-minded passion, between bouts at the drawing board and the stockholders' meetings, and he was conceived. Nine months of nausea and stretching pains and clumsiness climaxed with agony, and he was born. Two A.M. feedings. Changing diapers. Fondling and loving and dreaming over him; planning for the great things he would do. And the foetus becomes an infant, and the infant a child, and the child a man.

And the man—here and now—a scrap of bloody bone, unless someone pays a Mosaic price. But perhaps I won't have to do it, Norvell told himself desperately.

The earpiece of his hearing aid had slipped a bit. He looked around, still shyly, and prepared to readjust it. Then he didn't readjust it.

He didn't need it.

The shrieking crowd, the gloating, smacking voice of the M.C., the faint creak in the wind of the tower guys, even—it all, all came through.

He could hear.

For a moment he was almost terrified. It was the decision, he told himself, not quite knowing what he meant. He hadn't *wanted* to hear any of it. He hadn't *dared* hear any of it. He punished himself by not letting himself hear any of it—as long as he was a part of the horror.

But his resignation had been turned in.

Had he ever, really, been deaf? he puzzled. It felt the same as always. But now he could hear; and before he couldn't. He went to Norma Lavin and put his thin arm around the shaking shoulders. "It's going to be all right," he said. She cowered against him wordlessly.

"I've got a boy coming, you know," he told her. She gave him a distracted nod, her eyes on the tower. "And if anything happens," he went on, "it's only fair that they should be taken care of. Isn't it? Sandy and Virginia, and the boy. You'll remember?" She nodded without hearing. "There was this Field Day I heard about in Bay City," he chattered. "There was a high wire with piranhas, just like this. There was a judge up on the ladder to one of the perches, a little drunk, I guess, and he missed his footing; or something——" She wasn't paying attention.

He got up and joined Mundin. "If anything happens," he said, "it's only fair that Sandy and Virginia and the boy should be taken care of."

"What?"

"Just remember."

Shep was looking suspicious again. Norvell walked away.

The drumroll began and the M.C. fired the platform on which Don Lavin stood like a stone man. The crowd howled as the flames licked up and the boy hopped convulsively forward, his balance pole swaying.

The M.C. yelled furiously at the hecklers, "What the hell's the matter with you people? Toot! Chuck gravel! What are you getting paid for?"

One of the young toughs at the far end of the pool began to swing his rattle, glancing nervously at Shep. Hubble, beside him, snapped, "A hundred more, buster. Now calm down!" The tough calmed down and gasped at the wire-walker.

A foot, two feet, the pole swaying.

He has special slippers, Norvell thought. Maybe it'll be all right, maybe I won't have to do anything. And then I can go back to being comfortably deaf again, buying batteries for an act of contrition, turning this nausea, these people molded from blood-streaked slime, off at will.

Three feet, four feet, and the M.C. howling with rage. "Get in there and fight, you bastards! Blow your horns! Plaster him!"

Five feet, six feet, and the crowd noise was ugly, ugly and threatening. In one section a chant had started, one of those foot-stomping, hand-clapping things.

Six feet, seven, and the M.C. was breaking down into sobs. "We paid you to heckle and this is the way you treat us," he blubbered. "Those fine people in the stand. The reputation of the Stadium. Aren't you *ashamed?*"

Eight feet, nine feet, ten feet. Two-thirds of the way to the second tower.

Norvell hoped. But somebody in the stands, somebody with a mighty arm and a following wind, had found the range. The half-brick at the end of its journey sailed feebly *plop* into the tank, and white-bellied little things tore at it and bled themselves and tore at one another. The water boiled.

Suddenly ice-cold, all business, Norvie said briskly to Mundin, "They'll have him in a minute. Be ready to haul him out, fast. Remember what I said."

He strolled over to Willkie, who was watching the stubbornly silent hecklers in numb despair.

Another half-brick. This one hit the tower. Much flailing of the balance pole and a shriek from Norma.

"No nervous breakdown this year, Willkie," Norvell said chattily to the M.C.

"What? Bligh? Bligh, they won't *listen* to me," Willkie sobbed.

Twelve feet, almost there, and then the brick, unseen, that tapped Don Lavin between the shoulder blades and made him flail the pole, too hard; and the hecklers were out of control. Hubble and Mundin shouted and screamed and pleaded, but the "gravel" was in their hands, and they weren't listening; it was not only the piranha that were maddened at the first taste of blood.

Norvell took one last agonized look around the arena. But there was nothing. No chair, no table, no cushion, nothing to throw to the fish, but——

"NO!" bellowed Shep from behind him, and Norvell, startled, half-turned. Just for a moment. But the moment meant that it was Shep, not Norvell, who wrapped the sobbing Willkie in his arms; Shep, not Norvell, who lunged into the tank for an eternal instant; Shep—who had an "inpounding debt worry." And who paid his debts.

First the water was cool. And then boiling.

At the far end, the quiet end, of the tank, Mundin and Hubble yanked Don out in one heave.

Chapter Twenty-Five

"I WANTED TO DO IT," Norvell Bligh was saying in a cracked voice. "I was willing to do it."

Norma had her arms around him, in the cab going back to Belly Rave. "Of course you were," she soothed him.

Mundin, riding dazedly beside them, tried to rest his brain. That was a pretty good little man, he thought. Good thing

Shep took the play away from him. We'll need him. But of course he can't see it that way, not yet.

Hubble was chattering vivaciously away. "Really an adventure. But the big adventure's coming up, eh, Mundin? After the piranha, Green, Charlesworth. They'll make us wish we were back with the piranha, wouldn't you say?"

Don Lavin advised him, "Shut up." Something had happened to Don Lavin. He might have learned something on the wire, Mundin thought. Funny, how you grow up after a while—after a very long while, for some people.

Reminded, he picked up the phone and asked information for a number.

Hubble, eavesdropping and irrepressible, said, "Oh, of course. The Stadium infirmary. We plain forgot about old Ryan, didn't we? And we'll need him for the big doings—when are you going to let us in on the plan, by the way? Now that we've got Don back we've got the stock. But we'll never vote it. You know that; they'll tie us up in injunctions from here to hell. I suppose——" He broke off, warned by Mundin's expression as he slowly hung up the phone. "Ryan?" Hubble demanded in a completely different tone.

Mundin nodded. "Hemorrhage," he said. "He died on the operating table." He sighed.

War was never cheap, he thought. Shep—almost Bligh—and now Ryan. Give me one more victory such as this, and I am undone, he quoted to himself, as he began to plot the final struggle that Ryan had helped to shape, and would not see.

"You'd think," grumbled Don Lavin, "that ten hours' sleep would fix a person up."

Mundin said worriedly, "It's almost time for the bell. Do you see Norvie?" They were in the Stock Exchange, waiting for the start of business. The enormous hall was packed with its customary seething, excitable throng—but not quite the customary feeling of tension, Mundin thought, putting out psychic feelers into the crowd. It was a more somber mass of speculators than the last time he had been here, a worried bunch, fretful and disturbed. Their own publicity campaign, Mundin thought with a touch of satisfaction. There had been trading in G.M.L.; it was off a few points, over the last weeks.

163

Not much, but enough to shake, ever so slightly, the ironclad conviction of its stability. And if G.M.L. wasn't totally sound, the investors were wondering, almost aloud, what *was?*

They saw Norvie at last, inconspicuous against the far wall. He looked at them without visible recognition, then deliberately looked away. They followed his look; and there was Hubble, at a hundred-dollar window, chatting gaily with the investor at the window next to him. And then the bell rang for the first movement of the day.

"Your honor, sir," Mundin said formally to Don Lavin. Don acknowledged with an ironic bow and light-heartedly tapped out his first "sell" order:

333, 100 shares, market

The Big Board flickered and hummed, and the pari-mutuel computers totaled, subtracted, divided, and spat out their results. Mundin and Don had their glasses fixed to line 333; it flashed:

333, off ½

"Congratulations," said Mundin. "You have just thrown away a thousand bucks."

"My privilege," said Don, grinning. "Your turn, I believe."

The thirty-second warning bell sounded, and Mundin tapped out his own order—a hundred shares of Old 333, G.M.L. Homes, at the market. And they lopped off another half-point.

Don had been computing with a pencil and paper, thoughtfully. "At one movement every three minutes," he said, "and three hundred trading minutes in the day, at the present rate of progress we will bust G.M.L. right off the board in forty working days." They gravely shook hands.

A somberly dressed school teacher, showing her young civics class a first-rate example of The American Way in action, shepherded the kids past the line of betting windows where Don and Mundin were sitting. The investors on either side of the two conspirators were getting curious; the one next to Don leaned over and hissed, "Say buster—why pay the Exchange commission? You want to unload G.M.L. I can take you to a guy who'll make a private deal."

"Beat it," said Don, and punched out his order.

333, off ½

"Slow and steady," Mundin said philosophically.

164

A petulant little man, escorted by a grim guard, came stamping down the aisle. "K-81, K-82, K-83—oh, you must be the one," he counted. "You there, window K-85. And you. Are you aware of the penalties for non-delivery of stock sold through the pari-mutuel——"

"Take a look," said Mundin, shoving the stock certificates into his hands.

The petulant man looked, and giggled weakly. "Oh," he said fussily. "Well, of course—— Come along, Haynes. There certainly wasn't anything to *that* complaint, was there? Terrible how these stories get started. . . ."

Haynes paused and leaned over Mundin. "I'm watching you," he said. "The exit door is right over there—next to the cashier's area. I'll be there, when you deposit that stock." He lumbered, casually threatening, away.

"Green, Charlesworth," whispered Mundin, and Don nodded. What else? Green, Charlesworth themselves, or one of their satellites; just checking, so far.

And once they had checked, they would know.

The thirty-second bell was ringing. Mundin started to punch out his order; then pressed the cancel plate. "Better step it up," he said over his shoulder to Don:

333, 500 shares, market

They lopped off a full point that time. . . .

The Exchange had been going for half an hour, and already the buzz of whispers was louder than the calls of the speculators. Somebody was dumping G.M.L.

After the first drop, the market had firmed. Mundin, sweating doggedly over his punch keys, guessed that Green, Charlesworth's buying pool had orders to let the price drop a half point or a point at a time—no more. They could afford to watch and wait. They had plenty of time. And plenty of money. And plenty of resources.

And if the time and the money and the resources weren't enough—they had plenty of other ways to handle trouble.

Don Lavin was whispering something. Irritably Mundin looked up. "What?"

"I said, take a look at Belt Transport."

Mundin flicked his glasses over the Big Board. Belt Transport was off ten points, and he hadn't even noticed it. This was a hell of a time to get foggy-brained, he cursed himself. But he hadn't expected anything like that so soon; it had to be hunch players, two-bit investors getting worried and getting out. If that kept up, the big boys would be at the windows before long.

"You're right," Mundin told Don. "Give Norvie the nod."

Across the room, Norvie acknowledged the signal and began placing inconspicuous "buy" orders on the faltering stocks—all but G.M.L. He punched the keys as though he were punching Green, Charlesworth themselves, with a controlled, joyous rage. It had taken him a long time to realize that he was, after all, alive; and a longer time to get over the first wretched resentment that Shep had stolen his big scene, and died the death that Norvell had reserved for himself. But he was all over it now—and exulting at the chance to fight, however weakly, however ineffectually. . . .

Halfway through the second hour, they cued Hubble in, and he nodded, stopped piddling around with his two-dollar and five-dollar coppered bets and began following Norvie's lead. Mundin and Don Lavin had switched to thousand-share lots by now, more than a million dollars' worth of stock at every movement, and were sullenly hammering old 333 off a point, another point—a point and a half——

Three times already the conditioned cashier's messenger had come down through the aisles with the Exchange's certified checks, taking away stock certificates and leaving the money; the transactions were getting that big. He came again and Mundin, catching a glimpse of the amount the check was made out for, felt his eyes pop. All of a sudden things came into focus: Charles Mundin, tossing millions of dollars' worth of stock into the hopper every couple of minutes, Charles Mundin who ninety days before couldn't scare up the price of his monthly installments on the Sleepless Secretary! He almost panicked; he looked up wildly, staring around at the watching hangers-on, the touts, the fascinated investors who had abandoned their own windows, the guards, the children of the civics class and their sedate teacher. . . .

Something glinted and caught his eye. He hissed to the nearest kid, "Ixnay on the ottlebay!" The eight-year-old, squirming in his unaccustomed clothes, flushed and tucked the busted bottle farther out of sight hastily, but not so hastily that the eldest of the "class," a bony but sweet-faced thirteen, didn't catch it and move ominously closer. "Forget it, Lana," Mundin whispered. "Just keep them out of sight." He glanced at the "teacher," and then turned to the "teacher's" brother, beside him.

"How much have we dumped?" he demanded.

Don Lavin looked up from his penciled computations. "I make it just over eighteen thousand shares." A drop in the bucket, thought Mundin. They had started out with twenty-five per cent of G.M.L.'s entire stock issue—roughly seven million shares, in all, and their bloc close to two million. At that rate, he thought, they'd be there all year.

"Don," he said. "Don—both together, from now on. And twenty-five hundred shares at a time."

Fourteen billion dollars.

Fourteen billion dollars is massive, fourteen billion dollars has inertia; you don't shake it easily. Ram a Juggernaut into fourteen billion dollars. The Juggernaut crumples and spills its Hindic gods into the street; the fourteen billion dollars stands unmoved.

But fourteen billion dollars, or anything else that God ever made, has a natural rate of swing. Slap it with a feather, and wait; slap it again; slap it again. The oscillation builds. The giant construct vibrates and wobbles and sways.

And Don Lavin's twenty-five per cent interest was no feather.

The figures on the Big Board were plunging now—"333, off 10"; "333, off 6"; And even once, incredibly: "333, off 42." By working like dogs, Mundin and Bligh and Hubble and the Lavins had succeeded in cutting their collective fortunes in half, or just about. And it was time for something to happen.

Something did. "Hup, two. Hup, two. Hup, two." It was an eight-man squad of the City's Finest, and in their vanguard——

Del Dworcas.

He stepped coldly up to Mundin through a lane that opened in the slackjawed mob. "You," he said bitterly, "you cheat, you ingrate, you deadbeat, you!" Oh, no! thought Mundin, incredulously. Dworcas couldn't be——. "I hand you herewith," Dworcas said formally, "this Summons & Complaint—

give it to him, Herb—and attach all of your property pending adjudication thereof. Eight hundred dollars, Mundin! Loaned to you, to help you out, and you try to stiff me. With all the money you've got, too. Look at those stock certificates! Look at those checks! Boys, pick up his junk, and let's get out of here." He dried his eyes in a businesslike way and turned to go, as the cops reached for Mundin's and Lavin's stock.

"Hold it," squawked Mundin. "Del, listen—you're monkeying with something bigger than you are." Dworcas involuntarily stepped back away from him, glanced behind him, and looked nervously again at Mundin. He licked his lips.

"Yeah, mister," chimed in the sweet-faced thirteen-year-old by Dworcas's elbow. "Give the guy a chance. Go ahead."

Dworcas appeared to have trouble breathing. "Uh—all right," he got out. "Let's go, Herb."

"No, mister," implored the sweet-faced girl. "You don't want to go, just send the cops away. You want to stay here and watch that property, right?"

"Right," said Dworcas bitterly. "Beat it, Herb."

The big cop frowned and objected, "I give him the summons, Del. It says we got to take his stuff in pertective custody."

"Beat it, Herb!"

The cop shrugged petulantly and, gathering his squad, marched glowering away.

"Good work, Lana," breathed Mundin.

She shrugged. "All right, you kids," she said. "You can put the bottles away again. He'll stay put, won't you, buster?"

Fervently Dworcas choked, "Sure," watching the Wabbits with eyes as glassy as the bottles they were stowing away in their clothes again behind him.

Mundin turned limply back to the Big Board. He had missed a couple of movements, but—but——

He held the glasses rigid on Line 333 for long seconds. It said, 333, off 13.

"Don," he said unbelievingly, "Don, it's started. Somebody else is selling too!"

Coett? Nelson? Green, Charlesworth themselves? They never knew. But in a minute it was everyone. Old 333 plunged and plunged and plunged. Howling like maniacs, Mundin and

Lavin poured in ten thousand shares at a time, and other thousands appeared from hidden portfolios, from ancient voting trusts, from the very air, it seemed. Off 15. Off 28. Off 47. Off 61.

The whole market was churning now, and the Big Board's figures had little to do with what was happening then and there; they were minutes behind. Twice there was trouble, and the busted bottles came out, and a couple of bleeding hulks slid to the floor of the Exchange to be trampled into mush. But only twice. The density of the crowd protected them; Hitler's panzers could not have driven through that mass to get at Mundin.

This was the critical point, Mundin told himself desperately, hunched over his keys, punching out orders and waiting for the slow, the agonizingly slow, response of the once-instantaneous Big Board. This was when they had to feel the pulse of the market, and know when, quietly, to stop selling and when, invisibly, to begin to buy. A hand snaked over his shoulder and picked something up.

"Watch it, bud!" Mundin ordered hoarsely, glancing up. But it was only Del Dworcas, taking back the summons & complaint his man had given Mundin.

His face white but composed, Dworcas quietly tore the paper up. "Yours," he said to Mundin, letting the pieces slip to the floor. "I know when to get off a losing horse, Charles. And don't forget who put you in touch with the Lavins."

The judgment of a practical politician, Mundin thought wonderingly. It was like a voice from the grave, Ryan's voice.

And by it he knew that they had won.

Chapter Twenty-Six

THEY CELEBRATED THAT NIGHT in Belly Rave—there seemed no more fitting place. It was quiet but prideful. They had won, all of them together. And they all of them owned the biggest concentration of power the world had ever seen.

Even now, they didn't know the full extent of their holdings. Mundin and Norvie had made a laborious computation of their G.M.L. holdings—nearly seventy per cent. All of their own stock back, and probably Coett's and Nelson's and enough more to mean that they had dipped into the Green, Charlesworth reserves. But, wherever it came from, enough.

Enough to make the Lavin House—no longer the G.M.L. Home—what Lavin had meant it to be.

"Belt Transport Common B," sang out Hubble, "two hundred fifty shares." Don Lavin scouted through his lists, made a mark, called:

"Check."

Hubble carefully laid away the voucher and picked up another. "National Nonferrous—hey, that's Nelson! National Nonferrous, fifteen hundred shares." He scratched his head. "Did I buy those? Well, no matter. Tioga Point Kewpie Corporation—wait a minute." He stared at the Exchange's voucher. "Anybody here ever hear of a Tioga Point Kewpie Corporation? We seem to have picked up a controlling interest. Got *Poore's* around, Mundin?" Nobody had ever heard of it. Hubble shrugged, made a paper plane of the voucher and sailed it to Lana. "Here, kid. Looks like a doll factory. Yours."

Lana looked startled, then belligerent, then lost. She picked up the voucher and stared at it. "Dolls," she said, wonderingly.

Hubble threw the rest of the vouchers in his briefcase and slapped Don Lavin on the shoulder. "Hell with it. We'll finish tomorrow. It isn't exactly a balanced portfolio but——" his face was oddly young and eager when he smiled "—we put it together in kind of a hurry. Anyway, it looks like we own a little bit of everything."

"We'll need it," said Norma, nestled against Mundin's arm. "Those old monsters in their glass bottles. . . ."

Mundin patted her hand. "I don't know," he said, after a moment. "They're as good as dead, you know. They didn't have anything to live for but power, and when we broke the market we took that away from them. We——"

He stopped. The house shivered and sang. A white flash of light sprang up outside, turned orange and faded away.

"What's that?" demanded Norvie Bligh, a protective arm around his wife.

No one knew; and they all ran up to the battered second floor, where there was a window with glass—where there used to be a window with glass, they found. The glass was in shards across the floor.

Across the slaggy bay, luminous even in the evening light, where Old New York had stood and rotted—a mushroom-shaped cloud.

"Green, Charlesworth," mused Norvell. "I guess you weren't the only one who realized they were as good as dead, Charles."

They stood there for a long moment, watching the cloud drift out to sea, an insubstantial monument to the suicide of the Struldbrugs, but the only monument they would ever have. . . .

"We'd better get below," said Mundin. "We've got cleaning up to do."

ABOUT THE AUTHORS

FREDERIK POHL, is a double-threat science fictioneer, being the only person to have won science fiction's top award, the Hugo, both as an editor and as a writer. As a writer, he has published more than thirty novels and short story collections, including *The Space Merchants* (with C. M. Kornbluth), *The Age of the Pussyfoot*, *Day Million* and *The Gold at Starbow's End*. His awards include four Hugos and the Edward E. Smith Award. As an editor, he published the first series of anthologies of original stories in the science fiction field, *Star Science Fiction*, and for many years he was the editor of two leading magazines in the field, *Galaxy* and *If*. He is currently science fiction editor of Bantam Books. His interests extend beyond science fiction to national affairs (his book, *Practical Politics*, was a handbook for party reformers in the 1972 election year), history (he is the *Encyclopedia Britannica's* authority on the Roman Emperor, Tiberius) and almost the entire range of human affairs. He is currently president of the Science Fiction Writers of America, and makes his home in Red Bank, New Jersey.

CYRIL M. KORNBLUTH began writing science fiction for publication at the age of fifteen, and continued to do so until his early death in his mid-thirties. In his own right, he was the author of four science fiction novels, including *The Syndic*, a number of works outside the science fiction field and several score of the brightest and most innovative shorter science fiction pieces ever written. Some of his short stories and novelettes have been mainstays for the anthologists and have also been adapted for television production, such as *The Little Black Bag* and *The Marching Morons*. His collaboration with Frederik Pohl has been described as "the finest science fiction collaborating team in history." Together they wrote seven novels and more than thirty short stories. Among their works are such classics as *Wolfbane*, *Gladiator-at-Law* and *The Space Merchants*, which has been translated into more than thirty-five languages and has appeared on most lists of the most important science fiction novels ever written.